A Rogue By Birth

Mac's smile faded. Clearly he'd loved his mother a great deal. His feelings toward his father were more difficult to discern. There was anger, justifiably so, but for all his protests, Joanna recognized the haunted look in his eyes, one of disappointment and yearning. And yet Mac masked his life's pain with indifference and charm.

"Your mother would be very proud of you, other than the stealing and smuggling, of course," she blurted. Sweet Goddess, why had she uttered that observation? She stumbled again in their dancing, righted herself and added, "I mean there are so many other things you could do."

He burst out laughing as he spun her in a sweeping circle. "Do you mean to reform me, Joanna?"

"I spoke out of turn." She frowned. "I seem to spout whatever I am thinking when around you. Any other man would have abandoned me long ago for my impulsiveness."

"I'm smarter than they are. You need never keep your thoughts to yourself around me." He winked. "And under different circumstances, I just might let you."

Other Leisure books
by Peggy Waide:

MIGHTIER THAN THE SWORD
POTENT CHARMS
DUCHESS FOR A DAY

A Rogue's Promise

PEGGY WAIDE

LEISURE BOOKS NEW YORK CITY

To Kay, Robin, Janet, Sue, Teresa, Leslee and Alice,
who kept me somewhat sane and on track.

A LEISURE BOOK®

June 2002

Published by

Dorchester Publishing Co., Inc.
276 Fifth Avenue
New York, NY 10001

ISBN 0-8439-5022-6

The name "Leisure Books" and the stylized "L" with design are trademarks of Dorchester Publishing Co., Inc.

Printed in the United States of America.

Chapter One

London 1816

It paid to be cautious—especially in his trade.

MacDonald Archer balanced one foot on the skiff, the other on the marshy strip of land along the lower Thames, his hand resting on the butt of his pistol, his eyes and ears alert. The reeds rustled nearby. A wooden crate clunked against another. Slate-colored water licked the side of the small boat as a handful of Mac's best men transferred French champagne, cognac and lace to a nearby wagon.

Mother Nature played the smuggler's perfect accomplice. She had provided a black moonless sky, a cold wet drizzle, and a layer of fog so thick Mac could barely see the tips of his own boots. Another few minutes and the crew of the *Fleeting Star* would disappear into the shroud of mist several hundred pounds richer.

A dim circle of light shimmied along the narrow path from the road to the river and Knox, Mac's first mate, appeared. The man's knee was bent at an odd angle, the result of a hasty leap from a two-story building in a swift and irrevocable departure from his schooling at Oxford—made necessary by his penchant for thieving. Mac had found him, near dead, hiding from the constabulary in an abandoned warehouse. Eternally grateful, Knox had pledged his devotion to Mac. Six years later, the man still kept that promise.

"All done and accounted for, Captain. However, there seems to be one pestiferous aggravation." Knox jerked his head toward the man scurrying their way. "If I may say so, sir, Digger has the manners of monkey and a mind so infinitesimally small it is a marvel he can change his drawers."

Mac certainly didn't disagree with his first mate. Criminals littered the London docks, but most respected the unspoken code between thieves and smugglers. Digger was different. He'd sell his own mother for a profit. Though no one had proof, many sailors claimed he'd shot his last partner in the back. And he used his fists on ladies and young lads. Mac had no tolerance for disloyalty and even less for brutality.

Men like Digger had Mac rethinking his future. Still, it was hard to forsake a lifestyle you knew and understood—or one that was so lucrative. Mac had learned at an early age that money and information were power, so he'd carved his niche in the world by using what he had to provide the luxuries titled folk wanted and were willing to pay for. He knew their proclivities, their desires, and he did his best to fill them. It had indeed become a way of life.

In the beginning, the money, the adventure, and even the danger, had captured and held Mac's interest: A perverse part of him enjoyed circumventing the law. But now, as he stared out over the water, that murky thread binding his past and his future, he admitted the thrill of the game had ebbed, replaced by a nagging restlessness. He glanced toward Knox.

"I'll handle Digger," he said. "Prepare to shove off." He walked over to the distasteful man.

"You was to deliver fifteen crates," Digger spat.

"Considering our close proximity to London, and the increase in the Watch, I changed my mind. I took money for only twelve crates. Which is exactly how many you have on your wagon."

Grabbing Mac by the arm, the bearded rodent bared his yellow teeth. Mac glowered back, placing enough warning in his eyes so that even the beef-brain would understand. Digger quickly dropped his hand to his side and said, " 'Tain't what we agreed on."

"Too bloody bad. I don't like you, Digger. As long as you pay me well for my cargo, I'll deal with you— but don't press your luck. I'd just as soon shoot you as look at you."

"What am I to tell me customers?"

A prickling sensation suddenly trickled down Mac's

3

spine. Maybe it was the nervous whinny of the horses or the silence of the crickets, but whatever the cause, the feeling had saved his neck more times than he cared to count. He climbed into the boat. His men piled in behind him. "Tell them whatever you like, but if I were you, I'd get my goods and my arse out of here. I think we're about to have company."

"We ain't done yet!"

The pounding of hooves signaled the rapid approach of riders—in all likelihood the king's revenue men. Who else would be out in this empty wasteland on such a godforsaken night? Mac shrugged. "Alas, we are."

Torn between arguing or saving his ugly skinny neck, the man called Digger cursed then sprinted into the darkness, back toward his horses and contraband.

With one word, Mac had his crew put their backs into their oars. None of them wanted to spend the next few years in Newgate.

Chapter Two

Sweat, grease, and a dozen other equally unpleasant odors filled her nostrils. Mud and scraps of something that looked suspiciously like discarded chicken bones littered the taproom floor. Clouds of smoke hung in the air in wraithlike swirls.

Imagine—Miss Joanna Fenton thought with dismay, as she hovered in the doorway of the Pig-'N'-Whistle, a name in itself that made one wary—men purposely congregated in such places! The fumes alone were enough to give one pause.

Chang Li, her butler, self-appointed bodyguard and chaperon, stood beside her, his gaze darting from wall to wall. Though he valiantly tried to mask his feelings, disapproval edged with panic tensed every muscle in his bronzed and weathered face. At the moment, he surely thought her a bacon-brained fool.

Maybe she was.

The weather outside was absolutely inhospitable. Her hat drooped to one side, her parasol was practically ruined, water dripped from the bottom of her cape, and she stood in a tavern filled with men.

The memory of her first season flooded her mind. She'd thought herself in love and believed the particular gentleman felt the same. In a moonlight garden, she'd learned otherwise. She'd become a target of scandal. All hopes of a match evaporated. She never again wanted to draw the attention of the *Ton* to herself and knew she risked much by coming here.

She briefly considered turning around and going home. It did seem the most prudent thing to do. Unfortunately, she had no choice but to proceed. Desperation made her stay. Disaster had struck the Fenton household. And like all family matters, past and present, the problem had fallen upon Joanna's responsible shoulders. But this time she needed help.

She waved her linen handkerchief back and forth in a futile attempt to obtain a fresh breath of air. "What do you suppose we should do now?" she asked.

"Go and come back later? Maybe tomorrow or next day. Maybe not at all." Hope radiated from Chang Li in waves.

But if Joanna returned home empty-handed, her mother would praise divine intervention, claim all was well, then handle the problem as she always did: pretend it didn't exist. Her mother would hope the situation righted itself while she napped—which, of course, it would not. Joanna would be right back where she'd started.

Quite simply, Joanna had no choice. Time was of the essence if she was to save her family and her brother from scandal. "We shall ask our question at the bar," she decided.

Careful to keep her hands clear of the grime coating the wooden furniture, she threaded her way from the door around the tavern's trestle tables, benches and chairs. A bit of lye soap would do wonders for the place, she thought. Or a torch.

There was a gasp. A gentleman—Joanna knew she used the term loosely with the sailor—had noticed her presence, and his mouth fell open in shock. Good grief, you would have thought she stood here with a figwort planted on her head. The man spared a glance at Chang, and the butler's satin trousers and single braid. He blinked, then whirled back toward Joanna and continued to stare. He elbowed the fellow next to him. So on and so forth the elbowing proceeded until the entire taproom was aware of her presence. Heads swiveled and eyes bulged. It was as though she had just been caught witnessing some secret ritual.

Instinctively, Joanna shuffled backward—and smacked against the solid wood of the bar.

Chang, noting the crowd's reaction, moved forward in a protective stance. "We go now?"

Joanna considered. She knew the most basic defense tactics, taught to her by her father. Chang carried a pistol and practiced his own, fancier fighting techniques daily. He would defend her at all cost. But, considering the fact that she abhorred violence, that Chang was forty-four, and that they were outnumbered twenty-to-one, Joanna first opted for diplomacy. She pasted what she hoped was a congenial yet authoritative smile on her face, and spoke. "Pardon the intrusion, gentlemen, but I am searching for a man."

The crowd quickly recovered from its shock. Jokes and other rude comments—most of which she guessed were at her expense—flew back and forth. There came snickers and glares. One rude cretin actually burped in response.

"Lookee 'ere. An 'onest-to-goodness lady." A burly fellow with filthy black hair poking from beneath his woolen cap strutted forward. "Yep. Ye looks like a lady, right enough. We dun't never get no ladies 'ere."

"I wonder why?" she muttered to herself. "If I may—"

He sniffed at her. "Ye smells like a lady, too—so I guess *I'm* willin' to be that someone yer lookin' fer."

Joanna's heart pounded. Sweat formed on the palms of her hands. The muscles in her stomach knotted. Sweet Empress, the man had nosed her neck like a hound with a new bone: drawing unsettlingly close and inhaling air with a loud slurping noise. Several disgusting times.

Her sister would faint. Her mother would faint. But never in all her twenty-two years had Joanna fainted. She simply didn't have time for such theatrics.

She bit back her retort that the man needed to

bathe, shave, and burn his old clothes and replace them with something new—or in the very least, something clean. To be honest, most of the men now voicing their equally unsolicited and unwelcome opinions looked disreputable and unkempt. And the tavern maids weren't much better.

What had she expected? This wasn't a club on Pall Mall, but a tavern frequented by sailors and dockside workers.

"Thank you for your generous offer, but I am looking for a *particular* gentleman. A Mr. Archer."

Silence settled over the taproom, the heavy foreboding sort that usually preceded trouble. Joanna's pulse raced even faster. Then, as if Moses had risen on the very bar behind her and brandished his staff in the air, a path cleared between Joanna and the opposite wall. She gripped her parasol in her hands and waited.

By the Empress's ears! Her stomach plummeted to her toes. A shirtless man sauntered forward, power emanating from his muscular body. A dark rag, carelessly tossed around his neck, drew her gaze to his broad shoulders, the tanned muscles of his bare torso, the reddish-gold curls that dusted his chest, the narrow width of his waist. A strand of hair, loosened from the leather thong that restrained its brothers, hung beside the man's ear. A small scar intersected the dark brows that slashed low over his eyes.

Those eyes. Oh my. The color of his eyes reminded her of the lush green meadows of the lake country.

Buried in their depths lay curiosity, wariness and surprise. He appeared fierce, dangerous, a man to be reckoned with. And perfectly suited to the job she had in mind.

Chang tugged her sleeve. "Now we go?"

"Not just yet."

Refusing to wilt beneath the newcomer's burning gaze, Joanna locked her legs in place and met his bold stare with one of her own. At least she hoped she mimicked his boldness. "Are you Mr. Archer?"

"It depends on who's asking."

"If you are who you are, then why should who I am matter?"

"Depending on who you are and what you want, I may or may not wish to be him."

To Joanna's surprise, the man's voice was educated. Amusement, laced with an underlying insolence, sparkled in his eyes. Then the bare-chested rogue fisted the ends of a towel in his hands, revealing several red scratches along his knuckles.

Joanna felt a sudden urge to tend those scrapes. It was most alarming. After all, this wasn't a family member or stray mongrel who had wandered into her primroses. This was a complete stranger. True, he was one of the most handsome she had ever encountered, but still a stranger.

A raspy voice called out from behind a carved statue of an indecently clad mermaid, one she had tried not to notice, "Mac, dependin' on what the lady wants— and knowing you, I got a fair notion what that wantin' is—I'd be 'appy to take yer place. Me wooden leg's in need of sandin'."

"Aye," another sailor cheerfully agreed. "I've a 'ammer of me own that's eager for a bit of work."

"Even with yer bad luck lately, Archer," a deep voice boomed, "I'll trade ya places. I've an itch needs scratchin'."

Joanna's skin burned from head to toe. Scratching, wooden legs, and hammers, indeed!

Tense, but otherwise silent, Chang retreated. He seemed to want the same spot of floor where she stood. Poor soul. He was obviously unnerved by the giant standing before her. With good reason. Mr. Archer was a very, very, very big man. And all that bare muscle radiated raw masculine strength.

She offered Chang a reassuring smile, glared at the snickering faces of the nearest sailors, then turned back to the man she had come to see. "My name is Miss Joanna Fenton. If you do not wish to speak with me, please say so. Otherwise, let us confer quickly." She risked a pointed glance to the side, and the sniffing sailor who still lingered there, then she leaned forward and whispered: "Preferably somewhere private. It is quite urgent, Mr. Archer."

The man's gaze roamed over her.

Joanna froze, knowing he'd see what everyone saw: an ordinary female with no remarkable attributes— one who reminded men of spinsterhood, dependability or duty, or maybe even all three. As had happened many times of late, regrets and abandoned dreams of what could have been threatened to surface. She immediately dismissed them. They were silly notions, her nerves attacking her common sense.

The rogue's eyes lit with amusement. As his smile widened, emphasizing his full lower lip, a charming dimple appeared in his left cheek. "Most young ladies of the *Ton* are home readying themselves for a night at Almack's. I therefore have already assumed this matter to be of the utmost importance." He bowed like the finest of gentlemen. "William MacDonald Archer at your service—but call me Mac. All my close friends do."

As if she would dare to address such a man so informally! The fact that she could not remove her gaze from his bare chest was irrelevant. "Do you always go about in public without your clothes?"

"Only when attractive young ladies come calling." The wretch actually winked. "There was a wee brawl earlier. Rather than bloody my shirt, I removed it."

He turned to face the crowd of curious onlookers. "Enough, you scurvy dogs. It appears we have a true damsel in distress standing before us. And I, chivalrous fellow that I am, intend to play her shining knight. If you will excuse us." With that, amidst the groans and crude gibes of the crowd, he led Joanna and Chang to the darkest corner of the tavern.

He prowled rather than walked, emphasizing the solid muscles of his legs and back. She knew she shouldn't notice such things, but how could she not? He walked a mere three feet in front of her, naked from the waist up, his breeches practically sewn to his skin. It was sinful. Her mother's reprimand—had the woman been present—to turn away and look in the other direction flitted through Joanna's mind, but she ignored it.

She was on the edge of spinsterhood, not dead!

Mr. Archer reached the back table and grabbed a finely woven white shirt and a black woolen coat from a peg on the wall. He pulled a chair out for Joanna then sat across the table from her, facing the front door of the tavern. Chang placed himself between them, his back against the wall as well.

Joanna's gaze followed the upward path of Archer's fingers as he secured the laces of his shirt. His chest was really quite remarkable. Not that she had a point of reference other than her brother, but for some reason, Randolph's chest had never fascinated her so.

Belatedly, she realized someone was speaking to her—and that someone was Mr. Archer. The man wore an outrageous grin that indicated he knew exactly where she'd been looking and what she'd been thinking. It was bad enough to stare. It was far worse to be *caught*. What was wrong with her? She never behaved so foolishly. Silently cursing her behavior, she turned her eyes toward a dark stain on the wall behind Chang, and pretended she didn't hear Archer chuckle.

"So, sweetness, what can I do for you?"

Using her soberest voice, Joanna tried to put the rogue in his place. "Excuse me, sir, but since we just

13

met, it is impossible for us to be sweet anything. Shall we move forward with my business?"

"Whatever you like, my dear." Out of the corner of his eyes, the man studied Chang. "What's your name?"

"Chang, sir."

"Does your mistress often run amok on the London docks?"

Joanna raised a brow. Archer raised one of his own, then waited for Chang to answer.

"Of course not."

"And you brought her here tonight . . . ?"

"He had no choice," Joanna interjected, miffed that her companion chose to prattle on with her butler when she had more important matters to discuss.

"It best, sir. She stubborn. Hire coach and come with maid, Nixie. Nixie young and slow in head, and—"

"I understand." Archer held up his hand. He turned back to Joanna. "All right, Miss. I have another appointment shortly, so speak your piece."

She barely had time to settle her hands in her lap when a bow-legged man sporting bright red pantaloons, an earring, and a beard braided into three strands, rudely appeared and slapped both hands on the table.

"I've been looking fer ye, Archer. We needs to talk."

Archer leisurely continued to tie the laces of his shirt, a dazzling smile fixed on Joanna. "Don't mind him. He was born under a barnacle. Without the benefit of a mother, he never learned his manners. Go away, Digger. As you can see, I'm busy."

"Ye'll have plenty of time later to court yer whore."

Joanna felt the color drain from her face. A chilling silence fell over the table. A muscle quivered in Mr. Archer's cheek. "Mind yourself, Digger. You're in the presence of a lady."

The Digger fellow shrugged a bony shoulder, then proceeded to speak as if Joanna were not there. "You owe me one hundred pounds."

"Not according to my memory," Archer argued calmly.

"Yer memory's wrong. People expects me to pay them money or deliver a cargo. I ain't got neither. The king's men took my goods." The man was foaming at the mouth like a rabid dog.

"That's not my problem," Mac replied.

Digger reached behind his back. "I'm making it yours."

Before Joanna had time to breathe, let alone scream or climb beneath the table as she was so inclined, Mac had Digger by the throat with one hand and with the other had a pistol aimed right between the little man's beady eyes. The knife clutched in Digger's fingers clattered to the floor. Tension charged the air.

Joanna barely managed to swallow the brick lodged in her throat. "Gentlemen, please. Surely we can settle this without violence. Mr. Digger, if you would only wait, I will be on my way shortly." In fact, she could not complete her business soon enough.

Archer shot her a withering glare, then turned a

bland expression upon his prisoner. If not for the deadly intent in his eyes, she'd have thought he was discussing the color of his new waistcoat, not holding a gun to the man's head. "You fool. Stupidity and cowardice are a bad combination in business. I delivered the goods to you at the place you chose, at the time you chose. You paid me for the delivery. Don't blame me for your inability to escape the king's men. If you hadn't panicked, you could have buoyed your merchandise in the Thames and come back later."

"How did the excise men know the location of our meeting?" Fury and accusation filled Digger's words.

"I've wondered that myself." Archer's eyes narrowed slightly. "But danger's a part of the game. Take up embroidery if you're worried about the constable and his thugs." His voice dropped to a whisper. "Either way, patience with idiots is not my strong suit . . . so I suggest you leave before I change my mind and shoot you where you stand."

When Archer released his stranglehold, Digger tumbled backward. The man's lips curled into a snarl. "You'll be sorry. You ain't heard the last of me. We ain't finished." He shoved his way through the crowd and disappeared.

Joanna's clever plan was unraveling right before her eyes. She needed Archer to help her. Once her heart found a steady rhythm, she managed a whisper. "Dear me. You really should be careful. I think that man means you harm."

Archer turned amused eyes back to her. "A gnat is

more worrisome." He laid his gun on the table. "Now, what were you saying before we were so rudely interrupted?"

"I wish to hire your services."

"I assumed as much. But which services would you like to acquire?"

His question, spoken with a husky drawl and laced with innuendo, momentarily flustered her. No man had ever spoken to her with such familiarity. Though Joanna offered her sternest glare, the rogue continued to smile in a manner that suggested only the most wicked possibilities—those possibilities a decent young woman such as herself only heard about from the upstairs maid.

Joanna's stomach fluttered.

Sitting even taller in her chair, she added a prim edge to her words. "A mutual acquaintance, Lady Rebecca Kerrick, suggested I contact you. As a matter of fact, I feel I already know you. She has talked about you for months. When I mentioned my dilemma, Rebecca said you were exactly what I needed. Of course, she mentioned your tendency to follow rules of your own making. And she said that you could be alternately charming or intolerable—depending on the circumstances. But she also said that you were honorable and trustworthy, and that once you gave your word you would see a task to its very end."

"I'll be sure to thank her for the glowing recommendation."

"I sent you three posts over the last three days.

When you failed to respond, I visited your residence. A servant suggested I try your ship. A man there mentioned an inn called the Pickled Herring. The keeper at the inn said you were here."

Archer nodded. "I've been rather busy lately. You risked a great deal by coming here. You must be desperate, very brave or very, very foolish. It might be interesting to know which."

For the first time since she set down this path, Joanna relaxed. This was exactly the sort of man she needed: astute, compassionate and, aside from the fact that he looked a rogue of the most perilous kind, obviously capable of defending himself. And he had kind eyes. Everything was going to be fine.

"I will guarantee you fifty pounds," she offered.

His mouth thinned ever so slightly.

She quickly added, "I admit my ignorance in all this, but that seems a fair sum. I am prepared to pay one hundred, if need be."

"A mysterious lady spends a stormy afternoon tracking me down, then waltzes into a place she has no business being and offers me a large sum of money. Me, a recommended yet virtual stranger! Makes a man curious," he admitted. He studied the tips of his boots then Joanna. "I'm sure it must be a matter of the utmost importance. Yet there's no need to waste your time or mine haggling over a price. However intriguing, I'm afraid I cannot help you. I'm sorry."

Joanna clutched her sodden parasol to keep from wringing her hands. "That seems highly uncharitable.

A Rogue's Promise

At least hear me out. Rebecca assured me you would help!"

"I'm sure Rebecca meant well, but she has no right to speak for me."

"Where am I to turn now?"

"I have no doubt you'll eventually find someone willing to solve your little problem for you."

"My little problem?" she repeated, exasperated. Her voice was much too loud but she was beyond caring. The man sat there, smiling in that infuriatingly patronizing manner, as though her situation were as trivial as if she were having difficulty choosing the fabric for her bedroom drapes.

According to her mother, a lady never revealed emotion of any kind in public, especially anger. Unfortunately, Joanna's tolerance lessened every day her problems escalated. If she did not resolve her difficulty soon, she would become an ill-mannered shrew rather than the "sensible Joanna" everyone knew and expected. "Little problem? You have no idea the extent of my problem, because you refuse to listen to what I have to say!"

"It can't be helped." He shrugged his shoulders, an indifferent apology. "Come along now. I'll see you to your carriage."

"No, thank you. I have Chang. Besides, I would hate to inconvenience you."

The keen disappointment she felt was her own doing. She always believed in and hoped for the best in people. Chang had once said an evil person would

19

have to toss Joanna to the ground and stomp upon her battered body before she would grasp his true nature. She guessed this was one of those people. But Rebecca had spoken volumes about Mr. Archer and his fine ways. She claimed he had championed those in need many times before. Based upon that information, Joanna had risked her reputation and sought him out. And Mr. Archer, himself,—despite his open appraisal and innuendoes—had seemed so sincere and charming. She had been certain he would help.

Obviously, she was wrong.

She stood and marched toward the exit. Chang followed close behind. Conversation in the tavern waned, but it did not stop altogether.

Whatever was she going to do now?

One thing was certain, she had not come this far to face defeat. MacDonald Archer *would* help her. If only she could persuade him to listen to her proposal.

Stopping midway between Archer and the front door, Joanna squared her shoulders and rapped her parasol on the bar. Voices quieted. "Excuse me. If I may have everyone's attention." She rapped her parasol a second time.

All conversation ceased.

Joanna straightened her shoulders, stood to her full five feet four inches, and cleared her throat. Then she called: "I will pay one hundred pounds to the man I employ here tonight."

Chapter Three

The little hoyden's words caused an uproar. One particularly eager sailor leapt from table to table in his race to the bar, mindless of the food he sent flying. Pewter cups clattered onto their sides, chairs tipped to the floor, and another dozen desperate men with little to lose and much to gain abandoned their seats and ale and followed suit.

Mac hung his head and cursed. Twice. In two languages.

The little voice in his head screamed trouble as he again looked up in dumbfounded shock. Under other circumstances, he might have been inclined to see what the lady had to say, might even offer to help. But he didn't need this complication. Not now. He had problems of his own. Someone was determined to see him thrown in Newgate—or worse, dead. Miss Fenton could see herself in grave danger, if for no other reason than her association with Mac. Besides, he was scheduled to sail for Jamaica in a less than a month—his first legitimate business venture. He didn't need to borrow someone else's troubles, especially those of a featherbrained blue-blooded female member of polite society, a woman whose every whim likely centered on titles, matchmaking and social etiquette.

The subject of his ire braced herself for the onslaught of her prospective employees. Her companion planted himself in front of her, while she clutched her ugly green parasol like a sword. Fat lot of good that would do, thought Mac. If he had any sense, he'd walk right out the door. Then maybe, just maybe, Miss Joanna Fenton might learn a well-needed lesson.

It wasn't to happen. With eyes the size of two small portholes, the hoyden turned a pleading gaze in Mac's direction. There was no hope for it. He'd stolen from kings and commoners alike, shot men in self-defense, even beaten a man near to death, but never in all his life had he stood by and watched a woman suffer. Even if she'd brought it on herself.

"Step aside. Move your arse, Blick." Pushing and shoving men out of his path, Mac fought his way to the hoyden's side. He shot a glare in her companion's direction, just in case the man felt the need to intervene, then snapped at her: "I ought to let you hire one of these thugs and go about my business."

"They are eager," she agreed. He could hear panic threaded through her whispered words. "I had no idea so many men needed employment. But I would much rather hire you. As I said earlier, you come highly recommended. Also, I must confess, based on what Rebecca told me I knew you would come to my rescue."

"Not another word." Cursing again, because it eased his irritation and he felt himself justified, Mac thrust his hands in the air. "Sorry, fellows. There's no job here."

Blick, one of the sailors who had taken an earlier interest in Miss Fenton, lumbered forward. "That's not what I 'eard. She said she'd pay one of us a 'undred pounds."

Several men grunted their agreement. Mac flashed them a conspiratorial grin. "You know better than to trust a lady." He stared pointedly at Miss Fenton. "You don't want to take this job. You don't even know what she wants. I guarantee you it isn't what you think."

"I'd be willin' to do just about anything for a hundred quid." Blick grinned, exposing a mouthful of rotten teeth. "And maybe I can show her new things she wants."

Several other men agreed. They crudely offered up the use of specific body parts, their time, or both. Whatever the lady wanted, they said. They were willing, able, and above all, eager.

Bloody hell, why had the woman said what she had?

The circle tightened. Miss Fenton's chaperon took a step forward in her defense. Damn and blast, Mac thought. Reason wasn't going to work. Not with this group of lugheads. Hadn't the barroom brawl earlier proven that?

He eased his hand onto the pistol in his waistband and whispered into the hoyden's ear, "When I say, I want you to run behind the bar and wait beside that door."

The chit looked indignant, as if he'd asked her to strip and waltz naked on the bar. She probably didn't want to crouch on the floor in this place. Perhaps she wasn't such a hoyden, after all. Leave it to a *lady* to worry about her precious sensibilities when her body was in danger.

The chit's butler put his hands up to hold back the tide of sailors. Blick knocked him out of the way.

Mac lifted his pistol into the air for them all to see. Then, for insurance, he leveled the weapon at the crowd. "As I said, gents, the job is taken."

Grumbling and whispers spread through the throng.

Without waiting for them to gather courage, Mac swept Miss Fenton behind the bar to the narrow door he'd indicated earlier. It led to a private room. He figured her companion, who was too damn old with far too much starch in his silk trousers to be of any real help, was smart enough to follow.

Safely in the room, she ran her hands over her rumpled gown. "Was it really necessary to brandish your weapon?" she asked.

"Yes," he snapped. He was losing his patience with this . . . woman. For all he knew, the chit had just escaped Bedlam. Certainly no *sane* female would strut into a tavern with an ancient Chinaman as her sole protector. And Mac refused to consider that she might have a truly desperate problem. Likely she was what he had first surmized; a bored debutante, out for adventure.

Well, there was no time like the present to end such insanity once and for all. Mac crossed his arms over his chest, setting his mouth and narrowing his eyes. He'd used this particular scowl to intimidate his crew any number of times; it would send this chit scurrying back to where she belonged—in her polite society drawing rooms.

"Now listen well. Those men are nothing more than a parcel of cutthroats. You wouldn't last an hour in their care. I understand that you feel you have some great need, some problem that seems insurmountable, but I won't take the job. I don't care if the prince regent recommended my services. Nor will you hire any of those men out there. Go home, Miss Fenton. To your lace doilies, silver teaspoons and titled gentlemen, where you belong."

A tiny thing, she barely reached his shoulder. Yet she lifted her chin into the air with the same dignity of a queen of England, displaying more courage than most men he knew. He felt an unwelcome spark of admiration.

Then she did the unthinkable. She shook her head. "Not until you at least listen to what I have to say."

No one defied him when he was being so intimidating! Mac added a snarl to his already dangerous glare.

"*Please*," she asked.

Her whispered plea battered his resolve. Fine. He would listen to what she had to say, appease his conscience, then dump Miss Fenton and her companion in her carriage. He led her to the sole table and chairs in the center of the room. "Sit down."

"There is no need to be rude, sir."

"Pardon me, but I find such blatant manipulation offensive."

She seemed hurt by his accusation. "I would never stoop to such tactics without just cause. My friend said you were the one man who could help me. I asked for a simple favor, and you refused. I just thought if you knew more . . ."

Blast it! Mac disliked the thought that he'd upset her. He must be going soft in the head. He paced back and forth between the room's liquor cabinet and its small dirty window, wondering why he cared. It wasn't as if Miss Joanna Fenton was the usual type of female that attracted his attention. She wasn't quite like any type he'd ever seen.

She wore a drab olive-green jacket and gown adorned with numerous ruffles. Her matching parasol, as he'd noted earlier, was downright ugly. A wilted daisy was pinned to her lapel.

The color of her hair was hard to determine, because she wore a hat equally ugly as her parasol, but judging from a stray curl hanging about her face he guessed it to be honey-blond. A smattering of freckles dusted her nose and cheeks, adding a peach blush to her skin. Delicate brows arched over silver-blue eyes that reminded him of the wild seas off the coast of Ireland.

Except for those eyes, she had a quiet face. It was certainly not the kind one first noticed in a room full of beauties, but it was attractive nonetheless. If one took the time to really look.

Perhaps all that was why he was still listening; this girl was unique, a puzzle. And Mac loved puzzles almost as much as he loved women and the sea. One minute Miss Joanna Fenton seemed ready to battle Attila the Hun, the next she looked all bloody vulnerable, her gaze a mix of desperation and determination. Blast. He stood stock still, growing more afraid he was about to make her problems his. It was bloody annoying. "I said sit," he repeated. "Please."

With a nervous glance Miss Fenton removed her cape, then settled into the preferred chair with the same efficiency all young ladies of well-bred families perfected by the age of eight: a quiet swish of the skirts with no extraneous movements, her back ramrod straight, her hands folded in the lap. Her manners reminded him of her breeding. And of their current surroundings. What was this young woman doing here? Regardless of his own bloody rules, he found himself curious to know more.

He was *definitely* losing his mind.

"Excuse me, sir. Are you going to pace all night long, or shall I explain *why* I need to hire you?"

Mac poured himself a whiskey, crossed to the table and chairs, then sat. "Where's your husband?"

"I am not married."

"What about your father?"

"He died over a year ago."

The situation grew more worrisome by the moment. "Don't tell me your mother is dead as well."

"As a matter of fact—" When he scowled again, her expression turned grim. "I do have a mother, however she would have fainted before the carriage ever reached Ratcliff Highway. She is delicate. Mother also believes she can think problems into non-existence. Her primary concern at the moment is making a prosperous match for my sister Penelope. After all, good marriages are the cornerstone of London society."

Mac knew all about the *Ton*'s obsession with title. "What about brothers? Uncles? Cousins?"

"My uncles are far too old, my cousins too young. I do have a brother, but—"

"Why isn't *he* here, then?" Mac hadn't meant to bellow. It was just that he knew he was sinking deeper into trouble. Hers.

"My brother is the reason I am here. Randolph is missing." The chit pulled a handkerchief from the wristband of her dress. Without a thought, she dipped the linen in the alcohol he'd earlier poured himself and reached for Mac's right hand.

He yanked his fingers from hers. "What the devil are you doing?"

"Do you want those scratches to become infected? During his travels, my father discovered spirits were beneficial as an antiseptic," she answered.

28

He slowly slipped his hand back into hers. Let her play the nursery nanny and tell her story. Her kindness would not affect his decision.

"This will sting a little," she added.

He leaned back in his chair and watched the chit dab whiskey to his cuts with straightforward and efficient movements. It had been a very long time since a woman had tended his wounds. His ship's first mate usually handled such tasks. Mac decided he preferred the gentler touch.

Miss Fenton's hands were small with delicate fingers, the kind born to hold tiny porcelain teacups. By comparison, his hands were giant, tanned and callused and meant for hard labor. It reminded him again that she came from a different world.

Mac skirted the periphery of polite society. He smuggled their fancy goods to them and handled their particularly unsavory business details, entered their hallowed halls now and again, even had good friends among the *Ton*. But no matter how much money he possessed, he'd never be fully accepted. Not that he minded. His life suited him just fine.

He'd made the mistake once—fallen in love with one Lady Daphne, the daughter of a marquis—and learned his lesson: he hadn't a title, and therefore he wasn't a man a daughter of Society brought home to her father. After that, he'd contented himself to lust for the ladies of the *Ton*, but promised his heart to the sea. He'd been twenty. Still, the bitter memory lingered.

Sure, he bedded his fair share of the ladies: widows, bored wives whose husbands kept mistresses, women who knew exactly what they wanted from the likes of him. When they were willing, so was he. Virgins and young ladies fresh from the schoolroom were off limits, though. And Miss Fenton was as innocent as they came. That reason alone made him wary to hear her out. "A Bow Street runner would be better equipped to handle a missing person."

Miss Fenton shook her head. "I hired a runner. He did nothing more than spend my money. Money I do not have. Then he concluded that my brother was likely at the bottom of the Thames. After a great deal of worry and considerable thinking, I realized I need someone who lives and moves in less desirable circles. To be blunt, someone like you. You are after all . . . a thief."

Mac felt indignant all the way to his boots. He wasn't a common pickpocket! Not that it mattered what this lady thought. He pulled his hand free of hers, deciding her tender care was addling his brain. "I'm a free trader. I steal from no one."

"A minor point."

"Not to me, it's not."

"Then I concede. You are a free trader." She lifted her shoulder and muttered, "Though the last time I checked, a free trader is circumventing the king's law and is thereby stealing from him."

Mac managed to contain his annoyance. Barely. He leaned forward and lowered his voice to a whisper.

"Why don't you continue with your story."

"With nowhere else to turn, I shared my burdens with Lady Kerrick. Although you claim not to be a thief, she mentioned you have informants and the like throughout London who might have access to information I need. She also says you have some skills a thief might have, such as picking locks—though I hope we have no need for such trickery, because that would mean we were entering where we did not rightfully belong and I do not condone such—"

"You're rambling."

"Am I?" When he nodded, she whispered ruefully, "I tend to talk too much when unnerved."

He gave her a hard look. "Do I make you nervous, Miss Fenton?"

"As a matter of fact, you do. But nothing will stop me from asking you to help me. If you would only let me explain."

"You have five minutes more."

"That is hardly fair."

He pulled a gold watch from his pocket with his free hand. "You're wasting time."

Irritation flitted across her eyes before she buried the emotion in those stormy seas of blue. "My father was a historical scholar of sorts. Years ago, while visiting China, he happened upon an ancient artifact, a gold jeweled dragon, which he took. It was his prize possession. Unfortunately, in these last few years, our family has come close to financial ruin. We had several difficulties on the estate and one thing led to another, and now with father gone I find we are on the verge of bankruptcy. Selling the statue seemed the most logical solution. I scheduled an auction a month from today. Emissaries from the British Museum were even planning to attend. Unfortunately, the statue disappeared a fortnight ago. My brother vanished one day later."

Mac envisioned the chit traipsing throughout London, searching for her brother and her bauble, and shuddered. There was no doubt in his mind that she would do just that. Or hire scum like those outside. It was fine for him to fraternize with their likes, but her—she'd likely get herself hurt, or worse. He asked, "How do you intend to pay me the one hundred pounds?"

"I thought, perhaps, you might work on credit—until the statue is found and sold."

He took to pacing the room once again. "How old is your brother?"

"Twenty-four."

"I understand your concern, but many young men lose their common sense along with their allowances and the ability to hold their liquor. Many are stupid with it."

"I understand that—"

He continued, interrupting her: "Is it irresponsible? Yes. Nevertheless, it is a timeless male ritual—one even I practiced, thankfully for only a short period of my life. Your brother is probably too busy drinking, gambling and—well, never mind what else—to remember to come home."

Miss Fenton placed her hand on his elbow. "Randolph might use faulty judgment from time to time, is sometimes too idealistic for his own good, a bit gullible perhaps, but he is a kind man and the viscount. He would not just go off drinking and disappear. And I would never forgive myself if something happened to him. Too, it does not explain the disappearance of our statue."

"I know nothing of Chinese artifacts."

"But, if it were stolen, you would know where to look." The chit pulled a scrap of paper from her purse. "All the rest, everything you said about my brother, crossed my mind until I found this in his coat pocket."

The note was short and to the point, scripted on an ordinary piece of foolscap with black ink.

Deliver the goods or die.

A serpent coiled about a stake was stamped into a glob of red sealing wax at the bottom.

Chapter Four

The four-foot by four-foot cubicle that served as entryway for the rooming house smelled of mildew and urine. Mac glanced over his shoulder toward his longtime friend and all around good sport. Adam Hawksmore, the fifth earl of Kerrick, shifted a pile of rubbish with his polished boot. A rat the size of a soup tureen scurried from beneath the filth and disappeared through a hole in the wall. Thank goodness this visit would be short.

Adam's brow wrinkled with disgust. "Lovely accommodations. I assume you have a good reason for delaying our departure for the theatre?"

"Business."

"Of course." His friend paused then added, "I worry about you."

34

Mac veered toward the narrow stairway, gun in hand. "There's no need."

"That's why we're about to creep up an inhospitable nothing of a stairway in an unsavory part of St. Giles with pistols drawn? I feel so much better now that you reminded me."

Mac chuckled, though he felt anything but cheerful. After another thirty minutes of discussion with Miss Fenton, he had dumped her and her butler in their carriage with the promise to visit them tomorrow. He hadn't yet decided whether to keep the appointment. If Miss Fenton's brother had met with foul play, she was better off going to the authorities. The problem was, Mac knew she believed otherwise. His life suddenly seemed more complicated than it had been a few hours earlier.

Stopping by home, he'd changed into his evening clothes, then gathered Adam for one quick errand before they would go and suffer through the latest production of *Romeo and Juliet* where Rebecca would cry, Adam would console his wife, and Mac would wish he were back at the Pig-'N'-Whistle. "Well, don't worry about me. I'm smart enough to bring you along when I get into scraper, aren't I?"

"So you *do* expect trouble. Splendid. My wife can yell at us when we arrive at the theatre bloodied and bruised. Rebecca happens to prefer my body intact. As a matter of fact, since I retired from the military, I prefer the same."

Mac grimaced. "Though I have the utmost faith in your ability to soothe your wife should such a situation occur, I don't anticipate trouble. I need to have a short conversation with a sewer rat, nothing more. It just pays to be safe."

"Sounds even better."

Mac ignored his friend's sarcasm and slowly climbed the first flight of stairs.

Adam followed. "You need a new line of work. According to Knox, you barely escaped the revenue men the other night. That makes three times now."

"Keeping track, are you?"

"Someone had best, since you don't seem to care and since these incidents appear to be more than coincidental. What happened this time?"

Shrugging as if the whole episode had been an everyday occurrence, Mac said, "Same as last. We had barely unloaded the cargo when the constable and his men rode in."

"Have you considered that someone is setting you up?"

He gave his friend a hard look. "The thought crossed my mind. That's why we're here. I couldn't talk about it last time I saw this rat, but I mean to bait a trap tonight."

Adam raised an eyebrow. "If someone *is* setting you up, why bother? You could be caught or even killed. Forget this nonsense. You certainly don't need the money."

"A man who worked for me died a few weeks back

when the constable came. I hate unfinished business. If my luck holds, I will catch the bastard responsible just before I officially join the esteemed ranks of legitimate trade. It's a bloody shame, but thanks to Patrick Colquhoun and his ogglers, a man can hardly smuggle anything into the city anymore on the river. And the talk of fairer taxation won't help matters."

"The Prince Regent is pleased with Colquhoon's river police. Were you aware that Lord Dorridge is the one pushing for all the reforms in the House of Lords? He's requested more men and even participated in a few raids. One might think he hasn't forgiven you for bedding his wife."

"He hasn't forgiven me for proving him a coward," Mac agreed.

"Just be careful."

A smile curled Mac's lip. He and Adam were as close as brothers. They had saved one another's neck more times than either could count. When Adam returned from France last year and had been branded a traitor, they'd worked together to clear his name. Somewhere along the way, Adam had fallen in love with Rebecca—had toppled like a hundred-year-old oak. Now, he was a happily married man, determined to see that Mac altered his own lifestyle as well. He was worse than an interfering old woman. And his wife wasn't much better. And worst of all was Edward, Rebecca's father: He was a pain in the arse who hounded Mac constantly. "You sound just like Edward."

Adam hesitated mid-step. His gaze turned thoughtful.

An alarm sounded in Mac's brain. "What is it? Edward? That man has plagued me with questions and moralizing ever since I met him. What has he done now?"

Clearing his throat, Adam studied a brown stain on the ceiling overhead. "Edward believes he has found your father—a Lord Henry Belgrave, the earl of Fairfax."

"Everlasting bloody blasted hell! I don't give a shark's tooth about some stranger who abandoned my mother before I was even born. Who does Edward think he is, sticking his nose in my business? Blasted meddling—"

"If memory serves, you were thrilled to have Edward interfere in *my* affairs."

"That was different. You were trying to clear your name."

Adam snorted. "No need to cob on, my friend. And we don't know for certain if this Fairfax is your sire. If by some perverse twist of fate he is, well . . . maybe there is a reasonable explanation for his leaving your mother. Edward worries about you and would like to see you happy."

Mac buried his bitterness. Yelling at Adam accomplished nothing. "From the moment we met, that old man has badgered me about my heritage and my mother's birthplace. He keeps spouting nonsense about a familiarity to my features. Well, good intentions or no, he could present the king of England to me as my long-lost papa and I would turn about and leave. It is too late to play father and son with any man."

Taking the second flight of stairs two at a time, Mac added, "And everyone can bloody stop worrying about me. Let's finish this."

"Are you certain your man is here?" Adam called as he followed.

"The barkeep next door said he dragged a maid and a bottle out the door a short while ago. I imagine he's come home. Let's see what he's up to."

"Indubitably nothing of merit," was his friend's sole reply.

Mac stopped beside a broken window on the landing, glanced outside. "By the by, did you know your wife was going to recommend my services to a Miss Joanna Fenton? She went as far as to convince Miss Fenton that I was a common thief."

Adam laughed. "I'm sure it was difficult—considering you know all manner of thieves from the rookery, how to open locked doors with a pick, and how to deal in stolen goods. Did Rebecca tell Miss Fenton that you broke into a man's house not less than three months ago?"

"If I remember correctly, I was acting on your orders."

"And a smashing job you did, too." Adam leaned over and peered out the window Mac was staring through, then he added, "From what Rebecca said, I think you can help Miss Fenton."

Mac sighed. "What do you know?"

Adam shook his head. "Not much. Miss Fenton and my wife became friends while I was in France. I've only met her once, but she seems a nice young lady. I take it you know about her father's treasure?" He waited for Mac to nod. "Well, then you also know Miss Fenton was planning to sell it. An article described the statue in great detail and announced the auction in the *Times* weeks ago. Some say the piece is worth over three thousand pounds."

Mac tsked. "Every crook in London probably has an eye on that prize."

"To be sure," Adam agreed. "So, will you help her?"

Mac started up a third flight of stairs, more quietly this time. "I haven't decided. She gave me the distinct impression she would not take no for an answer. Perhaps I'll go tomorrow and at least hear her out."

He stopped at the top of the stairs and peered around the corner. Six closed doors lined the hallway. The muffled sounds of a man and a woman engaged in a shouting match drifted from behind the door nearest them. Cold air wafted through another broken window near the end of the corridor. He looked back and saw Adam pull his coat more snugly about his neck.

"Which room?" his friend asked.

"According to my sources, Digger occupies the room at the very end. Shall we see?"

The floorboards creaked as they walked forward,

flickering candles in cracked wall lamps lighting their way. Placing his ear to the final door, Mac heard muffled grunts and groans. Bracing himself, he tried the door. The knob turned easily in his hand.

The scene that greeted him epitomized Digger's ignoble existence: The man's bare ass vigorously pumped between a pair of plump thighs. The fool hadn't even bothered doffing his shoes or trousers, which were down around his ankles. The girl's dress was tossed carelessly above her waist.

Shaking his head, Mac cleared his throat.

The gyrating buttocks slowed then stilled altogether. Digger glanced over his shoulder. Realizing he had company, he rolled to the floor and stood, dragging his trousers up as he went. "What the hell do you want?"

Mac tossed a coin to the girl and jerked his head. She righted her clothing and scampered from the sparsely furnished room.

"Do you need any help?" Adam called from the doorway.

"Just keep your eyes open."

Blocking any escape, Adam braced his feet apart, his pistol aimed at Digger's groin. "Gladly."

The black marketeer glared from side to side. "What do you want? We ain't got no business to discuss right now."

"No warm welcome? No good-evening? Shame on you, Digger. Can't a friend stop by for a visit? Tell me, where did you go after you lost your goods last night?"

"Ain't none of yer business."

Slamming Digger against the wall, Mac aimed his pistol at the man's head. "That's where you're wrong."

"What's the matter with you? Where I go ain't your busi—"

"Since the king's men have tried to intercept my cargo several times, and since I lost one of my crewmen to them, I find I am suddenly concerned with all my business associates, their whereabouts and their friends."

"I ain't done nothing." Digger's eyes shifted nervously, then the fool stuck his chin out another inch. "Yet."

"Amazing," Adam said from the doorway. "Most people know to never threaten the person holding the gun."

Mac stared at the quivering criminal he held by the neck. If Digger knew more and was somehow involved, he'd hang himself soon enough. Mac tightened his grip on the man's throat. "You best be telling the truth. I intend to find out what happened, if I've been set up. I have one last shipment due to you at the end of the week, then I'm finished. Forever. If I find out you've done anything that affects my business, me, or anyone close to me; or if I find you have plans to see me in Newgate, Tyburn or Hell; you'll regret it." He thrust Digger away.

"Does this mean we can go?" Adam asked as Mac swept past. He followed, saying, "Please be sure to invite me again. What fun this was—though I have no desire to see another man's bare arse anytime soon. Especially one quite so ugly." They were halfway to the ground floor when he noted, "I liked the gun to the head, though. Nice touch."

"Stow it," Mac snapped.

At last, when tension finally gave way to laughter at Adam's continued commentary, two questions trumped the rest. Who was behind the raids on his shipments? And why?

"Were you frightened?" Penelope asked as she knelt before the row of brass bird cages hanging above the window seat in the parlor. She scooped small amounts of birdseed into porcelain dishes, her excitement palpable. And exhausting. "I still can't believe you went to such a place. Chang must have been absolutely green. Does Mr. Archer wear a patch over one eye? What color is his hair? Do you think he's stolen very much?"

Impatience joined the already present weariness tightening Joanna's neck and shoulders. She had slept little, knowing she must wake at the break of dawn to deal with a list of tasks before noon. She glanced from the brightly colored bird perched on her finger to her sister's eager smile, reminding herself that their current predicament was not Penelope's fault.

"Mr. Archer is not a pirate or a thief but a free trader," Joanna corrected. "They are altogether different." How they were different still mostly escaped Joanna, but her sister had talked about nothing else for the last hour. Joanna repeated Mr. Archer's very own words in hopes her sister would switch to another topic.

In anticipation of some grand revelation, Penelope leaned forward on the window seat, her chin tucked in her hands. "Is he handsome?"

The unbidden image of a tanned muscular chest and broad shoulders crept into Joanna's mind. She thought it best to keep her own heart-stopping reaction to Mr. Archer to herself . . . else Penelope would never change the subject. Besides, her sister needed to concentrate on respectable young men who stood to inherit money or property, or perhaps even both. At the moment, the marquis of Westcliff led the pack of candidates. "I imagine there are women with no common sense who think so."

Penelope sighed dreamily. "I wager he's divine."

With a kiss to the bird's beak, Joanna slipped the family's tiny nightingale back into its cage. "He is just a man like all others. A discovery you will make for yourself as you search for a husband is that no one is divine."

"They say a woman's love transforms a man," her sister proposed.

"Penelope, I do not believe you should enter marriage thinking to change someone. . . . Hopefully, you will find a gentleman who loves you with all his heart, and, if you are very lucky, you will feel the same for him—shortcomings and all."

"My husband shall be a veritable prince among men. And I cannot wait to meet Mr. Archer."

Joanna sighed. Her words of wisdom had proven ineffectual against the youth and optimism of Penelope's seventeen years. Men were men, though her sister did not realize it. So, why did her own stomach flutter at the thought of seeing Mr. Archer again? Goodness, she was being as silly as Penelope. She squelched the reaction and scanned the stack of bills she had yet to sort. "Mr. Archer may not even come today."

"But you said . . ."

"I know what I said. But the truth is it would not surprise me if he changed his mind and fled for the high seas this morning."

"Crumpet cakes!" Penelope waved her hand in the air. "You are absolutely the best person in the world. You always manage to right the wrongs."

Since she'd released much of the staff, the intended compliment only served Joanna as a reminder of the upstairs lamps in need of new wicks, the broken window in the servant's quarters, and the basket of sewing beside her bed. Not to mention the quarterly bills, the social invitations to accept and decline, the food selection for the dinner party they had no business hosting— Oh, bother! Joanna grew weary just thinking of all she had to do. There was no time to dally.

"Penelope? Time to go." Lady Caroline Fenton's impatient summons carried down the stairs and into the salon.

45

"Drat. I shan't be able to meet Mr. Archer," Penelope whispered sadly. "And I can already tell Mother is in one of her moods. She will parade me from one end of Mayfair to the other and back again."

Joanna crossed to the nearest table, gathered the scattered books there and stacked them into a neat pile. "She wants you to make the best possible match."

"I want that as well. She is just so—"

"Relentless?" Joanna suggested wryly.

"And tyrannical, tenacious, unyielding, presumptuous."

With a giggle, Joanna added, "She loves us."

As if on cue, Lady Fenton waltzed into the study in a cloud of silvery blue silk. The family cat, Confucius, was fast on her heels. He pranced in like the arrogant beast he was, a mouse dangling from his mouth. He rarely missed a meal or the opportunity to torment Joanna and Penelope's mother.

Lady Fenton muttered a crude threat, witnessed her daughters' grins, and frowned. "That cat is a brute. I should have buried him with your father when I had the chance. Either that or shipped him back to that Chinese prince fellow." She nudged the cat with her toe. "Shoo. Go away."

"He earns his keep quite nicely and enjoys sharing his trophies with you," Joanna said. "I think he wants you to praise him."

As if in agreement, Confucius plopped to the floor and dropped his dead mouse directly on Caroline Fenton's blue satin slipper.

Joanna's mother screeched, leapt backward, and glared at the cat. "Praise, indeed! Good kitty. Would you like a little arsenic in your evening meal?"

Penelope giggled. "Deep down, you know Confucius loves you."

"I wish he loved someone else and would leave me alone."

Gingerly sidestepping the mouse, Caroline Fenton tugged on her gloves as she crossed to her younger daughter. "Stand up and let me see." When Penelope stood and did a pirouette, Caroline beamed. "You look lovely." She turned to Joanna. "What do you have planned for the day?"

Joanna considered her answer carefully. Her mother surely preferred to know as little as possible about her errant son and the missing statue; dealing with problems had never been her strong suit. Joanna had lived with the behavior so long that she barely questioned it anymore. Her parents had married by arrangement.

Caroline had always been a socialite. She had accompanied her husband on his travels for many years, but deep down, she'd resented his inattentiveness and her own forced absence from London. She'd grown more and more withdrawn. Her older daughter had noticed. When her husband became the viscount and the family returned to England, she'd regained some happiness—and, in fact, vowed never to leave again. Her determination to earn a place in London trumped all else. Aside from the love of her children. She'd left all other responsibilities to her husband. Who had in turn been focused on his studies. It had fallen to Joanna to take care of much of the upkeep of the estate and the family finances—which was difficult since she couldn't not control her parents' spending.

Her father's death had exacerbated the problem, leaving Joanna with even more responsibility. The recent trip to London and Penelope's season had restored the spark to her mother's eye that had been absent since Joanna's own failed season. Of course, that meant Caroline had started spending once again. Joanna had been overjoyed to see her mother's happiness return, and had done her best to keep the family from bankruptcy.

But then Randolph had disappeared.

And the statue was stolen.

And creditors were beginning to bang on the door.

But it was better if her mother knew as little as possible about all that. There was little she could do that Joanna couldn't, and there was no point in her knowing the steps Joanna was taking.

Crossing the room, Joanna grabbed the dead mouse by the tail and made her way to the window. She sent the rodent outside with a flick of her wrist. Confucius followed, leaping out directly behind to intercept the treat in midair. Joanna slammed the window shut.

"Pity we weren't on the second floor," Caroline muttered.

"Shame on you." Joanna's scold gave way to laughter.

Her mother adjusted the flowered creation on her

head. "What have you planned for today?" she repeated.

"After I finish the additional invitations for our dinner party, I plan to visit Lord Tatterton. And Mr. Archer is scheduled to visit."

"I know you mean well, but your brother is like your father. He will return home when he is good and ready. I see no need of bothering to hire someone to help us. Instead, you should accompany us on our ride. Or to Almack's later tonight."

Joanna covered her worry with a smile. "Thank you, but I prefer not to."

Her mother patted her cheek. "I know you do. Pity. If only things had been different."

Joanna often wished the same thing. She felt the twinge of the envy that had plagued her since her failed season when she had been led astray by a lord with a golden tongue. Like sorrow for so many of her abandoned hopes, she willed the emotion away. Foolish daydreams were for young girls with choices left to be made. Her time had already come and gone.

Her sister, on the other hand, was touted as one of this season's young jewels by the lady patronesses of Almack's, and stood a good chance of securing a wonderful match. Joanna intended to do everything in her power to make that happen, which included keeping scandal at bay.

"I enjoy running the household," she equivocated. "Besides, you have enough to worry about with Penelope's social calendar. You don't need me tagging along."

Her mother sighed. "True. I intend to negotiate a magnificent match for your sister tonight." She marched toward the door, her smile bright and cunning as she likely considered some ploy to use on an unsuspecting matron. "We best be off then. One must be prompt, you know."

Chapter Five

Standing in the open doorway, unmoved by the erratic gusting of a cool April wind, Chang leveled on Mac a withering glare. "You have reason for being late?"

Mac eyed the Chinaman, trying to decide if the man were relieved by his arrival, disappointed by it, or was simply being a pain in the arse. Likely the latter. Mac had a distinct impression Miss Joanna Fenton's servant disapproved of her plan to hire him. He placed his coat upon Chang's waiting arm. "As a matter of fact, I was detained elsewhere."

"Confucius say, when summoned by princess, a great man start without waiting for carriage."

"Really. Well, according to MacDonald Archer, a loose-lipped fool usually wipes the floor with his face. Shall we?"

Bristling at the half-joking threat, the butler whirled on his heel and led Mac toward the back of the house.

As he walked Mac studied the tidy surroundings, fashionable though not lavishly decorated. Bright splashes of color were everywhere, and glimpses of China, India and Egypt. Two ornate vases on pedestals displayed grotesque creatures with bulging eyes and bulbous noses. If they resembled the missing statue, Mac thought, the Fentons might do best to leave their golden dragon stolen. The depicted creatures were enough to make a person ill.

All thought of stolen art vanished when Mac entered the conservatory. It was the size of a small shop on Bond Street, and flowers bloomed everywhere. In the corner of the room, surrounded by sunbeams, a dozen potted primroses and a walls of wisteria, stood Miss Fenton. Her nimble fingers pruned brilliant white blooms from a plant and placed them in a brass vase on a workbench beside her.

Hues of copper and gold flashed through her unbound hair which cascaded down her back. Her feet were bare beneath another faded gown. She turned, staring outdoors at a small bird. An enormous beige cat sprawled beside her locked his own hungry gaze on the same bird. Joanna's eyelids drifted shut, and she dreamily inhaled the perfume from the flower in her hand.

Mac's gut clenched at the vision. Rarely did people or situations surprise him. Today he was totally unprepared for his reaction. Miss Fenton had quite stolen his breath away. He gathered it again for a quip: "Why, I believe I've found a rose amongst the thistles."

Miss Fenton's eyes snapped open. Her vase of white flowers spilled to the floor, followed by a stack of papers and a book. Her hands hurried to confine her hair in a knot as she dropped to the floor, scrambling to gather the tiny spilled blooms. "Mr. Archer, you startled me! I did not expect you."

"If I remember correctly, we had an appointment."

"True, but when you failed to arrive in a timely fashion this morning, I thought you'd purposely forgot."

Pink tinged her cheeks. Though the admission obviously embarrassed her, Mac found her honesty refreshing. His past experiences with ladies of the *Ton* had led him to believe them all practiced liars.

Trying to make light of the situation, like a highflying nob he slapped a hand to his chest and trilled in mock outrage. "You wound me that you thought I would ignore your plea for help."

She looked skeptical. "I stand corrected. But if you recall, you were less than enthusiastic about my proposition last night. In fact, when we returned home, I told Chang you had probably agreed to come today just to be rid of us—and that once we removed ourselves from your sight, you would disappear indefinitely."

Mac nearly winced. That *had* been his original plan. Especially before talking to Adam. Somewhere between midnight and the early shades of dawn, though, while he tossed and turned, haunted by the vulnerability in this Miss Fenton's deep blue eyes, he had changed his mind. After that, he'd fallen asleep and slept like a babe.

When he woke, he'd excused his change of heart to the notion that searching out Miss Fenton's brother and her missing statue would provide an interesting diversion until he sailed for Jamaica—while he was also trying to discover who had set up his crew. Then, while sipping his Turkish coffee, he'd admitted he was bored. Restless. In a way, that had nothing to do with the events of the last few weeks. He had been for months. Which had led him to the main reason he'd decided to appear here at the Fenton residence today: Miss Fenton intrigued him in a way no female had managed for some time. Perhaps there was some way he could both solve her problem and keep her from being sucked into his.

He glanced toward Chang who hovered in the arched doorway. "This family's faith in me warms me to my toes."

The stony-faced butler nodded curtly. "I bring tea," he said, then disappeared.

Mac circled a small iron chair, then knelt on the bricked area beside his hostess. "So, what would you have done had I not come?"

"Tried to find you again and change your mind."

He moved closer to her. "I thought as much." A lone curl had evaded her hasty attempt to tidy her hair. He gently fingered the silky strand. "Beautiful."

The chit's eyes rounded in wonder and . . . something else. Confusion, astonishment or disbelief, maybe a little of all three? Mac wasn't sure.

"My hair is quite ordinary. Most people call it brown."

"Dirt is brown. London streets are brown. The hull of my ship is brown. Your hair is more like fine Scotch whisky."

"Please, Mr. Archer. Regardless of what you might think, such tactics—and I confess I do not understand their purpose—are wasted on me. I am not a vacuous female who swoons over unfounded compliments. There are women who deserve, believe, even desire, sweet words from men. In fact, my mother and sister are swayed by such rubbish. I, however, am not—"

"Miss Fenton!" Mac interrupted. He was surprised by her reaction. "*All* women need a compliment now and again—and mine was well founded. You *do* have beautiful hair. And I assure you, I know women and whisky."

"You obviously consumed an entire bottle on your way here," she retorted. "Either that, or one fell on your head. Perhaps that is the reason you were late today."

Amused by her vehemence, he winked. "Truth be told, I must admit that I had no intention of coming today—you were right earlier. So . . . I'm rather pleased that I managed to navigate my way here at all, considering." He paused. "My better judgment told me you were a handful, but curiosity forced my hand. You intrigue me."

"You will help me?"

"I give you my word."

Another curl escaped Miss Fenton's makeshift bun. Her cheeks glowed the same shade of red as the roses in another pot on the nearby table. Mac suddenly saw an intelligent, gentle-bred woman insecure in who she was and maybe even who she wanted to be. Devil take it, the girl had no idea what a fetching piece she was! Even more astonishing was the affect she was having on him.

He finished his explanation with, "If I choose, Miss Fenton, I'll shower you with praise at every opportunity."

"I did not hire you to shower me with anything."

"Nevertheless, I have decided to do just that. And there is little you can do about it. I'm no weak-kneed Milquetoast who feels constrained by society's hammer-headed rules. Sometimes, I know what a woman needs more than she does."

He was pleased to see that if her mouth fell open any farther, Miss Fenton would be able to swallow her songbird. He found himself grinning like a bloody fool.

Seeing the book that had fallen to the floor earlier, he reached for it. "Socrates? Lofty reading, but a tad boring for my taste."

Lines formed across Miss Fenton's brow as she frowned.

"Such shock," he continued, enjoying the response. "I'll reveal another secret. Even a few of we criminals

56

read. You surprise me, though. Few women in polite circles would claim to know *how* to read, let alone select subject matter other than the social pages of the *Times*."

"Perhaps I was using the book as a temporary desk upon which to write my correspondence," she snapped.

"I don't think so. Somehow this choice in reading material suits you."

She surprised him yet again by averting her gaze to the floor, but not before Mac noted a fresh spot of color darkening her cheeks. He cupped her chin in his hand and forced her face toward his. His earlier mischievous humor evaporated. He said soberly, "Curiosity and intelligence are never reasons to hide your eyes." He looked around at the room and the flowers she'd been cutting. "Now, what were you doing here?"

She glanced around. "Since many gentlemen have taking to wearing gardenias on a daily basis, I supply several of the shops on Bond Street. Their generosity allows me to maintain my hobby."

"Generosity, nothing. They're smart businessmen. You should probably double what you're charging." He looked at her surreptitiously. "These blooms are exquisite."

She was momentarily flustered, though pride shone in her eyes. Then Miss Fenton cleared her throat and said, "Thank you." After another moment she added, "The Chinese believe the gardenia represents feminine grace and artistry."

"Then *you* should wear one on a daily basis rather than that collection of sour-faced gents." He tucked a gardenia behind her ear. "Lovely."

He held a finger to her lips when she started to object, then glanced about the room. "So, all this is yours?"

"Aside from a small portion that Chang uses. He grows all manner of herbs for medicinal purposes."

As if summoned, the Chinese butler appeared over the edge of a settee, a tea tray in his hands and censure in his eyes. He obviously disapproved of their close proximity. "Most people hold conversation in chair. Tea ready."

"Guard dog *and* butler? A charming combination," Mac answered.

With a suspicious grunt, Chang deposited the tea service on the nearby table, pivoted on his heel and moved back to his vantage point at the door.

Chuckling, Mac gathered the balance of Joanna's papers as she collected her remaining spilled flowers. He stood, extending his hand. As she took it, he felt that several calluses covered the tender flesh of her palm. He'd wager her sister and mother bore no such marks. Admiration and irritation warred with one another.

Chang tapped his foot several times.

Reluctantly, Mac released Miss Fenton's hand. "I believe your chaperon dislikes me. Do you think the tea is safe?"

She cocked her head to the side. "Though Chang

grows several poisonous herbs, he has yet to kill any-one. Of course, I imagine there is a first time for every-thing."

"Well done, Miss Fenton. You managed to smile *and* tease me all in one breath. Or were you flirting?"

The chit sobered instantly. "I should say not. Green girls with no sense of propriety engage in such flirta-tions."

Joanna settled in a chair opposite the man respon-sible for the traitorous emotions laying siege to her good sense. Flirting, indeed!

Yet she had to admit he looked every inch the gentle-man, sitting there with one leg crossed over the other, his arm casually draped across the back of his chair. His tan breeches and finely cut sable coat, both obviously sewn by a skilled tailor, were simple, elegant and straightforward. Like the man himself. A leather string neatly bound his hair at the nape of his neck. The same wicked gleam in his eyes the night before had returned, and his mouth twitched with good humor.

Hard to believe, but in the light of day this man presented an even more imposing figure than he had the night before. Without saying anything at all, he seemed to dominate his surroundings.

Joanna's sister Penelope would have melted into the wooden floor like a glob of lard had she been present. And the girl would have flirted. Outrageously. And surely Mr. Archer would have fallen under her spell. Most men did. Still, such behavior was beyond Joanna. She simply wasn't capable of flirting, no matter what this daft man had accused. "Mr. Archer."

He crossed his arms across his chest. "Yes, Miss Fenton?"

"I think it best if we establish a few rules. During our relationship, it is imperative we maintain my family's reputation. Until Penelope bears a wedding band, a scandal of any kind is out of the question. As I said last night, Rebecca believes you to be the perfect solution to my problem—but she also readily admits that you are a handsome rogue who bends the rules to accommodate his wishes. I agree that—"

"You think me handsome?" the man interrupted. "I'm flattered."

"I did not say that." She wrapped her hands in the folds of her skirt.

"But you did. I heard you myself."

"I most certainly did not. I was agreeing with Rebecca's opinion that you obviously bend the rules to suit yourself. Thinking that a man of your nature is handsome, let alone uttering such an opinion, is highly improper."

He looked disgruntled for a moment, then his brow cleared. "Are you always proper, Miss Fenton?"

"Yes," she snapped. Liar, her mind screamed as the far-from-proper dreams of the night before resurfaced. Truth be told, buried beneath her upbringing and her need to find her brother, she was attracted to this man. She found him wildly exciting. He made her think impossible things, of dreams and wishes that only a young girl could possess before the hard realities of life destroyed them. He made her *want* again. Dream again. Her heart tripped over the scandalous notion.

And blister it, judging from the cocky grin on his face, she suspected he knew his effect on her. "May we proceed to the matter of my missing brother?" she asked.

He shrugged, then helped himself to a sugared biscuit from the tea tray. "As you wish. Assuming I agree to help, I'll have a few questions before I decide what's to be done next."

"But I thought . . ."

"What?"

"*I* have a few ideas on what must be done. I've already drawn up a plan—"

Archer waved his biscuit in the air, obviously annoyed. "There can only be one captain on this ship. As you so candidly pointed out last night, I am the one with the reluctant background. Since we're likely dealing with thieves, I am the one most qualified to make decisions regarding the procedure of this . . . investigation. Not some girl from a drawing room."

Joanna felt indignance flare up in her. "Yesterday you were not a thief. Today you are. That is rather convenient." She swirled her spoon round and round in her cup, searching for a ready solution. "I can see you intend to be difficult."

His expression grew serious, his voice implacable. "I promised to help you and intend to do what you have asked of me. I'll find your brother, your bauble, and keep you safe. My tactics may seem high-handed, but they're for your own good."

Control of the situation was slipping from Joanna's hands; she felt it. The situation was foreign and irritating to be sure, having someone dictate to her, a man she had hired! So much so, she barely refrained from stamping her foot. She had always prided herself on her even temperament, and most alarming was the fact that her irrational impulses grew stronger every day.

MacDonald Archer studied her over the rim of his cup, his sea-green eyes mesmerizing, probing, as if they saw far more than Joanna wanted to reveal to anyone. Heaven only knew what he was thinking. His ability to suddenly mask his expression was frustrating and even a bit frightening to her. With a sigh Joanna said, "You will need my help."

He nodded. "I wouldn't have it any other way. Now tell me about your brother."

"Randolph is a good person."

He seemed to believe her. "Good men make mistakes," he said, "often finding themselves in trouble with nowhere to turn."

Joanna felt a surge of emotion at his words. "I know. And if only I had been more understanding—"

Archer cut her off. "Your brother is a grown man responsible for his own actions. Don't waste your energy blaming yourself for things that may have happened. Now, tell me what you know."

A small sparrow fluttered outside the window, seeking entrance to this, Joanna's private sanctuary.

Amused by the irony, Joanna briefly envied the freedom the bird possessed. Duty and responsibility were all she knew. Responsibilities like her brother.

"When we first came to London," she explained, "Randolph understood our financial situation. He seemed content with his meager allowance. Then something changed. I barely recognized him. A month ago, when I realized we would have to sell father's artifact, Randolph was furious. He said I had no right. He also demanded more money. We had a horrible fight."

"Go on."

"The statue disappeared two weeks later. I found my brother that night, drunk, muttering he was sorry for everything. I thought he meant our argument. The next day, he vanished."

"You fear that he could be the very person who stole the statue?" Archer asked.

"Stole is such a harsh word. And though it seems the most obvious solution, I cannot believe my brother capable of such selfishness. He knows of the debts of our family."

Archer seemed willing to play along. "All right. For argument's sake, other than Randolph, who would want the statue badly enough to risk stealing it? Someone who might have easy access."

Though distressing to think of one's friends in such a distasteful manner, the same question had plagued her for the last few weeks. "Lord Tatterton, my father's old partner, coveted the statue for years. We should go look

63

at his collection. Then there is every other member of the Society of Historical Antiquities."

Archer gave her an odd look, then he sighed. "Did you report Randolph's disappearance and the theft of your father's statue to the authorities?"

"No."

He looked amazed. "Why the devil not?"

"Everyone would believe Randolph the thief. I have told you several times, we cannot afford the scandal. Mother will not allow one."

"Ah, yes. Penelope's need to marry a nobleman." An icy chill frosted his words. Then the rogue gave her an appraising stare. "Randolph's friends must wonder where he is."

"I fabricated an excuse. Everyone believes he is rusticating in the country. As his absence continues, though, I find it harder to find excuses. I'm beginning to fear I simply created another problem." Joanna opened her book, took out a piece of paper she'd stashed there, and handed it to Archer. "This was delivered last night."

The note, written in the same neat print as the one she'd shown him at the Pig-'N'-Whistle, read:

My patience dwindles. You cannot hide forever.
It is time to pay up, or else you will be sorry.

The same red serpentine seal ended the note.

"Short and to the point," Mac said after reading it. "Randolph obviously owes someone something. And by telling people he's in the country, you've managed to convince whoever wrote this that your brother's alive and well and avoiding his duty."

Mac toyed with the paper as he considered the ramifications of the second note. The soft patter of feet from the hallway broke the silence.

"Chang?" a female voice called. "Show yourself, you vexing man."

Joanna grimaced. "My mother."

"Chang," the woman called from the hallway again. Her footsteps stopped directly behind the Chinese butler, who guarded the closed door. Mac swore Chang grinned, but didn't open the door.

"There you are," Lady Fenton said, doing so herself. "Fetch me some tea. I had a dreadful afternoon. Lydia Litmore and her daughter were absolutely tedious to ride with. They're friends, but . . . my, my, what gossips. And the woman actually thinks Sylvia has a chance at snaring Westcliff. I have a feeling she'd stab me to do it, though. I know that's the way of the *Ton*, but . . . Have you found my string of pearls or that cat? I must find it before tomorrow night's ball," she finished.

"The cat?" the butler asked.

"Not the cat," Lady Fenton snapped. "I cannot very well wear *him* about my neck. I meant my pearls. He probably stole them. If they disappear like everything else, I shall take to my bed for a week. Where is Joanna?" A doll-like face peeked around Chang's right shoulder, then disappeared again. "Oh, hiding them

65

from me, are you? Some day I shall bind you and that cat together and pitch you into the Thames. Now go fetch our tea, move out of my way so I can greet our guest."

Chang strolled from the room to do as he'd been bidden, a satisfied grin on his face, and Lady Fenton was left alone in the doorway. Her blond hair was perfectly coifed with soft curls on the top of her head. Her gown mirrored her eyes, the same distinct blue as Joanna's. They were aimed on Mac. She floated across the floor. "Why Joanna, wherever did you find this handsome creature?"

Eager to meet this woman who yelled like a fishwife yet according to her daughter fainted at the least provocation, Mac watched Lady Fenton. Delicate, indeed. He recognized a skilled player in the game of manners and pretense. Lady Fenton was a master. Mac bowed. "Charmed, madam."

"Dear me, Penelope. Stop gawking from the doorway. Come and meet our caller."

Another female, fair-haired and slender, entered the room and stepped to Lady Fenton's side with the same elegant stride as her mother. Her pink muslin gown flattered rosy cheeks set on milk-white skin. She perched on the settee like a fragile china figurine, wearing the practiced look of innocence Mac had witnessed on many of the young ladies of the *Ton*. He imagined the hours of practice she must have endured—sitting, standing, walking, smiling—all with the sole purpose of attracting a rich titled husband.

Joanna, on the other hand, was all business—polished but practical, skilled, determined and purposeful. It was difficult to believe the three women were related. Aside from her eyes, Joanna shared no physical similarities with the other two.

She certainly didn't use the same dressmaker. Both Lady Fenton and Penelope wore elegant flattering creations. Joanna's gown was golden and had lace, but it turned her skin a pasty shade of yellow. It had obviously not been made for her. The fact annoyed Mac.

"May I introduce Mr. MacDonald Archer," Joanna said.

"Delighted." Lady Fenton removed her gloves and slipped onto the settee beside Penelope. "What a trying afternoon. Lydia Litmore babbled incessantly about the new saffron gown she bought for her daughter. We simply had to stop and order two new dresses for your sister. I refuse to have Penelope wearing the same color as Sylvia at our dinner party. Did you say *mister*?" The woman looked disappointed.

Joanna cleared her throat. "Yes, Mother. Mr. Archer is the gentleman I hired to find Randolph."

"Ah, yes. A waste of time if you ask me. Randolph will show himself soon enough." Lady Fenton's expression grew thoughtful. "MacDonald Archer . . . Are you, by chance, that friend of the duke of Kerrick?"

Mac nodded.

As quickly as a storm off the coast of South Africa, Lady Fenton's mood turned bright again. "I should have known. Always heard you were a handsome devil. And wealthy in your own right. Your reputation precedes you. Did you really shoot Lord Tisdale in the leg over a young widow?"

"Tisdale shot himself in the leg."

"Hmmm. And the rumors? Are they true or distorted by gossip?"

"I imagine that depends on with whom you talk."

"Mother," Joanna broke in, obviously unhappy with the turn of the conversation. "We were busy discussing—"

"One is never too busy for gossip." Lady Fenton laughed and batted her eyelashes several times. Then she turned serious. "Do you, by chance, have relatives within the *Ton* I might know? A duke or an earl? I'm not quite sure I know your family . . ."

Mac could all but here the gears of speculation and manipulation turning in the woman's mind. Rakish reputation or no, he feared he'd somehow just been tossed into the pot of potential suitors. Likely the bottom of the pot, but included all the same. He wondered whom Lady Fenton wanted for his bride. Lord Westcliff was the leading candidate for Penelope, so it was likely Joanna. Intriguing, businesslike Jo—

The effort was wasted, he reminded himself. He had no intention of marrying a female from society. Hell, he doubted he'd ever marry at all.

"Can't say that I do, Madam." And with that, he changed the subjects. "Now, I have question or two, if you would. You mentioned that other things have turned up missing lately. Mind telling me what?"

"Jewelry and trinkets. My favorite pearls, given to me by my dear deceased husband disappeared shortly before my son. Joanna's locket, as well. I blame Confucius. Like Chang, that cat lives to torment me."

Hearing his name the cat, who had been sleeping on a nearby chair, raised his head and looked in Lady Fenton's direction. Mac could have sworn the animal smiled. Shaking his head to clear it of such silly notions, he asked, "Where was everyone the day Randolph disappeared?"

Twirling a yellow daisy in her fingers, Joanna spoke up. "Mother and Penelope were at the modiste. I was visiting our solicitor. Several servants were about, but no one saw him leave."

Something in her answer pricked Mac's curiosity. "Why didn't *you* go to the dressmaker?"

"Joanna hates to shop." Penelope offered that tidbit in a voice as sweet as candied almonds.

Mac crossed his arms and looked at the older Miss Fenton. "When *was* the last time you bought a new gown?"

"My shopping habits and the stolen statue have nothing to do with each other."

"No doubt," Mac agreed, "but indulge my curiosity."

Joanna looked dismayed. "I prefer not to, thank you very much."

Chang appeared and poured tea into Lady Fenton's empty cup. "Miss Joanna no buy new gowns. Cook dye old gowns."

"I see," Mac murmured.

Joanna was afraid he did. The man had eyes. Her gowns were out of date, remade substitutes for new. For good reason. Fancy dresses would not change who or what she was—an unremarkable female destined for spinsterhood.

Besides, everyone knew this was Penelope's season and funds were limited. One by one she stripped the yellow petals from the flower in her hand. "There is nothing wrong with my wardrobe."

"Joanna prefers the jewel tones," her mother interjected. "Yet she refuses to spend the coin, afraid we might over extend ourselves. Which is nonsense of course. Both Penelope and Joanna have respectable dowries."

"Mother," Joanna managed between gritted teeth. "May we please return to the discussion of the statue? Or my brother?"

Lady Fenton's shoulders slumped like a child forced back to her lessons. "Oh, if we must. What other questions do you have, Mr. Archer?"

"Where was the statue kept?"

This was a subject easily managed, thought Joanna. "On a pedestal in the library on the second floor. Lung Wang Sun remained there for the last fifteen years without a problem."

"No matter that the thing could be sold for a bloody fortune? And still? Once the information was announced in the *Times* and every thief and burglar in the stews was coveting such a prize?"

"That never occurred to us, Mr. Archer," Lady Fenton answered disinterestedly. "As I explained to my daughter, Randolph probably borrowed Lung Wang Sun to impress some young girl or his gentlemen friends." She glanced at Joanna, then back. "Where do you reside, Mr. Archer? Mayfair? Green Park?"

"I consider my ship more a home than anywhere else, but I do keep a place near Green Park."

Joanna's mother leaned in, obviously delighted. "I don't recall anyone ever mentioning a *Mrs*. Archer."

"I should hope not. Marriage would not suit my lifestyle."

"Nonsense. You sound like my daughter. Where would the world be if everyone adopted such a ridiculous notion? Men are meant to marry and care for women. Women are meant to bear children, which means marriage. Marriage is an institution."

Obviously amused by the turn of the conversation, Mac smiled with merriment. Joanna, on the other hand, knew where this discussion would lead. Her mother still suffered delusions that some man would marry her eldest daughter. "Mother, please."

Lady Fenton paid her no heed. "Most people spout dribble about lifestyle when in reality they harbor some romantic notion of love or suffer from a bitter experience in courtship. Take my oldest, for instance—"

The daisy in Joanna's hand met a brutal death, torn up, and fell to the floor. She shook her head and stood. "Mr. Archer, I believe I promised to take you to Lord Tatterton's to view his collection? Perhaps it would be best if we did so now."

71

Chapter Six

Lord Harold Tatterton was a crack-brain.

That singular thought lodged in Mac's mind the instant Joanna introduced him. Yes, indeed. He was a portly, gray-haired, thin-nosed nutter, down to his flowing black satin robe covered with fancy colored birds; matching red slippers, their toes curling skyward; and his silk cap.

The man was a fanatical collector of Oriental art, both old and new. China figurines, vases, watercolors, rugs, squatty marble statues of men wearing loincloths, and jade fish-like birds and dragons covered every inch of space, floor to ceiling, wall to wall and corner to corner. Incense, sweet and pungent, scented the air. If anyone was obsessed with Chinese antiquities, this was he.

Blackmailer, kidnapper, or thief? Only time would

tell. Mac knew well enough to reserve judgment until later.

Joanna handed her bonnet to Chang, who scuttled from the foyer his assignment clear: mingle with Tatterton's staff. More often than not, a house's servants were privy to all the goings-on inside it. In case Joanna or Mac failed to gather some piece of pertinent information, Mac had no doubt that Chang would trick some poor soul into revealing it.

With apparent genuine pleasure, cooing and clucking like a mother hen, Tatterton kissed Joanna on the cheek.

"I hope you don't mind that I brought. Mr. Archer," she said, returning the old man's embrace with enthusiasm.

Tatterton clapped his hands in delight. "For what more could a man ask? Any newcomer presents me with the opportunity to impress him with my life's knowledge and remarkable collection. Prepare to be awed, young man."

"No doubt, sir." The goose-head had marked Mac as a lover of Chinese art, too. Well, Mac wasn't buying anything today except information. And, if he could help it, he had no intention of parting with any coin. He intended to ask questions, obtain answers and, in the end, try to understand the rumpus over this fourteen-inch dragon statue and form a list of possible suspects.

Mac was formulating the first question in his mind when a man he recognized all too well marched in his direction. Imagine that! Viscount Dorridge fancied Chinese trinkets.

Like many of the *Ton*'s lords, Dorridge appeared the portrait of a perfect gentleman. But buried beneath the well-polished veneer of nobility, proper manners and fancy clothes lay a man capable of profound treachery. Mac knew that firsthand.

The viscount bowed and greeted Joanna before he turned an icy glare on Mac. "Archer. I never would have taken you for a man versed or even remotely interested in antiquities. Your passions always veered in other directions."

"Funny. I always believed the same of you." Mac took a proprietary step toward Joanna.

Dorridge's lips thinned. "So, how is it that you and Miss Fenton know one another?"

Mac remained silent. Joanna glanced at him, an unspoken question in her eyes, before she pasted a placating smile on her face and answered. "We met before my father died. Mr. Archer and he shared many interests. Mr. Archer is anxious to view Lord Tatterton's collection."

The viscount gave her a smug look, then offered, "A word of advice, Miss Fenton. Mr. Archer is not what he seems."

"Careful, Dorridge," Mac snapped. "I'd hate to repeat the past. I might not be so generous next time."

Tatterton looked them all over. If he felt the animosity swirling in the air, he chose to ignore it. Or he tried to defix it with talk of art. "Tell me, Mr. Archer.

What particular period in history interests you?"

"Yes. Do tell," Dorridge agreed. He obviously didn't believe for a single instant that Mac had a legitimate reason for being here. The man had evidently forgotten how well Mac played these games of intrigue.

Eyeing the room and all the arranged exhibits, Mac asked, "What period is the Fentons' dragon from?"

"Approximately 900 A.D." Tatterton answered.

Hard to believe something had managed to survive so long. If Mac lived to be fifty or so, he figured Fate would have dealt him a decent hand of cards. Hell, if he made it through the next few weeks, he'd probably be lucky.

He stifled a laugh. One thing he knew for certain was that a dozen fancy lords wouldn't line up to study his bones, no matter how ancient. His life would be far from significant.

Well, he wasn't complaining and he had no regrets. Until the last few months, he'd felt at peace. The sea had given him that. Of course, recently he'd begun to feel something was missing from his life, but sooner or later he'd reason that through.

Tatterton smiled at Mac's prolonged silence. "I see the Dragon has won your admiration as well. I have tried to purchase, trade, bribe or win that prize for years, all to no avail. Joanna has proved to be as fierce a negotiator as her father. A pity."

"Not for me," Dorridge said. "I'm glad you never succeeded. There are many of us eager to bid on that artifact at the upcoming auction."

"Myself included," Mac added, to infuriate Dorridge. Also, it would be smart for the others to believe he was an interested collector.

Tatterton shook his head. "I figured as much. One more person to drive the price higher, I'm afraid. Well, come and meet the others. We were just about to begin our society meeting."

Men and a handful of ladies, all properly attired and coiffed, milled about the gallery. Some studied Tatterton's collection, but most watched one another. A few eyed Mac, an interloper invading their noble ranks. Money bought him the privilege of their company, but it would never buy their acceptance. He found some amusement, however, in the fact that here he was—a one-time thief and smuggler—spying on them, knowing that the real blackguard was probably one of their own and stood in this very room. The irony did not escape him.

Mac tapped Tatterton's elbow to get his attention. "What makes this Lung Wang Sun so special?"

"The artistry is utterly exquisite. Then, of course, there is the prestige of owning such an antiquity. And the legend, of course."

"The legend?" Mac asked.

Tatterton gasped. His already bushy sideburns seemed to stand on end. "Joanna, my dear. Have you neglected to tell Mr. Archer the statue's legacy?" When she nodded, Tatterton sputtered, his eyelid twitching. "If he intends to become a serious bidder, then we must rectify the situation immediately. As we should with many of the others here." He clapped his hands together. "Gather around, my friends. We have a special afternoon in store for us. I'm going to tell a story."

Everyone began to cluster about the fireplace, perching on dainty chairs or heavily sculpted benches. Viscount Dorridge hovered near the edge of the group.

Tatterton posed before a purple leather ottoman like a shepherd before his assembling flock. He crossed his arms, sliding his hands into the sleeves of his robe. Mac half expected him to pull a stone tablet, a hammer and a chisel from beneath his robe. Lord knew there was enough room in there.

Surprised by Joanna's sudden shyness, Mac ushered her toward the two seats nearest Tatterton. She actually tilted her head to stare at her lap, and toyed with a loose thread on her dress. Understanding, Mac felt a sudden kinship with her. A part of him wanted to demand she not hide her face from these people. The other part wanted to take her in his arms. To find and nuzzle the tiny spot behind her right ear.

Where in Hades had *that* thought come from? Shaking the lame-brained notion from his mind, Mac then found himself asking the question he'd wanted to ask ever since they'd left her house. "Why aren't you married?"

She looked offended. "A gentleman does not ask a lady such a question."

He waggled his eyebrows, making light of her displeasure. "I love it when you talk all stiff and proper-like. Your eyebrows arch in the most delightful manner. Now, please tell me."

"You are worse than a knee-biting four-year-old."

"I'll find out, you know," he threatened. The fire returned to her eyes, but she remained silent.

Well, even if she hadn't answered his question, Mac supposed her ire was better than her previous timidity. To defuse the tension he said, "Your friend Tatterton is three bricks short of a wall."

She took the bait. "Harry traveled with my father on several occasions. Together they established this society. Harry knows as much about Lung Wang Sun as my father did, and he loves to tell the stories. We might learn something of importance, something I have perhaps forgotten."

Mac doubted the lore was important. More likely the thief had been a common collector. "How well do you know Lord Dorridge?"

"Not very. He joined the society over a year ago. He also requested special consideration regarding the bidding at the auction. I refused, of course."

"Of course," Mac agreed. Then he added, "Stay away from him."

Mac's edict confirmed Joanna's earlier suspicions. Something lay between these two men. She quirked her head to the side. "Though you have no right to dictate whom I do or do not talk to, I rarely see the man and have virtually nothing in common with him— so you worry yourself needlessly. I might ask how *you* know Lord Dorridge."

The rogue held a finger to his lips, neatly avoiding her question. "Shhh. Crack-brain is about to begin."

He was incorrigible! Joanna barely concealed her laugh, and she turned her attention to her father's friend. Her skin began tingling with anticipation. Of all the tales and legends her father and Tatterton had brought back from the Orient, she enjoyed this particular tale the most. She wondered what Mac would think. His opinion would be interesting to hear after all was said and done, but she doubted he'd fall prey to the magic of this story. He seemed far too pragmatic, too grounded in reality.

She chanced a peek in his direction. For those who might be watching, Mac appeared as eager to hear the story as everyone else. But Joanna could feel the tension in the arm he'd casually draped over the edge of her chair. He reminded her of a Chinese tiger, lying indolent in the sun yet attuned to every scent and sound nearby. At the slightest provocation, he could and would kill to protect his domain, those he cared for. He could and would do so naturally.

Oddly enough, she felt no fear. She was more at ease with Mac than with any of the lords she'd encountered in her London season. Perhaps it was his clothing, which disguised him as any other gentleman. Or maybe it was the warmth she saw in his eyes when he looked at her, the easy way he smiled. His full lips were curving now—

To her horror, Joanna realized she'd been staring at him like a common tart. And the twinkle in Mac's eyes proved he'd noticed. Somehow, the man managed to incite her worst behaviors. Determined to ignore him, she folded her hands in her lap and stared at the front of the room.

Silence descended on the gallery as Lord Tatterton raised both arms in a sweeping motion. Then he sat cross-legged on the cushion. "Long ago in ancient China," he began, "dragons were believed to dispense the rain and create thunder. They brought prosperity or misfortune. Lung Wang Sun—the Dragon King of the Mountain—lived above the Yung Valley. He was a powerful sorcerer and immortal. The scales on his body signified universal harmony. Eighty-one scales were influenced by the Yang, goodness. The other thirty-six fell under the Yin influence of evil and misfortune. He was part protector, part destroyer. From the top of the mountain, he guarded the villagers. In return, they revered him."

For Joanna, within a few short minutes the spell was cast. Her father's partner captured his audience with the skill of a practiced storyteller, his deep-timbered voice laden with mystery and awe.

"One summer day, evil cast its shadow across the village. As its people celebrated their new growing season, a young woman tried to steal the dragon's treasure. Lung Wang Sun was furious. He believed the villagers had deceived him. He believed that they, too, had meant to rob him. In vengeance, he demanded a female sacrifice every year; if not freely given, the crops and the lands would suffer perpetual drought and blight." Lord Tatterton paused, a faraway expression on his face.

"Pray, do not stop now, sir," a young woman called.

Joanna knew Harry had no intention of stopping. He loved being dramatic in the telling of these tales.

Clearing his throat, he continued. "Twenty-five, fifty, a hundred years passed, and the villagers forfeited their daughters to the dragon. Their sacrifice was a small price to pay to keep their lands fertile. After all, daughters were not as important as sons."

Several women, Joanna included, muttered their opinions regarding that particular sentiment.

Harry chuckled. "Ladies, please. 'Tis not *my* way of thinking." He glanced at Joanna. "Would you care to finish the tale?"

Joanna shook her head.

He seemed unconvinced. "Of course you do, my dear. This is your favorite part—and since you now control Lung Wang Sun's destiny, your participation seems only fitting."

Granted, she probably knew the tale as well as Harry, and she often told it at the orphanage at which she volunteered. But that was altogether different. The children there were young and too appreciative of her attention to criticize her abilities as a storyteller. These people were her peers. Sweet Empress only knew what mistakes she might make. She had no desire to draw their attention.

Unfortunately, her father's partner looked adamant. He had no way of knowing that her reluctance stemmed from her first season when everything she did had been a disaster, every move a misstep, each effort upended in turmoil. And that had been before the scandal. She knew her fear of her peers had grown tenfold over the last few years to absurd proportions, but she was much more content to blend with the wall coverings. Unfortunately, her refusal would probably draw even greater speculation than any mistakes. She wished for a bolt of lightning to strike the house, but she knew she wasn't so lucky.

She shifted in her seat then gripped the arms of her chair. "Chin Ho," she said without turning around, "was a lone girl of twelve who possessed the courage to fight back."

To her dismay, she ended the sentence with a hiccup. She fell deathly silent for a long moment. Nearby, Joanna saw Mr. Archer turn amazed eyes upon her. He saw her mortification.

His hiss filled her ear: "I cannot believe you are the same woman who waltzed into a tavern filled with cutthroats and demanded I help her." He edged closer. "Do not cower before these people, Joanna. You are strong. You are worth all of them. If it helps, look at *me*. Tell *me* the story."

His words were commanding, and they lent her a shield of confidence. Granted, her legs still trembled like a newborn foal's beneath her dress, but Archer's words and his warm presence eroded her hesitation. She drew a deep breath, sought every ounce of pride she possessed and smiled.

"Chin Ho had a plan," she said at last. "She visited the ancient wise man beneath the river falls. He gave her many jewels—pearls, sapphires, emeralds, and a heart-shaped ruby—and a magical spell to defeat Lung Wang Sun . . . along with a final warning. The spell would defeat the dragon only if the bearer were wise and brave and had the purest of hearts."

Joanna saw Mac at her side, smiling, and it was as if she were sitting in the sunlight next to her roses. Her voice grew stronger, bolder. "At the first kiss of dawn, Chin Ho crept up the mountain to his cave. She lured Lung Wang Sun to the entrance with the beauty of her song and the brilliance of the ruby. She stunned him with the innocence of her face.

"Lung Wang Sun lumbered forward, his teeth bared, his fetid breath singeing her long dark hair. Chin Ho flung the two sacred pearls into the dragon's eyes to blind him. The beast roared with pain. Chin Ho lodged the heart-shaped ruby into Lung Wang Sun's breast. The dragon screamed with fear. Chin Ho threw the golden powder to shrink his body and turn him to stone. Finally, she cast thirty-six sapphires and eighty-one emeralds into the air. They settled like scales over Lung Wang Sun's body to bind him within the statue for eternity. The village was saved; Chin Ho became their savior, married the young prince and lived happily ever after."

"What happened to the statue?" one fellow three chairs back called.

Lord Tatterton answered. "In order to remind its

people of their earlier unfortunate greed, the village built a temple where it kept Lung Wang Sun. Another hundred years passed. Celebrating their continued good fortune, the villagers planned a grand party. That day a terrible rumbling shook the ground. The earth split and swallowed the entire village. They say Lung Wang Sun, embittered and angered by the villagers' joy, somehow caused their destruction."

"So, how did Lord Fenton find the statue?" another man, sounding a bit awed, asked.

"Like any good historian or archaeologist: a good map, a fine guide, skill, determination, belief, and of course . . . luck."

"Speaking of Chinese magic," Viscount Dorridge spoke up. "I once heard mention of the Red Scroll of Incantations—something about the statue and a rite of immortality. Do you think such a ceremony ever existed?"

Joanna herself had wondered if Harry purposely forgot to mention that part of Lung Wang Sun's legend. Then she wondered how Lord Dorridge had come by the information. It wasn't exactly common knowledge—or at least she hadn't thought so. She must have flinched, because Mac shifted and studied her intently.

Seemingly surprised by the question, Lord Harry hesitated then answered, "Indeed the scroll did exist. Saw it myself. Unfortunately, it disappeared when Lord Fenton died."

"And its fabled powers? Were they real?" Dorridge pressed, his eyes glittering.

"That remains to be seen. One must first possess both Lung Wang Sun and the scroll."

"Rubbish," Mac called from beside Joanna, crossing his arms. "Granted, so much gold and so many jewels must be worth a fortune, but the rest—it's only a statue. Books of spells? Immortality? No insult, sir, but I have difficulty believing such nonsense."

With a wave of dismissal, Lord Tatterton opined, "The Chinese are an ancient culture with a past laden with mystery and legends. Who knows exactly where truth begins and fantasy ends? However, trust me when I tell you there are those who would kill for this statue—and those people believe in the promise of immortality, eternal youth and unlimited power."

"Would you?" Mac asked.

Lord Harry did not shrink away or wince. "Perhaps once, when I was young and foolish. Over the years, I have learned two things. Little in life is worth killing for, and power of such magnitude usually brings about more harm than good."

"What would *you* kill for, Mr. Archer?" Dorridge asked, nastily.

Joanna felt Mac place a proprietary hand over her own, then he said, "For starters, anything or anyone under my protection."

If anyone in this room was intending to hound Joanna or her family, they had been duly warned. MacDonald Archer had slipped sufficient steel into his words to make his point: He was her protector.

Joanna shook with rage. Where before she'd been

pleased at the man's assistance, now she was furious at his lack of subtlety. They had come today to ask a few questions, not plaster a message on the wall for all to see.

Dorridge's gaze lit with disdain. "How plebean."

"Why, Joanna," her father's partner drawled, "you've found yourself an absolute brute. How lovely."

"He is not *my* brute." She aimed every word at Mac, willing him to silence.

He merely shrugged his shoulder. "Brute or not, I intend to buy that statue at the auction."

So much for tact and guile. And Joanna had been worried about drawing attention to herself. Great Mother, Mac might well have stood on the chair and yelled. The man was purposely behaving like a spoiled tot, and Joanna had no idea why. She pressed her heel down on his toe and shot him another warning glance.

After a moment of stunned silence, Lord Tatterton burst out laughing. He rose. "I like your enthusiasm, young man. But do not be too certain that you will be the victor. Much can happen between now and the auction. Come. Let me show you something." The historical society began to disperse. Whispers began amongst the lords and ladies as it did.

Joanna saw Dorridge level a final narrow glare at Mac and slip from the gallery, then she and Mac followed Harry to a wall of porcelain bric-a-brac.

Stopping before a bronze statuette of a woman seated on a throne, Lord Harry said, "Mr. Archer, for

centuries man has sought a way to control his destiny—in other words, sought immortality. Something
which Isis here is renowned for having found. All the
world seeks it. From here in the Empire, Dr. John Dee
spent his life searching for the Philosopher's Stone, a
substance that supposedly cures all illness and prom-
ises immortal life. He didn't find it. Throughout the
world, others are searching even now. For many, Lung
Wang Sun is the answer to that insatiable craving."

Mac spoke up: "If the legend is true, and if Lord
Fenton possessed both the scroll and the statue, why
is he dead? Why didn't he use the powers of Lung
Wang Sun to save his own life?"

Lord Harry looked sad. "He was killed unexpect-
edly—in a riding accident. However, even if he knew
death was imminent, I doubt he would have used the
scroll and Lung Wang Sun. My partner was the ultimate scholar. Notoriety within the world of academia
meant more to him than immortality."

"Hmmm." Mac smiled. "Well, I myself will think of
the statue as a very expensive piece for my mantel."

Lord Tatterton accepted his words with a laugh.
When he was finished, he turned to Joanna. "I hoped
Randolph might come today. I wanted to talk with him
again."

Joanna was shocked. "Randolph came to visit you?
When?"

"Over six weeks ago. That was why I was so surprised to hear about the auction. He hounded me with
questions about the Red Scroll and your father's jour-

nals. He brought that Ashford chap along. Though I found his friend rude, I must say I was thrilled that after all these years your brother has finally seemed to develop an interest in your father's studies. You seem surprised."

Tatterton's second revelation was more than a surprise; it was astounding. Her brother despised her father's relics. He always had. But more worrisome was the fact that Randolph had brought Ashford with him, and the fact that he had kept the visit a secret. "Randolph failed to mention it. He is rusticating in the country now. Some business on our estate."

"Will he return before the auction?" Tatterton asked.

She smiled at Mac. "I am certain of it."

Chapter Seven

Joanna peered out the carriage window. The bank of dark clouds promised rain, likely a torrential downpour if the moisture clinging to the air was any indication. Nevertheless, she inhaled a deep breath, relishing the rare taste of freedom. Freedom from what seemed like constant worry. She'd needed to take a break. Now here she was near the Thames.

All morning she had transplanted cuttings from her roses for delivery to the flower shops. Every pence benefited the family coffers—a fortunate excuse to maintain her flowers, the one selfish pleasure she allowed herself, the one luxury that had been enough to keep her happy these last four hopeless years.

Until MacDonald Archer plopped into her life.

In a few short days, he'd managed to plant the seeds of dreams and wishes, of desires and wants, all over again. The desire for a family of her own. And that affected other parts of her life. She wasn't an immature miss easily swayed from her responsibilities anymore, but when Mac had arrived on her doorstep that morning, promising to go scour the London pawnshops, she'd quickly asked to go. The bills and daily chores would wait until she returned.

Now here she was. Ships floated by their carriage on the river outside; people bustled along the docks, carting crates and boxes of all shapes and sizes; and wagons stacked with cargo fought for space in the narrow lanes. A young girl clung to her mother's hand, waving toward a distant ship. Memories of the ports Joanna had visited and the people she had met while traveling with her father came to mind. She had never thought to miss the life of a vagabond, but this bustling activity had her smiling.

She turned to find Mac staring at her. Lost in her thoughts, she had rudely abandoned their conversation. "Sorry. I was daydreaming. I had forgotten the anticipation and humanity that surrounds these docks."

He nodded, seeming to understand. "Did you travel with your father?"

"Until I was ten and his older brother died. Mother refused to pack another bag, so we settled in Suffolk where she gleefully adapted to her role as lady of the manor. Father came and went, depending on which way the wind blew or which legend captured his interest."

"Do you miss it—the traveling, I mean?"

"I was thrilled to have a room of my own and swore never to set foot on a ship again unless kidnapped by a band of wild pirates." She smiled at the memory. "Remember, I was only ten. I suppose there are moments like today that I feel a tad nostalgic, but solid ground suits me just fine. Father brought me parts of the world when he returned from his later trips by bringing me flowers to add to my gardens."

Mac fingered the sprig of tiny white blooms pinned to her cloak. "What are these?"

"Yeh-his-ming."

He quirked a brow.

"Jasmine," Joanna teased. "Supposedly Vasco da Gama brought the first plant back from China in the sixteenth century. The Chinese name was too difficult to pronounce, hence jasmine. The flower brings good luck."

"Do you think we need extra luck today?"

"I should think so, to find my brother."

The road narrowed as the carriage turned away from the Thames and rolled past a two-story warehouse. It stopped before an ordinary brick building with bars covering its two small windows. This was a part of London Joanna had never seen. "Someone doesn't trust his neighbors."

"Though you'll still want to guard your purse, most of the riff-raff stay away during the day. Night is altogether different. Annie walks a thin line between running an honest business and dealing in stolen goods, but she's no fool—she prides herself on her inventory and prefers to keep her bounty intact. Come on."

He opened the carriage door and lifted her down as if she were no heavier than a small cat. Joanna tried not to notice the easy way he managed the feat, the way his hands fit about her waist, or the heat his touch aroused through the fabric of her dress. His eyes moved over her face, settling on her mouth. A thrill shivered its way to her toes. She knew she should demand he put her down. It was the proper thing to do. The most prudent.

Yet, his hands felt so wonderful. She found herself smiling at him, silently begging him to pull her closer. His thumbs moved ever so slightly, a tad bit higher and closer to her breast. To her mortification her nipples ached. It was a sensation she'd never before felt, a dull, persistent, wanting sort of throb. She drifted closer to him of her own accord.

Had Chang not cleared his throat from his perch atop the carriage, she just might have purred. Mortified by her behavior—and having been seen—Joanna ducked out of Mac's grip and moved away.

The rogue actually chuckled.

She might have kicked the door of the pawnshop open, had it not been at least six inches thick and had Mac not been watching. Instead, she opened it and marched inside with all the dignity she could muster.

Stale perfume mixed with wood shavings and lamp oil hung in the air. Floor-to-ceiling shelves crammed with a variety of tools, jewelry, silver tea sets—the list was endless—lined two walls. Cabinets were scattered about the center of the room. Another door opened behind a counter in the back.

A large woman of indeterminate age sauntered out carrying a small velvet box. She leaned her elbow on a glass counter, a cigar dangling from her lips, and fell into negotiations with a dark-skinned sailor. When a floorboard creaked she glanced up, saw Mac, and cackled. "Now ain't this a grand day. Are you buying or selling?"

"I'm in need of information," Mac replied.

"Buying then. Give me a wink."

Joanna wandered the aisles, studying the assortment of goods. Gold watches, a silver tea service, brass spyglasses and other heirlooms filled the shelves. Stolen or bartered, she wasn't sure. "How awful it must be to discard the past."

Leaning over her shoulder, Mac fingered a small pearled coinpurse. "Such shops serve their purpose. Some of these items find their way here by way of a pickpocket or a thief, but many others come from owners who found themselves in trouble. And while many a man or woman, lord or servant, has fallen on hard times honestly, most of the fools forced to deal here gambled their monies away. Don't pity them. They got what they deserve."

It was exactly what her brother might have done. Joanna's shoulders slumped at the thought.

"I'm sorry," Mac said, obviously realizing the direction her thoughts had taken.

"If my brother acted in such a manner then I would have to agree with you. There is no excuse for such irresponsible behavior."

Mac lifted a brass sextant from a shelf. "How did your family's financial problems land in your lap in the first place?"

"My mother abhors anything resembling a ledger or mathematical equation. My father understood numbers, but he was caught up in his adventures so was rarely around. Our solicitor handled matters until I grew older, then one thing led to another until I had assumed complete control."

His gaze skimmed over the instrument in his hands and settled on her face.

She fidgeted with her collar. "How odd you must think me."

"On the contrary, I think you're quite remarkable. What has your brother been doing all this time?"

"What all young lords do. Attending school and looking to find his place in the world. Other than spending his allowance, he cared even less about the family finances than my mother."

Further discussion was cut short as the pawn shop's proprietress sashayed over, swinging her ample hips. She clasped Mac's face between her hands and pulled him down for a loud kiss. "It's been awhile, luv. Where've you been 'iding yerself?"

"Here and there."

"Blimey. A nasty rumor says yer starting a legit shipping company with legal papers, cargo and all."

"So it would seem."

She chucked Mac in the chin. "I always knew ye was a bright one. Business is changing. Do whatcha must." Drawing on her cigar, the woman eyed Joanna. "And what 'ave we 'ere?"

After making introductions, Mac explained the reason for their visit. Annie whistled through the gap in her two front teeth. "I heard talk of that statue. Every crook in London would love to lay his 'ands on it. Another rumor says it don't exist."

Joanna was surprised. "Why would someone think that?" she asked.

"According to a bloke that visits me from time to time, someone took a special interest in the ditty and decided to pay his respects—out of curiosity, of course. He said 'tweren't hide nor 'air of the thing."

"In other words," Mac cut in, "someone tried to steal the statue, but it was already missing."

Joanna barely contained her shock. "You mean someone broke into our house and I never knew?"

"So it would seem," Mac said. "What else, Annie?"

"A few months back a young man started coming about, selling trinkets. A pocket watch, a fancy brooch, maybe a necklace. Three weeks ago or so, he came back. Asked me about a fancy statue from the East, wanted to know how much I would give him."

"What did he look like?" Joanna asked, a sense of dread settling in her stomach.

"Fancy clothes. Average height, blond hair."

"You just described half the gentlemen in London," Mac said. "Would you happen to have any of those trinkets still here?"

"Sorry, luv. It was prime stuff." Mac withdrew a sketch of the seal that had been on the threatening notes Joanna had received. "What do you make of this?"

Annie gave him a serious look. "How'd you come by this, luv?"

"The where doesn't matter. I'm interested in who and what."

As if the walls had ears, Annie glanced from side to side. "That mark's been seen in the Rookery the last few months. Usually on a dead body. Rumor has it someone's starting business down by the docks. Nasty business."

"Such as?"

"As long as they leave me alone, I don't know and don't want to know."

Joanna shuddered. She doubted Annie scared easily.

Mac placed a gold coin in the proprietress's hand. "If you hear anything, leave a message for me at the Pig-'N'-Whistle. Someone will find me."

Annie studied the coin. "You realize that statue's worth more to most rumblers if'n it's in pieces?"

He nodded. "I'm not convinced I'm looking for your average thief, but if so, I'd like the statue back whole." He paused. "And Annie . . . if that young man comes back, his name would be worth some gold—his whereabouts more."

"Of course, luv. Have I ever disappointed ya?"

"Only a half-dozen times to someone who paid a higher price. But I guarantee I'll make this worth your while."

Annie's laughter followed them from the shop as Joanna and Mac left. A chilling rain poured from the sky, carried on a brisk wind that had people scurrying for shelter. Her illusions and hopes waning, Joanna barely noticed. "My brother *is* of average height and has blond hair."

"I figured as much," Mac said with a grimace. "I think it's time I meet Randolph's friends."

Joanna nodded. "The Westcliff ball is tomorrow night."

"Let me see if I understand you," Adam asked Mac. "You want me to introduce Miss Fenton to eligible gentlemen who are financially solvent, generous with their scratch, affable, on the intellectual side, and between the ages of twenty-six and thirty-five? Is that correct?"

Staring at his long-time friend's bewildered expression, Mac nodded. It seemed a simple enough task. Nevertheless, he folded his arms across his chest, leaned his shoulder against the gold plaster wall, stared across the Westcliff ballroom, and reconsidered the qualifications he had listed. After a moment he added, "And a sense of humor."

Obviously still perplexed, Adam asked, "Why?"

"Because she's far too serious."

"I *meant*, why should I do this? And what does Miss Fenton have to say about the idea?"

Hadn't he explained this once already? Mac stared past a waterfall of flowers, a whirl of dancing couples, and a melting ice sculpture of a unicorn to where Joanna sat with her family.

Dressed in a classic peach silk gown, Joanna's sister Penelope was polished to perfection and artfully placed at the forefront of a group of young ladies guarded by their ever-present mamas.

Joanna, on the other hand, looked like . . . Mac hated to even think it, but, wearing a drab umber dress, she resembled the apple left at the bottom of the barrel after six weeks at sea—the one no one wanted. Her wardrobe was obviously sparer than he'd first thought. And she sat by herself, practically ignored.

It was a travesty.

Somehow or another, while finding the chit's damn statue, Mac meant to rectify this situation. He simply needed Adam's assistance. "Ever since the Fentons arrived, Joanna has hidden in that corner. She's like a bloody vine—clinging to the wall, and speaking only when someone *happens* to trample her toes on the way to greet Penelope or her mother. She's retired to spinsterhood and doesn't deserve to be there. She needs a man to watch out for her, to give her a home of her own and babies."

Adam raised his left eyebrow an impressive inch, then fixed his gaze on the object of Mac's passion. "You seem to have taken more than a business interest in Miss Fenton."

"Not at all. I'm still interested in finding her brother and that statue, it's just that I've just never met someone so bloody self-sacrificing. Her mother dotes on Penelope while Joanna worries about everyone and everything else. I'm already involved with the family—I might as well see to the girl's happiness if I can."

Adam snorted.

Mac felt as surprised by his notions as his friend. He had never planned on playing nursemaid to a female of the aristocracy, yet here he was. And he certainly hadn't expected to like her.

To want her.

Oh, how he wanted Joanna naked and beneath him—more than he had wanted any woman in a very long time. That was reason enough to find her a husband. He had no intention of bedding the chit. She was a bloody virgin—a type of female he avoided at all costs. And he certainly wasn't going to marry her!

But there was no reason he couldn't act her champion. And if ever there was someone who needed a champion, it was the honorable Miss Joanna Fenton.

"You must have become fast friends, if you are already on a first-name basis with Joanna," an all too familiar voice sounded from behind Mac.

With a grimace, he glanced over his shoulder to find Adam's meddling wife smiling as if she'd just done something extraordinary. "I thought you were talking with Lady Archibald," he snapped.

"I was," she answered sweetly. "I am back. And a good thing, too. You are keeping secrets from me."

"And *you're* interfering in my affairs," Mac replied. "And eavesdropping."

Nestled in the crook of her husband's arm, Rebecca continued: "If Joanna so needs a husband, why not apply yourself to the position?"

Bloody frigging oysters! What an idea. A ridiculously idiotic idea. Mac recognized the gleam in the woman's eyes, a particularly frightening glint of female cunning that sent wise men scurrying for the darkest corner of a room or the solace of their club. Women were legendary for scheming, and Rebecca was no different. Their objective was usually the loss of a man's purse, his bachelorhood or his common sense. Sometimes all three. Adam was living proof—no matter how happy the man thought himself.

"Forget everything you are trying," Mac snapped. "You have already done enough by recommending Joanna hire me."

"What was wrong with that?" Rebecca asked, without the least bit of remorse. "I am confident you can help her. And, as you search for her brother, if you happen to develop a mutual attraction, so much the better. The two of you are perfect for one another."

Rebecca had just confirmed Mac's suspicions. He gaped at Adam, who merely shrugged.

And these people called themselves his friends!

Rebecca's thinking was not that surprising. She believed all sorts of nonsense about women's rights and social reform, that a member of society could marry an untitled bastard such as himself and survive the scandal. Her father was living proof.

Nevertheless, Mac wasn't about to become one of Rebecca's charity cases. He was totally and unequivocally wrong for Joanna. The distant horizons and endless oceans were his only love. And like her roses, Joanna needed dirt and roots to flourish. She needed a settled sort of lord, one of her kind. Certainly one with a title and a heritage to pass to her children, someone who knew how to become part of a real family.

Mac snared a glass of champagne from a passing servant. "I don't want or need a wife, so stop playing matchmaker."

"Perhaps I will and perhaps I won't. Joanna may not even fancy you, so do not fall into a snit just yet."

"Women have snits," Mac explained. "Men simply shoot the person irritating them." He gave her a pointed look. "Besides, even if I did want a wife, I'd not go searching in polite society."

"What, pray tell, is wrong with the ladies of the *Ton?*"

"You know as well as I that most are empty-headed bauble-brains who want one thing only: a titled lord with a fat purse."

Rebecca slid further into the curve of her husband's embrace. "What of me?"

"You are an exception and well you know it. Even so, both you and Adam come from rare good stock."

Rebecca smiled. "And what if we discovered the stock you come from?"

"Everlasting bloody hell! I told you to tell Edward to stop this nonsense," Mac said to Adam. A nearby gasp alerted him to the fact that he'd raised his voice. He glared at the offended couple, who hustled away to another corner of the ballroom.

"Quit throwing a tantrum," Rebecca said. "My father is only trying to help."

"Careful, darling," her husband cautioned. "This particular subject tends to put Mac on edge."

"Any subject contrary to a man's opinion puts him on edge. I should know."

Enjoying the fact that now Adam had been cast into the same black kettle as himself—men and their wrongful ideas—Mac grinned.

"Don't be too quick to believe I'm wrong-headed in everything," Adam warned. "Nothing would make me happier than to see you married and reunited with this Lord Fairfax, if he is your father. That nonsense of not needing or having a family is just that: Nonsense. You and I have been one another's family ever since our parents died."

Mac sighed. "Be that as it may, if and when I marry, it will not be to a lady of nobility. I nearly made that mistake once already."

Rebecca placed her palm on his cheek. "Lady Daphne was a fool. I wager there are women in this room who would forfeit a title for love any day. A title is merely a piece of paper. I cannot believe such a minor obstacle would keep *you* from taking a woman as your wife."

"If I wanted that particular woman," he agreed. "At any rate, perhaps there *are* women that would throw caution to the wind for the promise of love. Perhaps Joanna Fenton is one of them. I have no intention of finding out. Either way, I know *most* ladies place their existence on a title and the status it affords. And if they don't, their mamas and papas do."

With those words, Mac affectionately clipped Rebecca under the chin. "And, no matter what your father thinks, not only do I lack a title, I lack the benefit of a respectable birth. Nothing will change the fact I was born a bastard. You had best be remembering that before you continue this game of yours. I like my life just fine. A wife and a family would change everything I know. I'm not sure I'll ever be prepared to take such a step."

Mac knew Rebecca had no ready response, no matter how she might wish otherwise. The Season, the marriage mart, the very foundations of society rested on carefully chosen matches with established families. Love was a minor if nonexistent factor in such decisions. And there was nothing she could say about his love of freedom.

With Rebecca temporarily silenced, Mac relaxed. He chanced a glimpse across the room.

"For heaven's sake," his friend complained. "If you

continue to stare at her like that, people will talk."

Mac shrugged, an attempt to ease the tension from his shoulders. For four days, he and Adam had sought leads to Joanna's brother's disappearance, all to no avail. He'd come tonight to meet Randolph's friends. So far, none had arrived. What the hell else was he to do but watch Joanna? "Look at her. Sitting in the corner like the matrons and other spinsters while her sister courts fools. Joanna has yet to dance, and there are no prospects in sight."

"Why not ask her yourself?" Rebecca's question was clearly a challenge.

"And start tongues wagging? You'd like that, wouldn't you." Mac shifted his weight as he saw Adam studying him intently. "What are you staring at?"

"Actually, dancing might be just the thing." His friend paused, mind busy formulating some sort of strategy. "Do you remember the mare at Tattersall's a few months back, that haggard roan they tried to sell for weeks?"

"Yes, though I see no bearing on that to Joanna."

"People overlooked the pitiful creature until Wellington came along and gave the horse a nod. Then everyone took note. If I remember, Lord Kirk bought it for a tidy sum."

"Miss Fenton is not a horse, nor is she for sale."

"You are being purposely obtuse," Adam complained.

"And you used to be an intelligent man. Marriage

has addled your brain. *I* am not the sort of interest she needs."

Adam chuckled. "On the contrary, my friend, your exploits with women are legendary. The men may not openly acknowledge or relish that fact, but they hear and discuss things just like the ladies. What do you suppose the eligible men here will think when a man like you suddenly notices Miss Fenton? They might ask themselves what you see in her. They would speculate on this and that. Who knows? Perhaps one would even strike up a conversation with her. A dance here or there. So on and so forth. It certainly couldn't hurt. Of course, you must be careful not to let anyone believe she's your mistress."

Rebecca placed an exuberant kiss on her husband's lips. "What a brilliant idea! You should dance with her as well. That will help."

Shaking his head, Mac grumbled, "I always said society sustains itself on misperception and perfidy."

"Such is our life," Adam agreed. "But it may be moot. It seems Miss Fenton is taking matters into her own hands!"

Mac whirled about. Joanna was approaching at an alarming speed. It was not part of the plan. He distinctly remembered telling her to stay clear of him tonight. He scowled in her direction, hoping she would correctly interpret the signal and take her derriere elsewhere than where he feared she was taking it.

She kept coming, briskly striding across the parquet floor.

Mac cursed.

Adam laughed.

Mac quieted him with a glare.

Joanna stopped directly before Mac. She glanced nervously from side to side, then said, "Do stop scowling. People will wonder what I did wrong."

"Let me tell you. We decided you and I would not openly talk with one another tonight."

"We decided that?" she asked Mac. "On the contrary; *you* decided that." She smiled at his friends. "Good evening."

Rebecca giggled and Adam grinned.

Idiots surrounded him. Knowing there was no hope for it, Mac moved to Joanna's side. "Then by all means, let us all talk. That is, if my friends can stifle their amusement enough to hold a conversation."

Adam recovered from his fit of laughter and said, "You chose well to hire Mac."

"It was on the advice of your wife, and so far I have to agree with you." She turned to Mac. "We have been to several places I would never have known to look. Now we are waiting for my brother's friends. I have no idea where Ashford and Hayes are. They should be here by now."

In the silence that followed, Rebecca spoke up: "While you are waiting, why don't the two of you dance?"

Damn her manipulative hide! Was Adam's wife ignoring everything he had said? Mac knew Joanna didn't deserve to sit in a corner, had no idea why she'd allowed herself to be put there in the first place—surely she had her reasons—but her decision to play the spinster wasn't his concern. Not really. No matter that she possessed more character than the majority of the men or women in the room. He swallowed the remark on the tip of his tongue.

"That is not necessary." Joanna spoke to the tips of the brown slippers that peeked from beneath her gown.

Damning the consequences, Mac extended his arm. "Actually, I believe it is."

Chapter Eight

Anxiety poured over her: the fear she might trip or somehow make a fool of herself, drawing the scrutiny of the *Ton*'s gossips as she had in her first season. The notion was utterly ridiculous, of course, highly illogical. No one cared about Joanna Fenton anymore. No one paid her attention. She had purposely seen to that. And even if someone happened to do so, noticed her dancing with Mac and targeted her for the rumor mill, she doubted she could be more humiliated than she had been those few years ago.

Even so, the urge to flee spread to her limbs. Her hands fisted at her sides. Her feet refused to budge. When Mac gave her a curious look, hating herself for being cowardly, she whispered, "I have not danced in a very long time. Perhaps we should wait until later."

"Later . . . or never? Relax, Miss Fenton. I've not lost a partner yet."

He settled the matter with a tidy bow and a grin. He swept her into his arms, his hand steady and firm against her back, much like the man himself. And he danced as he did everything: effortlessly, elegantly, in complete control.

He would not allow her to stumble.

Joanna's panic slowly ebbed, replaced by the novel pleasure of being held by a man so handsome and compelling that he garnered feminine giggles and fascinated stares, yet who paid them no mind, his sole attention focused on her. Nor would he chastise her if she stumbled. Tension eased from her shoulders. She relaxed her grip on his hands.

"And what flower are we wearing tonight?" he asked as they spun through the room.

She glanced to the pink bloom on her shoulder. "A peony. The Chinese believe it gives one the ability to keep a secret."

"What titillating secrets could you possibly be keeping, Miss Fenton?"

His breath teased the sensitive skin of her neck. A quiver shot down her arms to the very tips of her fingers. Fire spread across her cheeks. Her growing attraction to this man was most alarming. They merely danced, and her breath quickened and her heart tumbled like a leaf in the breeze. Imagine her reaction if he happened to kiss her!

Not that he would ever have a reason to take such liberties, she reminded herself. Nor would she want him to. Not really, unless she considered her recent far-from-proper dreams as a sign of her true feelings.

He wanted to know her secrets! At that thought, her face flamed the same color as the bloom she wore.

"You really must stop blushing every time I speak to you," Mac said. "People will think I've said something wicked."

They swirled by her mother, who stared, mouth open wide like a costermonger hawking her wares. Three nearby matrons wore similar expressions. And Lord Beasley was there as well, scowling.

She tried not to think about Beasley. The vile man had once courted her, but she had set her sights on someone better, thinking she actually had a choice in the matter. In that first season, she'd been so naive, believed that one of the handsome lords who spouted flattery in her ear, promised the moon and the stars, would actually marry her. She'd realized too late that the prevaricating wretches had only wanted under her skirts. Even worse, Lord Beasley had witnessed one such debacle then belittled and scolded her, humiliated and harangued her before her peers. Nasty rumors had surfaced. Aside from being clumsy, Joanna had been marked as fickle and shrewish, a woman not to be trusted, perhaps even loose with her favors.

How ironic it was that she'd never felt anything of desire with those other men—not like she was feeling for Mac now. She looked up at him.

"Your mother looks faint," he teased. "Shall we stop to catch her or leave her to the other ladies and Lord Beasley."

Nothing good could come from a conversation between Beasley and Joanna's mother, even if Beasley did have the confidence of Lord Westcliff. Self-doubt surfaced and lingered. Joanna stumbled.

Mac reassured her, correctly interpreting her misstep. It was amazing how the man could read her! "Forget them, each and every one. They can only hurt you if you let them." Determination, along with his brilliant, satisfyingly male smile, bolstered her confidence. An intoxicating mix of selfish pleasure and abandon moved her feet. She felt a rush of anticipation, long buried and nearly forgotten. Laughter spilled from her mouth.

"I take that to mean we leave them to their own devices." Mac winked at Lady Fenton and, in a quick swirl to the side, they left the little group behind. "You should laugh more often. The effect is lovely."

"Perhaps I shall," she agreed, a warmth settling dangerously near her heart.

"Perhaps your reaction is the result of dancing with such a handsome man," he proposed. A small, reticent smile graced his lips.

"An arrogant man," she retorted. *But dashing, kind, charming.* A man any woman would claim. MacDonald Archer was an enigma, more complex than the puzzle box her father once brought home from Beijing; and he fascinated her.

"May I ask you a question?" she asked. When he nodded, she continued, "How is it that a man of your background . . . I mean to say . . . How do you move within society and tolerate their scrutiny?"

"Without being thought a complete fool?"

Her face flushed. "I simply meant—"

His eyes twinkled with mischief.

"Shame on you. I am nervous enough without your perverse sense of humor making matters worse."

"Nervous? For reasons I don't understand and sincerely hope you will someday explain to me. You're doing fine," he whispered in her ear. "So, if I understand your question, you want to know how a charming no-account free trader of low birth learned to properly behave in society."

"I admit some curiosity."

He pulled her closer and spun toward the center of the dance floor. "When my mother was sixteen, she met a sailor and fell madly in love. Unfortunately, he took to the high seas after a few months, pledging to return. She waited three months for him. He never returned. Pregnant, abandoned by her father and ashamed to stay in Glasgow, she packed her meager belongings and left home. I was born and grew up in a speck of a town in the middle of nowhere on the eastern coast of England called Lynmouth."

His words seemed practiced as though he had repeated the same speech time and again. "Your mother must have been terrified," she said.

"I imagine so. Yet in all those years, she never complained. I heard her weeping late at night, but it wasn't until I was older that I understood. I believe she was most pained that I was treated as a bastard by others. I remember the first time I heard that word, felt its sting . . ."

"That must have been very hard."

"Yes, but it also taught me a valuable lesson: Whatever I would get from life would depend upon what I was willing to do. I had to make my own way in the world."

They twirled past Rebecca and Adam, who both grinned like co-conspirators. Joanna couldn't shake the feeling that she was somehow the target of their plotting. "How did you meet Lord Kerrick?"

"One summer afternoon I encountered Adam, all pompous and lordly, trying to rescue a downed seagull. I helped him succeed and, odd as it seems, we became inseparable. Caused quite the stir. The village bastard and the noble. Adam decided that, if he had to suffer his lessons, I should suffer right along with him."

"That was very generous of him."

"I didn't think so at the time." He grinned. "But their cook made the best custard this side of heaven, so I relented in order to eat. That early education and training has served me well over the years." He gave her a dour look, then. "Of course, my association with Adam also gave me a false sense of belonging. That was a lesson I learned when I first came to London. Thanks to his friendship and my money, I hover at

113

society's edge—but I'll never truly belong."

He spun her, then added, "I accepted that fact years ago. Rich or not, educated or not, friend of an earl or not, in the eyes of society, I will always be an untitled bastard."

Joanna found herself shocked by the self-demeaning way he spoke. "Bastards line portrait galleries of many of the *Ton*," she argued.

He laughed. "True. And many possess less than admirable qualities. Even so, in the eyes of the *Ton*, a title eradicates the sin."

"Where is your mother?"

His smile faded. "She died when I was eleven. She had a kind heart and worked herself to death providing what little we had. Adam's parents moved me and my meager belongings into Kerrick Castle. At fifteen, I signed on as a cabin boy on a ship. I've been at sea ever since."

"And your father?"

"I don't even know his name—and I don't care to. I have no use for a man who left my mother to suffer such a fate."

His eyes were misty. Clearly, he'd loved his mother a great deal. His feelings toward his father were more difficult to discern. There was anger—justifiably so— but for all his protests, Joanna recognized the haunted look in Mac's eyes, the look of disappointment and yearning. It mirrored an expression her father sometimes wore at the end of a long quest that had ended in failure. Mac masked his pain with indifference and charm, but Joanna suspected his ignoble birth was a wound deepened by his father's rejection. And society's. People could be exceedingly cruel; she knew from first-hand experience.

"Your mother would be very proud of you—other than the stealing and smuggling, of course." Sweet Goddess, why had she uttered that observation? She stumbled again, righted herself and added, "I mean, there are so many other things you could do."

The man burst out laughing as he spun her in a circle. "Do you mean to reform me, Joanna?"

"I spoke out of turn." She frowned. "I seem to spout whatever I am thinking when I'm around you. Any other man would surely chide me for my impulsiveness."

"I'm smarter than they are. You need never keep your thoughts to yourself around me." He winked. "And under different circumstances, I just might let you reform me."

Having no ready response to his suggestion, Joanna fell silent. Reform him, indeed. Even if a man like Mac were capable of being changed, she doubted she would try. He behaved as honorably as any gentlemen she knew. He was compassionate, unpretentious, good-humored, and certainly more charming than most of those born of the noblest blood. Someday a very lucky woman would call Mac her husband, share his bed and raise his children. A pang of envy struck her.

From the corner of her eye, Joanna noticed two men standing at the top of the marble stairs that led into the ballroom. Thankful for the distraction, yet reluctant to leave Mac's arms, she forced herself to step away from his heat, his masculinity, which drew her closer, she feared, toward heartbreak. "Lords Ashford and Charlesworth have arrived," she said.

Mac glanced across the room. "I feel a sudden urge to make new friends."

As they circled the room, Joanna noted the expressions of those they passed: speculation with a splash of disdain from the men, curiosity from the women. She cocked her head in the air and glided toward the stairs.

Both of Randolph's friends had brown hair cut in a similar style. They stood the same height and were very close to the same weight. But the similarities ended there. Charlie liked bright colors while Ashford leaned toward somber clothing. Ashford had a rigid countenance. Charlie constantly fidgeted, his gaze flitting back and forth across the ballroom. He seemed unable to stand still. In truth, they were unlikely companions.

His usual cheerful self, Charlie beamed. He snagged two glasses of champagne from a servant. "Jo, my dear. How dazzling you are tonight."

She smiled, accepting the compliment quietly. Charlie tended to overstate the facts. She thanked him and introduced Mac.

Ashford, grim as always, nodded. "How is your brother? Is he back from Suffolk?"

"Not yet. I expect him in the next week or so."

Charlie turned sullen. "Pity. I miss the chap. How are the plans for your auction coming along?"

In the past, conversation with Charlie had come easily. Now Joanna found herself pondering his every question for a response. "Fabulously," she said at last.

"Are you a potential bidder?" Mac asked from where he leaned against a marble pillar.

"Egads, isn't everyone?"

Ashford frowned. "I say, I was surprised to hear that Randolph decided to sell that statue after all. I thought he liked the piece."

"Not really," Joanna replied. "Father was the only one of our family fascinated by Lung Wang Sun."

"But what of those magic powers and all?" Charlie asked. "Wouldn't you like to live forever, Jo?"

"One lifetime will suffice. And you, Lord Ashford? Do you believe in magic spells like Charlie? Do you have hopes of living several hundred years?"

Ashford tugged on his lace cuff. "Admittedly, the possibility is intriguing." Then he turned away, his attention caught by something else. He asked at last, "If you will excuse us, I should like to play poker. Come along, Charlie."

From where he stood against the pillar, Mac smiled. He rubbed his hands together. "Mind if I join you?"

Somehow or other, Joanna found herself at a small sidebar, sipping punch, staring at the array of desserts and pondering her future. The reason was not so hard to come by. The moment Mac had deposited her at her mother's side, matrons bombarded her with questions.

Lady Pifsom wanted to know if she had a penchant for sweets. Another woman asked if she liked children. They discussed all Joanna's attributes and tastes, even her shoe size!

Oddly, she had been asked to dance again. Three times. Her mother hadn't stopped babbling about it for fifteen minutes. Yet most disconcerting was the fact that Lord Beasley had sidled up beside her, offering his opinion on her choice of dance partners. The wretch had actually questioned her relationship with Mac, then in the same breath, mentioned he was in the hunt for a fourth Lady Beasley. If Joanna were humble enough, sufficiently pliant and docile, he might reconsider her as a potential candidate.

And her mother might one day tolerate the family cat.

Shocking herself and Lord Beasley, Joanna had simply walked away.

She nibbled on a honeyed apple when Lord Dorridge stomped in her direction. Judging from his expression, he was not the bearer of good tidings. Unfortunately, escape was impossible.

"I see you ignored my advice."

So much for pleasantries, she thought. "Good evening, sir. Which advice was that?"

"Mr. Archer is only concerned with himself. I'm sure he is hovering about you only to gain some edge in the auction."

A lord and lady stared from the corner of the room. Joanna tasted a moment's apprehension. She certainly did not want or need a scene, but she refused to bow to Dorridge's intimidation. Her nails bit into her fisted hands. "Do lower your voice. I assure you, Mr. Archer is no concern of yours."

Dorridge's eyes narrowed and his jaw clenched. "He is not a gentleman but rather a rude wastrel who preys on women to gain notoriety."

As she knew, Dorridge had just described himself as well. "Obviously you and I have different opinions of Mr. Archer. Excuse me."

Without warning, he grabbed her wrist, his face twisted with anger. "Only because you're a woman. You cannot see beyond the charming veneer he sports. If you refuse to listen to reason in that venue, perhaps you will be more reasonable regarding the statue. There are considerations a mere woman cannot understand. I would be willing to pay double what anyone offers if I am given the piece."

"I cannot do that. Everyone will be given the same opportunity."

The viscount leaned within an inch of her face. "There are forces at work that you do not know. Do not say you were not warned." He stormed from the room then, furious.

A tremble shook Joanna's body. She suddenly wanted, needed, to see Mac; but in the card room he sat with Charlie, Ashford and Lord Kerrick, engrossed in a card game, doing exactly what needed to be done.

Disturbing him now because of an ill-tempered cretin like Dorridge seemed pointless. Dorridge was a prig, and certainly not deserving of her fear. She took a deep breath, forced herself to relax, and sought a quiet place to gather her thoughts.

She slipped up the stairs toward the ladies' retiring room. Fresh air wafted down the dimly lit hallway, drawing her forward. She barely managed a deep breath when a reed-like woman wearing a diaphanous gown and a smile that guarded a multitude of secrets floated from the shadows. Set against pale porcelain skin, her black hair shone. An elaborate golden hairpin contrasted to its dark color. Her eyes glittered with excitement. "He is extraordinary, is he not?"

Wonderful, Joanna thought. Would no one give her a moment of peace? She did not know whom she was talking with, but she suspected she knew whom she was talking about. Her one dance with Mac had created quite the stir. Perhaps if she feigned ignorance the woman would simply go away. "Pardon me?"

"Mr. Archer, my dear. I certainly wasn't talking about Lord Beasley. That man is an insect. Mac, on the other hand, is an angel. The memories that seeing him stir . . ."

"Are you and Mr. Archer close?"

"Close?" The woman coughed. "You could say we were very close at one time. Let me introduce myself. I am Lady Dorridge. And you are a very lucky girl."

Lady Dorridge. *First the husband, now the wife?* Her evening seemed to get better and better. At least

Lady Dorridge didn't look ready to expire from an apoplectic fit—and the opportunity to discover the reason for the obvious dislike between Lord Dorridge and Mac was too enticing for Joanna to ignore. "Why, exactly, am I lucky?" she asked.

"There is no need to play coy . . . Though I do not blame you. I remember a time I would have locked Mac in a tower and kept the only key for myself. Pity he felt differently. Near broke my heart, but he was never one that was content with only one female for any length of time."

Shock and disappointment came with the dreaded truth. This woman and Mac had been—well, there was no delicate way to put it—*lovers*. And Lady Dorridge thought that Joanna and Mac were the same. Piffle! The notion was laughable. Joanna was not the sort of woman whom men seduced. In response, she could only stare open-mouthed.

"Could it be you've managed to keep the wolf at bay?" Lady Dorridge keened. "How novel—though I can hardly fathom such a notion. The man is an absolute satyr." She tapped her finger to her painted lips. "In that case, I assume you wouldn't mind sharing him."

Joanna managed to recover her voice along with her indignation. "I assure you, madam, Mr. Archer and I have shared nothing more than a dance."

"Mac rarely attends social functions without sufficient reason, which is usually female in nature. Considering the way he watched you tonight, I assumed you were his newest source of entertainment. I apologize if I spoke out of turn. Perhaps his motives are altogether different."

"Mr. Archer's sole interest in me is regarding an artifact that belonged to my father. My family is holding an auction in a week or so, and Mac intends to place a bid."

"The dragon statuette?" Lady Dorridge shuddered. "My husband has spoken of nothing else for the last year. He's determined to possess the thing." An unidentifiable emotion sparked in her eyes. "Tell me, do you believe all the stories about its magic powers?"

"I honestly cannot say," Joanna answered, relieved by the change of topic. "According to my father's journals, *he* believed in the possibility."

"Journals, you say? Do they explain this rite of—" She waved her hand in the air.

"Immortality?"

"Yes. That's it."

"The notes are sketchy and useless without the Red Scroll of Incantations."

"My husband certainly believes in the statue's powers. But he mentioned nothing about the scroll being sold with the statue."

"Unfortunately, the scroll was misplaced." An uncomfortable silence settled between the women.

After a moment, Lady Dorridge pulled a handkerchief from her sleeve as another cough racked her body.

"Are you all right?" Joanna asked.

"A slight cold, nothing to worry about. I considered staying home, but my husband insisted I come. And I do so usually enjoy a party." The viscount's wife turned to leave, hesitated, then faced Joanna once again. "A word of advice, Miss Fenton, as one woman to another—sisters, so to speak, in a world dominated by men. A woman should answer to no man. In fact, she should tempt and control men, which she can always do if she but uses the right methods. She should get whatever she wants. Speaking as a voice of experience, you might rethink your decision regarding Mr. Archer if you were telling the truth about putting him off. You'd not be disappointed. A woman must grasp her destiny with her own two hands. She must find what pleasure she can. Good night." And with that, Lady Dorridge left.

By the Empress's ears. A complete and utter stranger had just suggested Joanna take Mac to bed! Discreet liaisons outside of marriage were common enough, though society pretended otherwise; but one didn't go about discussing them as one might a sunny day. This conversation was, by far, the oddest and most unexpected Joanna had ever had. Totally and utterly dumbfounded, she watched Lady Dorridge melt down the corridor with liquid grace and swishing hips.

Unbidden, she compared herself to the woman. Lady Dorridge was certainly attractive, if you liked the fragile willowy sort. But beneath the beauty was an underlying glimmer of ill-spirit.

Yet she had been Mac's lover. He had likely showered her with compliments as he had done with Joanna. *Lud!* Fool that she was, Joanna had wanted to believe him, had nearly done so. She was still as gullible as she had been four years ago. Only this time a new emotion swirled in the mix: Jealousy. Raw, painful jealousy. She was simply another woman to the likes of MacDonald Archer.

Fine. She would simply fortify her heart to his wicked tongue.

At least now she understood the reason for the men's animosity. And if Lord Dorridge was as obsessed with the statue as his wife claimed, he was a definite suspect in the disappearance of Lung Wang Sun. It would be interesting to hear what Mac had to say on that subject.

She wandered further onto the balcony. The night air cooled her skin. She closed her eyes and inhaled a deep breath. The candle in the hallway sputtered and died. A floorboard creaked.

"Lady Dorridge?" Joanna called.

No one answered.

"Hello? Anyone there?"

Again nothing. The moon slid behind a cloud, masking the last of the light. Her solitude suddenly felt oppressive, dangerous. Inexplicably, Joanna knew she wasn't alone. It was the most illogical conclusion to make, but she had never felt so certain of anything in her life.

A large hulking form slid through the open doorway. Instinctively, she stepped back. Her legs pressed against the marble balustrade, the rail the only barrier between her and the stone walkway far below. "Who are you? What do you want?"

The intruder grabbed her shoulder. "I gots a message for yer brother."

"But my—"

The shadow's powerful grip tightened painfully. "Shut yer mouth. Tell Randie me boss is tired o' waiting. Consider this 'is last warnin'. Deliver the goods."

Without warning, he gave her a shove. She toppled over the stone rail.

Chapter Nine

Over the cards in his hand, Mac eyed the man directly across the table. The young Earl of Ashford was an ass, a high-flying nob with few admirable qualities. Charlesworth wasn't much better. He was a bloody bosky who acted Ashford's errand boy and court jester. On several occasions, Mac thought Adam might knock young Charlie from his chair.

Adam sat beside Mac, using his soldier's instincts and skills to quietly assess the situation and the players. It would be interesting to see what he had to say about them. But Mac himself was discovering where they played their lordling games.

He downed another shot of whisky, discarded a deuce and drew an ace of spades. "I agree about a few of the places you mentioned, but when a gent wants an especially fine time—if you know what I mean—

the place to go is Nellie's in Southwark. Top drawer, in my opinion."

Ashford added two pounds to the growing pot as if he hadn't a care in the world. "I suppose."

"I wager Faust's has the best hazard tables in London," Adam added. He tossed his cards into the middle of the felt-covered table.

Shaking his head, Charlie added two coins to the pot. "There's the Keeping Room and the Gargoyle, but you haven't seen anything until you've seen Eden. Not for the faint of heart, though." He named several other hells, listing their attributes before Ashford shot him a glare. Charlie halted his catalogue mid-sentence.

But not before Mac had a list of haunts to investigate.

The fools liked the rougher side of London. It wasn't uncommon, but such youthful stupidity deserved to be taught a lesson. Ashford and Charlesworth were both cocky youngbloods without a whit of sense. If these were the fellows Randolph ran with, the boy was in serious trouble.

Chewing on his cigar, Mac slapped Charlie on the back. "I imagine Randie had a fine time at these places."

Ashford frowned—at the cards or the comment, Mac wasn't sure.

Mac took a drag on his cigar. Smoke floated toward the ceiling. "Odd though," he added. "With the auction of that fancy statue in a few weeks, I figured Randolph would want to be in London."

True to form, Charlie chirped some inane comment, which garnered another furtive look from Ashford. No doubt these two shared secrets. But Ashford kept Charlie on a tight leash and Ashford wasn't talking. Mac would discover nothing more tonight.

He resigned himself to a few more minutes of play.

A scream rent the air. And, damn if the voice didn't screech his name.

Mac stood and dashed from the room toward the sound. Up the stairs he went, Adam on his heels. He imagined Charlie, Ashford and half the guests were following as well. Darkness greeted him at the landing. "Joanna?" he called.

"Careful," Adam warned.

A muffled cry came from the end of the hall. Mac sprinted forward. "Joanna, where are you?"

"Down here."

He followed her voice. Joanna balanced on a narrow ledge three feet below the balcony and thirty feet above the ground. One hand gripped a trellis on the right that was ready to splinter at any moment, the other a small brick protruding from the side of the house. Panic ripped through Mac. He forced himself to remain calm. "Stay perfectly still," he said.

"What do you think I'm doing?" she snapped.

He straddled the marble balustrade. "I want you to hold on to the trellis with one hand and reach for me with the other."

Fear glittered in her eyes. "I would rather not."

"If I join you on the ledge, I could very well shove you off. Or you, me. Trust me, darling."

"I trust you. This scrap of wood is what's worrisome. You promise not to drop me?"

"And risk losing my one hundred pounds? Never." He turned to Adam. "Brace me." He leaned far over the railing, then, his hands within inches of Joanna's. All she had to do was grab hold. "Come on now. You can do this."

A minute passed. An eternity. He waited, saying nothing, willing himself to be patient. Finally, she clasped her hand in his. He yanked her up into his arms and over the balcony.

"Someone pushed me," she said, her voice muffled by his jacket.

He tipped her face toward his. "What?"

"Someone pushed me."

"Are you certain?"

"I certainly did not leap over the railing for fun!" Joanna shuddered in his arms. "Can we go, before someone else finds us? The questions would be too difficult to answer."

Too late. Drawn by Joanna's scream, a sizable crowd had already gathered. Mac didn't give a damn about the group of gossipmongers, he simply wanted to hold Joanna until his heart started beating again. But Joanna wanted privacy. He supposed he understood.

Hovering at Mac's side, Adam said, "Another moment and the entire ballroom will be here."

A variety of interpretations and speculation would run rampant amongst the ranks of society tonight. There would be hell to pay tomorrow. But while Mac didn't care, Joanna did. Nothing could be done now except spare her the embarrassment of answering any questions. Mac met Adam's murderous glare, which likely mirrored his own. "Have your carriage brought 'round. I'll take her home."

He swept Joanna down the hallway, past the gawking crowd of nobles and out the front door, refusing to release her until the carriage pulled up.

Fury boiled in his veins.

Safely tucked inside the carriage with curtains drawn and lamp glowing, Mac kept Joanna balanced on his lap. The scent of lavender surrounded him. He knew he should release her, but he couldn't quite bring himself to do so. Especially when, obviously still shaken, she shivered and burrowed deeper into his chest. And with good reason. Watching her dangle thirty feet above the ground had cut years off his life.

And he was bloody furious.

"Are you all right?" he managed to ask.

"I twisted my ankle. And my hands hurt."

His coat muffled her answer. Another tremor shook her body. Judging from the quiver in her voice, she was near tears.

"Let me see." Mac pulled her body from his. He removed her torn gloves. Blood and scratches covered her palms with one nasty thorn still embedded in her skin. "This thorn must come out."

She yanked her hand free. "No. We should wait until we reach the house. The pain is gone. Truly."

"You're a terrible liar. Your hand will feel better once I remove the thorn." He gripped her hand again. A quick pinch with his fingers and the nasty spine slipped free. Using his handkerchief, he covered the wound.

The single tear sliding down her cheek tore at his heart. He wiped Joanna's cheeks then studied the damage to her hands. His temper, never really buried, rose again. He wanted to beat someone to a bloody pulp. Unfortunately, no one deserving of his wrath was available. Joanna certainly didn't deserve the brunt of his temper. He unclenched his fist and stroked her back.

"I'm behaving like a tot," Joanna said, her voice soft and vulnerable.

"Good Lord, Joanna. Weep, scream, or cry. You're entitled. I'd worry if you *weren't* frightened. There are grown men afraid to climb the main mast of the *Fleeting Star* for fear of falling such a height as you almost did. Most women would be hysterical by now."

"Hysteria is overrated." She smiled. "Besides, I knew you would find me once I managed to scream."

Amazing! The chit reassured *him*, the person she'd hired to protect her in the first place. The gesture infuriated him. He'd be damned if she assumed responsibility for this incident like she did everything else. *He* was to blame. Pure and simple.

Joanna apparently noticed the gaping tear in her

dress, which exposed her entire lower leg. Small holes littered the front, as well. "This was one of my favorite gowns," she said.

"It was ugly," he argued. When she gasped, he snapped, "It's the bloody truth. It should have been turned to rags long ago."

"I may not wear fancy dresses like other women, but there is no need to be rude!" One moment she was near tears, the next she chastised him like a tutor schooling him in manners. He found it endearing.

He pressed her head against his shoulder, afraid if he continued to stare at her mouth and tear-filled eyes, he might do something foolish. So foolish it bore no consideration.

He wanted to kiss her. He'd wanted it since that first morning amongst her flowers and sunshine. The absurd impulse had struck again while they danced and she'd looked at him with such unconcealed admiration and trust—as if he could single-handedly scale a hundred-foot wall. The sudden urge to mold his mouth to hers was almost irresistible. Especially for a man of his sexual experience.

He studied her hands, those delicate fingers that had no business being bloodied or torn. He raised them to his lips and placed gentle kisses on each palm.

Not a good idea. His arousal grew.

She trembled again. Fear still governed her body. Definitely this was not the time to kiss her. It was beyond stupid. He blew air from his mouth like a well-run horse. "Can you tell me what happened?" he asked.

"I wanted some fresh air, so I ventured upstairs. Suddenly, this huge shadow with a horrible voice was there. He said, 'Tell Randie we're tired of' waitin',' and then he said something about a warning."

She exhaled, choking back her tears, and sent a whisper of air across Mac's cheek. He felt his desire more keenly.

"I thought it the oddest thing, since I was surely going to die. How could I possibly give my brother a message?" She looked up at him with wide blue eyes. "Have you ever believed you were going to die?"

"There's been a time or two."

"I remember thinking I was glad that you and I danced. You're a wonderful dancer. Then I envisioned my poor mother in black once again. She truly hates black. So does Penelope. Chang doesn't mind so much. I would have ruined all their plans for a match with Westcliff." Finally Joanna's tears began to fall. She buried her face in his shoulder. "I could have *died*."

"But you didn't," Mac reassured her. His hands drifted up and down her spine. He kissed her brow, her cheek, tasted the salt from her tears. Knowing it was an idiotic, undisciplined thing to do, telling himself he simply offered comfort, he lowered his mouth to hers.

He meant the kiss to be brief, a small measure of reassurance. But then his lips touched hers and his good intentions fled like a thief stealing a parcel of fruit. He settled in and, in that moment, decided Joanna possessed the finest pair of lips in all of London.

Lips that parted beneath his.

He slowly thrust his tongue into her mouth. Sensing her hesitation, he retreated only to return once again. One moment caution ruled, the next he plundered.

This was insanity. He knew he should stop, retreat to the other side of the carriage and gain his equilibrium. Hell, the only safe place would be on a street corner at the other side of London.

One more kiss and he would pull away.

Joanna wrapped her hands about his neck and such thoughts blew away like rain in a summer squall. He slid his hand higher, felt the weight of her breasts. Then he was cupping their fullness, teasing the tender flesh. Her nipple pebbled against his palm.

He knew he should stop.

"Joanna," he whispered against her ear. "You are so bloody sweet."

Until today, she had thought her name ordinary, much like herself. When spoken in Mac's husky drawl, her name sounded almost pretty. Then Joanna remembered where she was, what had happened. The smug smile of Lady Dorridge flashed in her mind. Their conversation. A cold dose of reality jerked Joanna back to her senses. She pressed with her hands against Mac's shoulders.

He pulled back enough to study her from beneath

heavy lids. "What's the matter, sweetness?"

"Do not call me that! I should never allowed—" She averted her eyes, unable to face him and admit she had welcomed his kiss.

"What? Let me kiss you? I don't remember giving you a choice. But passion is nothing to be afraid of. In fact, it's quite common after an experience such as tonight's." He gently rubbed his finger across her lower lip. "There is nothing wrong with sharing a few kisses."

Sharing a few kisses? Hah! Her heart had tilted precariously close to initiating something altogether different. His calm demeanor only made her feel even more wretched. Unlike Mac, Joanna was not in the habit of sharing such intimacies. And she certainly had no desire to be another notch in MacDonald Archer's bedpost. Unfortunately, she feared his kisses were already a permanent part of her.

"We must not do that again," she said. His acquiescence came too slowly. "Do you hear me? I do not need your kisses any more than I need your compliments. Save them for your other women."

He looked insulted. "What are you insinuating?"

Her tears threatened to return. What was the matter with her? She never lost her composure so completely. "I would rather not discuss the subject any further."

"I'd rather we do."

She gave a sigh of annoyance. "Do people always do as you wish?"

"No. But I will not let you make the comment you did and then ignore it."

He *had* told her she could always speak her mind. She intended to find out if his open-mindedness was real. Joanna folded her hands in her lap. "I met Lady Dorridge this evening. She enlightened me about your past liaison."

"That was a long time ago." When Joanna frowned, Mac dragged his hand through his hair. "I never claimed to be a saint, but what does Lady Dorridge have to do with what just happened between you and me?"

"I have no desire to be manipulated, then cast off like a withered floral arrangement."

His gaze, hot and languid only moments before, turned to ice. "Is that what she told you? That I discarded her without a care?"

"More or less. That you were a master at seduction. That she was but one of many ladies you seduce."

He moved to the seat across the carriage. "And what did you say?"

Ignoring the loss of warmth his absence brought, she said, "I told her the truth, that our relationship is strictly business and that I already understand your feelings on women and marriage."

"Let me clarify something for you. If Lady Dorridge were the last woman on Earth, I would not accept her favors."

"Your affairs are none of my business," she rejoined.

"You tossed her name into the discussion, not I, so I feel compelled to explain." Leaning back against the seat, Mac crossed his arms. "Lord Dorridge flaunted his mistresses in front of his wife, so Lady Dorridge decided to teach him a lesson. I was the pawn in her little game. What better way to exact revenge than to take an untitled bastard to her bed? Don't mistake me—I went willingly, as I'd done on any number of occasions with an endless stream of widows and matrons. The difference was that Lady Dorridge ran to her husband, eager to reveal her sins."

"There is no need to tell me all this."

He shot her a baleful glare that clearly reminded Joanna that she had broached the subject, not he. "The outcome was not what Lady Dorridge expected. She paid for her indiscretion with a lengthy sojourn to the country. Lord Dorridge challenged me to a duel, but the coward took his marks early, humiliating himself before his friends. Which is why he hates me. Now you know the entire sordid story." He leaned forward and cupped her chin. "Do not, ever, compare yourself to Lady Dorridge or any other woman I have been with."

Confused and frightened by his words and the intensity of his emotion, Joanna sought safety in her dignity. "I see no reason for you to be angry with me."

He stared out the carriage window for the longest time, saying nothing. Then, "I'm angry with myself."

"Because you kissed me?"

A wry smile twisted his lips. "That is the one thing I'm not angry about."

For the moment, the storm had passed. She cocked her head. "Then why are you angry?"

"First and foremost I am angry with myself. Because you've done such a fine job of convincing everyone that Randolph is simply avoiding his duties and not missing, I should have anticipated the threat to you. The mistake won't happen again. Tonight's fiasco proves how desperate these people are, which shows your brother owed them something that they want very badly."

The shift in topic offered Joanna no comfort. Until tonight she had hoped and prayed that Randolph was somehow uninvolved in what was happening. After the episode at the ball, she knew Mac spoke the truth. "Do you believe Randolph stole the statue for these people?"

"It is a definite possibility."

"I wish I had found a way to give him the money."

"Don't you dare take responsibility for his actions!" Mac snapped.

Joanna thought for a moment, then asked, "If he stole the statue as we believe, why did he disappear? Where did he go? And why didn't he deliver it?"

Mac shrugged his shoulders. "If the boy gambled with his friends at the hells and lost, there's no telling. When it comes to collecting debts, creditors don't politely ask for their money. Maybe Randolph decided to pawn the statue to pay gambling losses. Or perhaps someone was trying to blackmail him."

"So you definitely think it was my brother?"

"Until we either find the statue or Randolph, or learn who is behind those notes, I'll discount no one, including Lord Tatterton and Lord Dorridge."

"Lord Dorridge warned me to stay away from you. And he wants the statue—even his wife said so. I think we should move him to the top of our list of suspects. He is not a very nice man."

"On that we agree."

The carriage rolled to a stop. Lights flickered in the Fenton townhouse's windows, small beacons that normally offered solace from inhospitable weather. Tonight, returning home only served as a reminder of her brother's probable deceit. "It seems we are running in circles."

"Not really. We know your brother pawned your father's watch, which means as of a week ago he was still alive. There is, as yet, no word on the streets of precious gems being sold or a statue being pawned. Which means your brother likely still has possession of the dragon."

"What of private collectors?" she asked quietly. "We would never know if . . ."

"We may consider such a possibility if nothing else pans out. When I mentioned your brother, Charlesworth grew nervous. Ashford became even more taciturn. My instincts tell me they are somehow involved. Tomorrow night I'll venture to their haunts and perhaps learn something useful. With a bit of luck, those two will be there."

"What do you want me to do?"

"Stay home. After tonight, you surely realize these people are dangerous."

"I have no intention of taking unnecessary risks," she agreed, then placed a hand on his arm. "But only I can recognize the man who threatened me tonight."

"He's likely only hired help. We may not see him again. Anyway, I want the person in charge."

"Mr. Archer, please do not worry. I have you to protect me."

"But who will protect you from me?"

The heat of his gaze startled her. "I was not aware I needed such protection."

He glanced out the window, and she thought she heard him say, "Perhaps more than you know."

Chapter Ten

Hells like Eden promised it all.

Sheltered beneath the towering warehouses east of Ratcliff Highway, two small lamps marked the entrance at the bottom of a steep flight of stairs. The stench of dead fish and stagnant water hung in the air. Malevolence filled the shadows. Yet carriages rumbled past, depositing those arrogant or foolish enough to risk their coin, all in the name of sport, desperation, or a taste of excitement.

Mac frequented such establishments from time to time, but none as uninviting as Eden. Which proved what he already knew: Randolph and his cohorts were beyond stupid.

Jumping out of his carriage, Adam studied their surroundings like a general strategizing for battle. "Charming. So far, we've been to the Keeping Room,

Purgatory, the Gargoyle and the Lair. Who do suppose thinks up these names?"

"Some clever businessman eager to raid the purses of we who are stupid enough to try our luck at such places."

Adam laughed. "Take my wife's advice. Allow Miss Fenton to rescue your misguided soul and settle down. You might live to the ripe old age of thirty-five."

No matter how many times Adam broached the topic—it seemed to be once every half hour—marriage was the last thing Mac intended to discuss. Especially marriage to Joanna Fenton. They were cut from altogether different cloths.

She needed brick walls and mortar. He preferred open skies and endless horizons. She sought to satisfy everyone. He answered to no man. She wanted a family. To him, family meant all things unfamiliar: Responsibility. Compromise. Abandonment of the only life he knew, trusted and understood—the one thing in which he felt truly on equal ground with the rest of the world.

Not that the idiotic idea hadn't crossed his mind the last few days . . . which was absolutely absurd since he'd known the woman only a week. The memory of her passionate response in the carriage reminded him of how badly he wanted her in his bed. And she had wanted him. He was sure of it. Her allure grew stronger every day they spent together. The dainty manner in which she slipped her fingers into her gloves fascinated him; the compassion she showed street urchins warmed his heart, and the way she worried her lower lip when she felt unsure of herself made him want to wrap her in his arms and kiss her senseless.

He kept telling himself a quick tumble with one of Maddie's girls would vanquish any and all lusty impulses toward her. For one reason or another though, he hadn't managed to find time to visit the whorehouse. Instead, he and Joanna, Chang in tow, had scoured the pawn shops, visited galleries, questioned jewelers and dissected her father's library and journals. In the evenings, Mac visited the hells Ashford and Charlesworth claimed to frequent. He had discovered nothing more than the fact that Randolph had poor taste in entertainment.

The balance of his time had been spent tending to his shipping business. He'd arranged a potential buyer for his first cargo, hired three new crewmen and charted his course to Jamaica. Decks were scoured and supplies ordered. His final delivery of cognac was scheduled. Each of the tasks served as anchors to the life Mac knew and understood, that of a seaman. He and Joanna would part ways the minute he found her brother and the statue. Even if Adam and Rebecca thought otherwise.

Glancing in both directions, Mac studied the dimly lit street before Eden. "I'm not a family man destined to have a dog at my heels and slippers by the fire, Adam. And, if you remember, Miss Fenton is the reason we're visiting this lovely place."

Peggy Waide

His friend shook his head. "If I can be a happily married man, there is hope for you. If you live long enough. When do you make your last delivery?"

"Three more days."

"I'll say it one last time, though I know you'll ignore me—it's not too late to change your mind."

"Exactly," Mac agreed. Then he marched down the steps and knocked on the door to the hell.

Someone peered through the small wicket before, ever so slowly, the door opened. A man with shoulders the size of Westminster Abbey and a jagged scar crawling across his cheek blocked the entry. Bouncer, protector, proprietor, or all-around nasty-person-to-deal-with, he guarded the door with the effectiveness of a cavalry troop. Crossing his arms, he asked, "What's your pleasure, gents?"

"An acquaintance suggested we might like what you have to offer," Mac said. "We thought to give it a go."

"And who might your acquaintance be?"

After glancing about the room, Mac met Scarface's question with perfect aristocratic disdain. "Lord Fenton. I was hoping to see him tonight."

Recognition or perhaps wariness flickered in the man's eyes. Mac would have missed the reaction had he not been carefully watching.

Scarface scratched his ear. "Don't recall the name, but we gots a lot of customers, so I'll take your word for it. The ladies are willing, gamble as long as you gots the blunt to cover the bets, and no cheating."

As the man retreated to the shadows, Mac whispered to Adam, "Cheerful fellow. I wager cheating is reserved for the dealers." He handed his overcoat to the young boy of twelve or thirteen who appeared to take it. "And he was lying. Fenton supposedly came here several times a week. Not only would Scarface remember Randolph, he'd welcome the youngster with open arms. So let's have a look-see."

Below the raised entryway, lords, sailors, common workers, even a few women, crowded around the various gaming tables. Men and scantily clad females drifted up and down the staircase at the far side of the room. The furnishings were decent, the lighting subdued. Smoke shifted with the moving bodies. Servants bearing trays laden with glasses bustled through the crowd.

A mural, aptly titled "Temptation," covered much of the back wall. A voluptuous Eve, wearing a calculating smile and nothing else, tempted her mate in the Garden of Eden. Satan, himself, formed the body of the tree with one of his arms curving into a green-eyed serpent that leered over Eve's shoulder. This first scene blended into a second, which Mac considered a particularly twisted version of Man's fall from grace. Nymphs cavorted in a variety of acts of sexual dominance over men. It was enough to make him shudder.

"I'd say we have a solid connection between the serpent design on Randolph's notes and this place," Mac said as he glanced toward the gaming tables.

Adam nodded, then pointed.

Ashford played at a hazard table. And sunk in a

leather chair below Satan was Charlesworth, a scantily dressed female draped across his lap, no doubt doing her best to convince him to spend his coin on her.

"You take Ashford," Mac said. "I think Charlesworth needs to be rescued before that whore swallows him whole."

Noting the faces in the crowd, Mac crossed the room and dragged a chair opposite Charlesworth. A young girl slid beside him, offering a drink along with a glimpse of breasts covered by a melange of sheer red scarves. Shaking his head, Mac said, "I'll have what this chap's having. Charlesworth, old boy, your glass is empty. Shall I buy you another?"

"That . . . would be grand." Charlesworth's words were slurred. "You're the fellow from the Westcliff ball, the friend of Randie's."

"Exactly. I hoped Randolph might be here with you."

"Not so far." Charlesworth shot a furtive glance toward the doorway where Scarface lurked.

"Who's the big fellow?" Mac asked.

"Jinx. He's a raw one. Don't much like him."

"You're not supposed to like him." Through the smoke and cacopharous noise, Mac studied Charlesworth. Sullen, the boy was. No surprise. Though alcohol flowed freely and women were plentiful, this hell reeked of desperation.

When the serving girl delivered their drinks, Mac placed an extra coin in her hand and tossed another to the doxy on Charlesworth's lap. He followed his generosity with a tip of his head. Both girls drifted away like swirls of smoke. Sipping his drink, Mac asked, "So, tell me. How did you find this charming place?"

"Ashford brought me. Said it would be fun." Charlesworth stared at his drink, his eyelids heavy. "But I don't think I've had fun for a long time."

Mac leaned forward in his chair. "Why do you suppose that is?"

"Don't know what you mean."

"Come now. Don't be shy. Consider me your newest and best friend. I can help, but you have to trust me."

"There's . . . nothing to tell." The boy looked miserable.

"No?" Mac grabbed him by the coat. "You're up to your balls in trouble, boy. You're either too stupid or too scared to admit it. I think Randolph is in even bigger trouble. Now, I intend to have some answers."

"Ashford won't like it." Charlesworth's voice was a whisper.

Mac moved his hold to the young lord's elegant cravat. "You won't like what I do to you, either. Let *me* worry about Ashford. Tell me about Fenton."

Like a trapped animal, the young noble glanced from side to side. "Randie lost a lot of blunt. When he knew he was in too deep and Jinx started pressing for payment, he became real scared. Ashford said he had a way for Randie to even things out. Then Randie up and disappeared. And I don't think he took to the country like his sister says. Ashford is bloody furious."

Once Charlesworth decided to talk, his words had come out in a flurry. Mac processed them while he asked, "Why would Ashford care?"

"I have no idea. I swear. And I don't know where Randie is, but I hope he's all right. He was always nice to me. Ashford isn't so nice anymore." The boy's eyes filled with tears.

Mac felt disgust well up in him. He had little sympathy for spoiled children. "What else do you know about the Fentons' statue?"

"The dragon?" Charlesworth shook his head. "Nothing. Honest."

"Do you want it for yourself?"

"No."

"Desperation clings to you like a second skin. Why, Charlesworth? Have you lost a lot of blunt, too?"

"No." Panic filled the lad's eyes. He blinked several times. He was obviously terrified. Unfortunately, interference in the hulking form of Jinx ambled in Mac's direction. Loosening his hold on Charlesworth, Mac finished, "A word of advice. Go home, pack your bags, and leave London before you find yourself at the bottom of the Thames. These people don't play around."

Jinx cleared his throat. "Problem?"

"Not at all." Mac gave his most charming grin. "Charlesworth and I were simply deciding whether or not his cravat was worth ruining in our dispute over a tumble with one of your girls."

"I see." Jinx studied Charlesworth for several seconds. "Come along, sir. Your friend's waiting."

Jinx gathered the young lord and guided him toward Ashford who waited at the front door. These fellows were taking no chances with the loose-tongued lad. Hopefully, the boy would take Mac's advice to heart and leave town—but not before Mac had a chance to speak with him again.

Waiting for Adam to finish a card game he'd begun, Mac sipped cognac. The girl draped with scarves descended the stairs, plopped into Mac's lap and wrapped her bare arms around his shoulders. She nipped his ear. "Are you Lord Fenton's friend?"

"That depends."

"If'n you'd try looking a bit interested so Jinx don't wonder what I'm saying, we might be able to see if we got anything in common. What do you want with Randie?"

The girl was either genuinely concerned or Jinx's snitch. Given his lack of leads, Mac was willing to take a risk. He tipped her chin as if studying the merchandise. "Fenton's been acting rather odd lately. His sister is worried. She asked me to help. I understand he lost a lot of money."

"They cheat at the tables here. I warned Randie, but he ignored me. He didn't have the money to pay."

"Did he say what he planned to do?"

"Said he had a way to fix it. Said he'd come back when he did. But that was weeks ago. He gave me this to keep in a safe place." She slid one hand over Mac's chest, slipping something into his coat pocket.

149

"What about Charlesworth? Does he owe Jinx money?"

"All's I know is he gambled, too."

"Thank you." He kissed her forehead. "If you hear from Fenton, send word to MacDonald Archer at the Pig'-N'-Whistle."

"If'n it will help Randie. Tell 'im I miss 'im." She placed a smacking kiss on his lips, winked and sashayed over to a portly fellow who eagerly accepted her offerings.

Adam leaned over the top of his chair. "Lucky you. You always did have a way with the ladies. What did the chit have to say?"

Mac explained what he'd learned, then added, "I doubt we'll discover anything else tonight. Let's get out of here."

Seated inside Adam's carriage, he pulled a scarf of red silk laced with gold threads from his pocket. Embroidered in the corner were two serpents twisted to form the letter E. He gave the scarf to Adam. "A similar theme. What do you think? E for Eden?"

"That would be the logical deduction," Adam said. "E for evil fits nicely. Then there's Eve. And of course the serpent contains the letter E." He grinned. "Why do you suppose Randolph gave this to the girl?"

"He must have thought it important. We know Randolph owed these people money, which explains the blackmail notes. When he disappeared and Joanna fabricated an excuse for him, they changed their tactics to threats. Based on what Annie said, I wager Randolph stole the statue, intending to sell the thing."

"He could have hocked the statue, paid the debt, claimed he was innocent and gone on his merry way. Why disappear?"

"Perhaps Randolph is at the bottom of the Thames." Mac took back the scarf and rubbed it between his fingers. The stitching of its logo might have been sewn anywhere, but the silk was exquisite and, hopefully, easily traceable. "I believe Joanna and I are going shopping tomorrow."

Lush velvets, cheerful muslins and exquisite Indian prints lined the walls of one of the smaller dress shops near Bond Street. A violet-blue satin that reminded Joanna of delphiniums lay on a shelf in the corner. The fabric was absolutely stunning. Without thinking, she rubbed the material against her cheek, imagining the feel of it as a gown against her skin.

"You would look beautiful in that," Mac said.

She let the satin slip from her fingers. "Perhaps, but I have no need of a new dress."

"True. You need a dozen or so."

She ignored his remark—the sixth he'd made today, but who was counting. Chang had been no better. He had elaborated on the dismal condition of her wardrobe, which only fueled Mac's determination to torment her.

A part of her was thrilled that Mac had taken an interest in what she wore, a negative interest it seemed, but an interest all the same. Another part feared he was like all the other men who thought the pretty package defined a woman. Yet the other night in the carriage, he hadn't seemed the least concerned that she wore a gown that was three years old. He had still kissed her senseless. Days later, the memory still brought a flush to her skin and a pulse in her loins. It was most disconcerting. Thank goodness a short slender woman with a cheerful countenance saved Joanna from considering the matter any further.

"Good afternoon. May I help you?"

Joanna pulled from her purse the silk scarf Mac had given her, prepared to offer the same explanation she had used at the seven previous shops: "My cousin and I found this scarf, and it is obvious someone went to a great deal of trouble to have it sewn as a special gift. Surely they are distraught at such a loss. Perhaps you could help locate this person?"

The seamstress studied the scarf and her face brightened. "I remember this. Exquisite, is it not?"

Joanna noted the excitement on Mac's face. Feeling a similar rush, she nodded.

"I believe my Nellie did this embroidery. She has a fine hand. If I recall, a gentleman purchased the scarf as a gift . . . along with a robe."

"Marvelous," Mac said. "If you would be so kind as to check your records and see who placed the order? We would love to see the scarf returned to its rightful owner."

"Let me think for a moment." The seamstress circled around Joanna, an artist studying a canvas. She shook her head, clucked a time or two and loosed a calculated look on Mac. "I believe I still have that particular record. Perhaps you and your cousin would like to look at fabrics for a new gown while I check. The blue satin would be lovely."

Joanna planted her hands on her hips. "You cannot expect us to—"

"What an excellent idea, Madame," Mac cut her off. "My cousin could actually use several new gowns."

"There is nothing wrong with my gowns," Joanna argued, pleased that she had managed to keep the irritation out of her voice. Barely. Mac knew she couldn't afford new clothes, so why was he putting her in such an awkward position?

The dressmaker tsked.

Grabbing Joanna's arm, Mac moved a discreet four feet away and whispered, "We need the name of the person who bought this scarf, and since we're here, you might as well do as the woman suggests."

"She's asking us to—that is outright blackmail."

"More like bribery." When she frowned, he added, "Think of it as a charitable donation. Do you want to find your brother?"

"How can you suggest otherwise?" She glanced over her shoulder and smiled at the seamstress who pretended to sort through a stack of fashion plates. "I simply see no reason to allow this woman to manipulate us into spending our coin. Surely there is another way."

"There is one. I can break into this shop when everyone leaves. Of course, I could be caught and tossed into Newgate. The owner may very well take her records home with her and—"

Joanna held her hand in the air. "Do not waste your breath. You know I won't allow you to take such a chance. But I would be as frivolous as my mother if I spent money I do not have on a new gown."

"Take the cost out of my one hundred pounds."

"I certainly will not. That would make me . . . well . . . the same as . . . never mind." Mac scowled. "It would not be proper," she finished lamely.

"Good Christ, Joanna. I'm buying you a bloody dress, not asking you to my bed, not that the thought hasn't crossed my mind a few dozen times."

His voice was too loud, and the dressmaker gasped.

What exactly did one do with information such as Mac had just imparted, Joanna wondered? She had no previous experience and certainly no answer. She stared at Mac blankly.

Snarling, for that was the only way to describe the manner in which Mac's lips curled, he yanked the blue satin from the shelf, dragged Joanna to a place before a mirror, and draped the fabric over her shoulder. "Listen to me. For once in your life, aside from the fact that we need the information, think about yourself."

Joanna stared at the fabric. There was no denying its beauty, but the last thing she wanted to do was wrap herself up in a fancy package and then see disappointment in Mac's eyes when he compared her to other women. She'd come to believe, even after her conversation with Lady Dorridge, that he liked her. At least a little, even without the trimmings of wealth.

Tears pooled in her eyes, an embarrassing display of emotion that seemed to happen frequently these days. She handed the fabric back. "I will not accept your charity. Nor will I allow myself to feel indebted to you. Offer the woman a few coins for her information and let us go home."

She managed three steps before he whirled her about and backed her against the wall. "We're not leaving until you have a new dress."

The seamstress stared at them. "Is everything all right, sir?"

Mac shooed her away. The woman went into her office.

"Good heavens, you're causing a scene," Joanna hissed.

"I don't give a damn, nor do I understand the problem. Most women would leap at the opportunity to buy a new gown!"

"I am not most women."

He dragged his fingers through his hair. "Trust me, I am more aware of that fact than you can possibly know. You're keeping something from me—now, what is it? And don't try to lie. You're horrible at it."

She nudged her chin up. "If people cannot see beyond a fancy dress, then why should I bother trying to please them? I am what I am. A fancy gown will not make a difference. I am not Penelope, my mother, Lydia Litmore or Lady Dorridge."

"And your point is?" he asked.

Mercy, however had they worked their way to this particular topic? Mortified to have to reveal what she considered one of her greatest flaws, but determined to end this nonsense once and for all, she blurted, "I am plump." Her cheeks flushed even as she spoke.

Mac flashed a devastatingly irresistible grin. "Only a dog likes a bone, Joanna. Most men, myself included, like to know they've a *woman* in their bed."

He was either being kind or cruel; Joanna wasn't sure. She wasn't sure, but it looked like she would have to bare her entire soul. "And I'm plain."

He rubbed his chin, considering, adding to her discomfort as he continued to stare. She suddenly wished for a blanket to hide beneath.

"First off, you are lovely inside and out—though somewhere along the line you decided to hide yourself in brown sacks rather than pretty paper with ribbons." He turned her around to face the mirror. "Secondly you've a fine figure, but the clothes you wear will make anyone wonder whether you know it, even yourself."

She watched her reflection in the mirror as his gaze floated down her. She felt her knees wobble under his bold assessment. He tossed her hat to the floor and loosened the pins in her hair, sending it down about her waist.

"You have beautiful hair, but you need a style that is soft and alluring." To demonstrate, he fashioned her curls into a loose knot at the nape of her neck and freed a few about her face.

"And you have fine breasts, but the gowns you wear conceal every curve."

She looked at him, stunned. "You must not say such things!"

She might as well have been talking to a wall for all the good it did. The man was determined to prove a point. He tugged her dress lower to reveal a fair amount of bosom. Joanna's heart pounded against her ribs as his gaze settled on the flesh he'd uncovered. Then his hands slid downward as he described the rest of her figure with a carnal honesty that was wholly improper and filled her body with tremors. He even complimented her feet. Her feet, for goodness sake!

She wanted to believe him.

All her life, she'd been reminded that she resembled her father. She had her father's hair, his skin, his tendency to hold flesh. She wasn't soft and pink like Penelope or her mother. She'd lived with those subtle observations all her life only to have the same beliefs reinforced during her first season.

It was odd to see oneself through a man's eyes—one who, for the first time, seemed to find you attractive. A tiny whisper of hope settled in her stomach and grew.

Then the conversation with Lady Dorridge surfaced, along with Joanna's insecurities and all the reasons not to buy the gown. Penelope and her mother had a closet full of new dresses—and with good reason. This was Penelope's year to find a husband. And her mother defined herself through her wardrobe. Which didn't leave much money for her.

But this once she wanted to be selfish. She wanted Mac to buy her the gown. But prudence reared its unforgiving head.

"I appreciate the flattery, though I have no doubt it is unfounded. And I have some question why you are interested."

Mac felt his own bewilderment. "I'm as baffled as you are. All I know is that it *matters*." Maybe he wanted to see her smile, make her happy. Maybe he wanted to dress Joanna in a manner he hadn't been able to dress his mother. Maybe he wanted to see her in a new gown to please himself, so he could fantasize about her in it. And if she thought he was behaving like a bully, he didn't care. She wasn't leaving without a bloody gown!

He'd seen her expression, the longing, the wanting, then the pride she had. If given the chance, she'd likely offer up a dozen more excuses to refuse the dress. Fine. He'd keep her mouth closed until she agreed. He tipped her chin with his hand and kissed her brow, her cheek.

"Mac," she whispered.

He nibbled his way to her lips, then hesitated a scant half inch away. "It's just a dress, Joanna."

"This isn't at all proper."

"But proper isn't near as satisfying."

No longer caring where they were or even their purpose, Mac kissed her. Thoughts of fabric and gowns and scarves became a distant memory. He settled into her softness, her breasts pressing against his chest. A heart pounded—his or hers, he wasn't sure and didn't care.

Her tongue touched his as light as a soft summer breeze. Passion flared instantly. His hand cupped her breast as he pulled her against him. She moaned and he swallowed the sound, pressing closer, absorbing everything she offered.

Somewhere in the dim recesses of his mind, he chided himself. He was standing in clothes shop, acting wanton and thinking of nothing but making love to Joanna. He felt the urgency of a sailor on dry land after six months at sea.

He lifted his head. Joanna's eyes were heavy with desire. The emotion quickly faded, replaced by her infuriating little look of propriety. Now she would lecture him on their fall from grace. He placed a finger to her lips. "Before you tell me once again that we have behaved improperly, let's settle this once and for all. Your rules mean nothing to me. I wanted to kiss you, and you wanted me to kiss you. We can both think on that and decide what to do. As for the dress, we need the name. The woman has it. Take what I offer with no strings, no ties, nothing. A gift."

Her sigh of resignation came from deep in her chest. "I will make a deal with you," she agreed. "You may pay for the gown, but only because I have decided I *want* the dress, and only as long as you accept my voucher. When the auction is over, I intend to repay you every pence."

A smart man knew when to capitulate—or at least to pretend. If Joanna thought he'd ever take her money, she was sorely mistaken. He'd be halfway to Jamaica before she had a chance to repay him.

Allowing her no time to change her mind, they ordered a pink muslin day gown, chose a design, and paid. And they had the name of the person who'd bought the scarf.

Ashford.

Mac felt more than satisfied with the day's events.

Chapter Eleven

The curtains were drawn on Ashford's austere three-story townhouse even though it was well past ten o'clock. The temperature was climbing, and the sun valiantly fought through the morning fog. Joanna glanced at Mac and Chang. Their clenched jaws coupled with the rigid set of their shoulders punctuated the two men's frustration. And *they* had called *her* stubborn.

"Sweet Empress. I am here and intend to stay, so the both of you may as well wipe the scowls from your faces."

"So that you might convince yourself I'm pleased you forced my hand?" Mac poured his irritation into pounding the brass knocker on Ashford's front door. The noise echoed down this quiet street just north of

St. James Park. "A sensible woman would have done as I asked and remained at home."

"You continue to forget that I know Ashford better than you, and will more likely recognize any falsehoods he might tell. Besides, Ashford can tax a *patient* man's temper. You would likely strangle him within the first five minutes of this visit . . . if I weren't here to keep you civil." She felt a certain amused fondness for Mac's fits of temper.

Mac's eyes narrowed. "If I discover he had anything to do with your 'accident' the other night, nothing will stop me from knocking him into the ground. And quit looking so pleased with yourself."

She matched him glare for glare, a hint of a smile making her lips twitch. Until recently, such open defiance was beyond her. Whether good or bad, she liked the change.

Mac pounded on the door once more. "Where the devil are the servants?"

"Ashford is likely still abed," Joanna answered. "His friends rarely call this early in the morning—I know, as his friends are my brother's. But his servants should answer. . . . Maybe we should come back later."

"Maybe," Mac said. He took the doorknob in his hand. It turned easily. "Maybe not."

Her astonishment blended with wariness, Joanna grabbed Mac's elbow. "What are you doing?"

"Since the door is unlocked and since we're already here, I say we look around."

"Absolutely not. How would we explain our presence should someone find us wandering Ashford's halls?"

Mac smiled irreverently. "Come on, Joanna. You wanted to come along. Live dangerously."

She stood firm. "You cannot enter a gentleman's home unannounced. Such behavior is beyond the pale. Chang, tell him."

Chang crossed his arms over his chest. "If urn lack character of urn, why call it urn? Ashford no gentleman."

Mac slapped the butler on the back. "Well said. I'm going in. Feel free to wait in the carriage, Joanna." And with that, he disappeared into the shadows of Ashford's foyer.

"You'd like that, wouldn't you," she whispered to no one in particular since Chang had followed Mac. And the men claimed *she* lacked common sense. She tiptoed after them. "Should I land in Newgate, my mother will never forgive me."

"Shhhh," Mac called from the bottom of the stairway curving up to the rooms above. "Listen."

She froze mid-step, half expecting a platoon of servants to come marching down the stairs. All she heard was the beating of her heart. There was no shuffling of feet, muted conversation, rattling of pans, or sweeping of floors sounding from anywhere in the house. "There is no noise at all," she remarked.

"Exactly." Mac pulled a pistol from his coat.

"Why do you have a gun?" she asked. "You said you only meant to talk with Ashford!"

"I simply keep prepared for the unexpected. I carry a weapon most everywhere I go, especially when accompanying females who lack the sense to stay home where they belong. Relax. Nothing is going to happen—unless of course, you're caught with the silver service beneath your skirts."

"Your attempt at humor escapes me," she complained. "And quit pouting because I made you bring me along."

"Be quiet then, and don't make me regret my decision. I would just as soon look around before we're arrested."

The dining room, typically busy this time of day, was devoid of activity. No tantalizing scent of breakfast fare lured the master from his bed. The front parlor was just as empty, just as silent. Two chairs and a table were positioned before the fireplace; otherwise the room was empty.

Joanna slid her hand across the back of one threadbare chair. "Evidently Ashford spent his coin elsewhere than on furniture."

"Likely the gaming tables."

Joanna peeked through an arched doorway. The closed window curtains washed the next room in shadow. Floor-to-ceiling shelves loomed on three of the four walls. Ashford liked books, it seemed—a surprising discovery since the man was such a bore. "What are we looking for?" she asked.

"Anything remotely tied to the statue or your brother," Mac answered. He slid to her side, pointing to a pair of black boots jutting from behind the desk in the corner. "Chang, come here. Joanna, stay put." He crept across the floor and peered over the top of the desk.

Ashford lay crumpled there. Spittle trickled from the corners of his mouth. His eyes, dilated and unfocused, stared upward, but the heavenly chorus of angels painted on the ceiling could do little for him now. His body convulsed. Air poured from his mouth with a wheeze, then ceased altogether.

"Is he dead?" Joanna whispered from behind Mac, her words raw with panic.

Every muscle in Mac's body tensed. "I told you to stay put."

Chang moved to Ashford's side, lifted the man's eyelids and studied his lips. "Poison."

"Are you sure?" Mac asked.

Chang nodded.

"The poor man," Joanna whispered. "We must send for the authorities."

Dragging his fingers through his hair, Mac shifted his gaze from Ashford to Joanna. All color had disappeared from her face. Her hand braced the corner of the desk as she swayed to the side. Damn. She was going to faint. And it was his fault for allowing her to come in the first place!

Well, there was nothing to be done now but keep her safe. Gripping her shoulders, Mac steadied his voice. "And tell them what? That we just walked into Ashford's house and happened to find him dead? Pardon my cynicism, but I have little faith that I won't end up as a permanent guest in Newgate." He added the other reason she would want to avoid the authorities. "If nothing else, think of your mother and sister. Imagine the questions that would be raised if we were involved in such a scandal."

"We cannot leave him here," she answered quietly.

Her voice trembled, along with her hands, evidence that the gravity of the situation had began to sink in. Still, Mac was amazed at her control thus far. She'd just watched a man die and hadn't run screaming from the room. The woman had mettle. He liked that.

"Yes, we can. There is nothing we can do for him except perhaps discover the identity of his murderer. And we must save your brother the same fate. Someone will find his body soon enough."

He needed to get her moving. Rubbing his hands up and down her arms, he asked, "Would you rather wait in the carriage, or help Chang search the bookshelves?"

"I'd rather not be alone." She stumbled toward the shelves, her shoulders slumped.

Mac wanted to sweep her away to somewhere safe, to remove the sadness from her eyes. But the best he could offer was the resolution of her problems: he must find her brother and that blasted statue! He set to work on Ashford's desk.

An empty glass sat on the corner, a plate with a sliced apple nearby. Another glass, likely belonging to some guest, was on the mantel over the fireplace, which had not been lit. There were no signs of forced entry or a struggle. As far as Mac could tell, Ashford had known his murderer. They'd sat, shared a friendly drink, a little food, and talked. All while the poison killed him. Very neat and tidy.

Several papers littered the desktop: general correspondence that had no relevance to Lung Wang Sun or Randolph. The desk drawers contained ledgers, ink, sealing wax, stationary but little else. Mac turned his attention to the dead man lying at his feet.

His pockets were empty. A white linen handkerchief, steeped with some herb, lay on the floor beside his shoulder. A small gold object stuck out between the fingers of his fisted hand. Mac pried Ashford's fingers open, thankful that Joanna stood on the other side of the room. Upon closer inspection, he realized the object was a gold serpent with a single red ruby as an eye. "I'll be damned."

A floorboard creaked from somewhere near the dining room.

Granted, it might be a servant returning from wherever they all were, but Mac had his doubts. And even if it were a servant, he had no desire to be caught kneeling beside a dead earl. Also, Joanna's safety superceded all else.

Mac tucked the gold serpent and the handkerchief in his pocket to study later, grabbed Joanna's hand and motioned for Chang to follow. He opened and slipped through the study window, then caught Joanna about the waist as Chang helped her out the same way. At last the butler leapt through, landing on his feet with the same agility as Confucius. He shut the window.

Behind them, the back door rattled.

They spun and crouched behind a hedgerow of privet in full bloom just as a man wearing a dirty black coat stepped outside. A hat pulled low on his head covered most of his face.

Joanna gasped. "Randolph!"

The man whirled in the direction of the noise, then fear gripped him. In a moment, he was sprinting across the garden toward St. James Park.

An order for Chang to take Joanna to the carriage flew from Mac's mouth even as he gave chase. He called twice to Randolph, but to no avail. A thick patch of shrubs swallowed the lad before Mac could catch up.

Glorious color flowed from bloom to bloom. Sunshine warmed the conservatory, kissing new buds into life. Yet all Joanna felt was a bone-chilling cold. They'd stopped by Charlesworth's house on the way back, but he had not been there. His servants had told them nothing.

All Joanna could see was death. Ashford's. No one deserved such a brutal end to his life, even a lost soul with a weakness for cards and alcohol. Tucked away in the recesses of her mind, she harbored uncharitable gratitude, thanking God that it hadn't been Randolph on Ashford's parlor floor. But the possibility her brother had administered the poison that killed Ashford was too much too bear. And where was Charlie? Trembling, she fought the inclination to slide into Mac's arms and instead burrowed into the corner of the settee.

Mac placed a glass in her hand. "Drink this."

"I do not drink spirits."

"Today you do."

She started to protest. Hs brow arched high on his forehead in a manner she now recognized. Arguing was futile. He meant to have his way, and at the moment she simply hadn't the energy to debate the issue. One sip sent the liquid burning down her throat. Heat spread from her chest to her limbs.

Kneeling before her, Mac asked, "Are you all right?"

Such an absurd question. She doubted she'd ever be the same again. "Let me think. I found a dead body today; saw my brother dash through St. James Park as though Xing Tian, the Headless Giant, gave chase; his other friend is missing; my mother thinks I have lost my mind; my family is on the verge of bankruptcy; and the one heirloom that can save them is missing."

Mac rubbed his hands up and down her arms. "Could be worse, though. . . ."

Ashford's hollow eyes flashed before her, his final shuddering breath. She doubted she'd ever sleep again. Mac, on the other hand, seemed capable of a nap. She found his composure most frustrating. "I imagine dying bodies litter your past."

He gave her a hard look. "You make me sound like John Williams of Ratcliff Highway." Then he added,

"I've seen my share of death, yes. But it's never an easy thing, no matter the circumstance."

"I should never like to see another," she said. She closed her eyes and inhaled a deep breath. "And I feel so guilty."

"For God's sake, why? *You* certainly aren't responsible."

"I keep thinking it is better that Ashford died than Randolph. Doesn't that make me a horrible person?"

"It makes you a sister who loves her brother."

"How ever will I manage tea with Lady Litmore and her daughter this afternoon? My mother will be furious."

"You'll do fine. If need be, plead a headache and leave the social chatter for her and Penelope. And Chang will help. He seems to be very good at that." After a moment, Mac handed a white linen handkerchief to her. "Does this mean anything to you?"

A noticeably sweet scent caught her attention. "This handkerchief has been drenched with peppermint."

"Yes, I noticed."

Unwrapping the linen, Joanna stared at a golden serpent. A ruby eye glared back. She shuddered. "Where did you find this?"

"Ashford was holding it."

She nearly dropped the object to the floor. Considering whom had last held it, she hesitated to even touch the thing. Without a doubt, the piece was artfully crafted and terribly expensive. "Mac, I swear I have seen this somewhere before."

"Really? Where?"

She rubbed her temple. "I cannot remember. But look here, a piece appears to have broken off. I believe it is from some sort of a pin."

Mac took the serpent from her. "It could very well belong to Ashford, a stick pin for his cravat, perhaps. Either way, a piece like this would be easily remembered. I'll have my man Knox start questioning jewelers today." He stared at a small bed of hyacinths, his voice calm but his body tense. "Considering what happened today, I need you to do something for me. I have a meeting tonight and cannot be distracted by worrying about you. Promise me you'll stay home. These people are obviously desperate enough to kill now."

"Hiding in his house did little good for Ashford," Joanna said. Then she sighed. "I apologize. Snapping at you certainly will not help."

He seemed unperturbed. "Snap all you like. You're entitled. You've seen a lot today. For what it's worth, I've done some thinking. I believe Ashford expected his killer. He likely sent the servants away and was waiting for someone he knew and trusted."

"Randolph?" she asked.

"Do you honestly think your brother capable of murder? Poisoning, no less?"

No, she thought. Regardless of Randolph's shortcomings, she believed him too moral for such an act. Shaking her head, she asked, "So why was he there? I do not understand why he hasn't come home or sent a note. Something to let me know he's alive. He hates violence. He barely tolerates hunting. Truly. And now Charlie has disappeared, as well." Sweet Empress, she was babbling like Lydia Litmore. Kneading the back of her neck, she asked, "What about Penelope and my mother? They'll want to go out."

"Ask your sister to feign a headache, a bellyache, anything. We can decide what's to be done tomorrow. Just stay home tonight."

Apart from her time spent with her father, Joanna had always considered herself an average female, her life quite predictable and boring. The last few weeks had been anything but. A quiet evening at home sounded divine, the perfect opportunity to sort through her turbulent emotions of late, and the inexplicable draw of Mac. She'd been so rebellious and wild lately, felt the ridiculous return of all her youthful dreams. Yes, indeed. A bath and a book were the perfect antidote to restore her sense of balance. Then she had a thought. "Where exactly are *you* going tonight?"

He hesitated ever so slightly before answering. "Bit of business, certainly nothing to worry your pretty blue eyes over."

"Flattery will not deter me," she snapped. "Are you dealing smuggled goods tonight?"

He looked annoyed. "If I am?"

"Are you so eager to risk landing in jail—or worse, die—all to turn a profit? Rebecca said you were finished with that smuggling nonsense. You sat in this very room and claimed you were starting a legitimate trading company. Was it a lie?"

He looked pained. "No. This is my final delivery." After a moment he added, "If something does happen to me, though, contact Lord Kerrick. He'll help you." He squeezed her shoulders and grinned. "I've managed to live this long. Everything will be fine."

A sense of urgency overwhelmed Joanna. Maybe the image of Ashford's dead body triggered the reaction, or her own feelings of despondency. And her growing affection for Mac no doubt encouraged the impetuous behavior. Either way, she was consumed by a sudden need to merge her lips with his, the desire to feel the heat of his embrace.

She never behaved so boldly. Being kissed and allowing it was one thing; kissing him was another thing entirely. Yet her feet moved to where he stood. She slid to her toes and pressed her mouth to his.

He obviously favored the idea as well. His arms curved around her, dragging their bodies closer. His embrace was a fusing of passion and security, an intoxicating aphrodisiac to erase any and all of Joanna's misgivings.

His kiss was everything she'd remembered and more. Tenderness. Heat. A sensual assault that battered her heart and ravaged her emotions. His tongue traced a path across her lips. Further recklessness coursed through her. Logic, all rules of comportment, her beliefs of right and wrong, all vanished. Surely such want was wrong. Ladies weren't supposed to possess such strong physical attractions, yet here she was clinging to Mac like the unwieldy vine of a honeysuckle wrapped about the solid trunk of a tree.

Her hand feathered across his cheek and cupped the nape of his neck. One kiss became two. Two became four. Heat burned between them, enveloping her in a fog of pleasure.

Mac at last lifted his mouth from hers. His thumb rubbed across her lower lip, his gaze locking with hers. "What am I to do with you, Miss Fenton?"

His tenderness rendered her speechless. But he was gone before she could muster a response.

Rain pounded on the wooden roof of the warehouse Mac was in. This was a perfect spot for a clandestine rendezvous—secluded and abandoned. Adrenaline pumped through his veins. With the benefit of several torches, he fixed his gaze on the back door, one of three ways to escape if trouble came their way.

And Mac anticipated trouble. Hoped for it. He'd been on edge ever since leaving Joanna. Pounding a few heads seemed an excellent outlet for all his energy, since taking Joanna to bed was out of the question.

Damn, this was not the time to be thinking about Joanna. No woman had ever distracted him so. At some point, he was going to have to consider a solution.

He'd brought six men with him on this mission. Knox transferred cargo from one wagon to another, with the aid of two crewmen. They had specific instructions: In case of trouble, snuff the torches, forget the goods, scatter, find the nearest tavern, and blend with the riffraff. One crewman hid outside, waiting to follow Digger after the transaction was complete. Another kept watch from the roof, and one more stayed with the horses behind the building next door.

Tonight's drop wasn't about money. Mac hoped to catch a rat. And he wanted to catch the rat's master, too. The rat in question glanced over his shoulder every other minute. He looked guilty as hell.

"Relax, Digger, one would think you were expecting company the way you're watching the door."

"Can't be too careful," the man said.

Mac smiled wryly. "No, you can't. But we've never used this particular drop point, so the only way the authorities could find us is if someone gave them the information. Relax. Have you found a new source to get your goods?"

Digger made a face. "As if I believe you intend to quit the trade. It's in your blood."

"A wise man knows when to watch his back and when to move on to a new venture. What about you? Where will you turn when the authorities tighten the screws on the docks and the harbor? Or do you already have a connection to protect you?"

"I ain't got nothing." He was silent a moment, then said. "We won't miss each other, that's for sure. I don't like you and you don't like me."

"Truer words were never spoken," Mac agreed. He crossed his arms. "We about ready, Knox?"

"Aye, Captain. All done."

"Already?" Digger said. "Now wait just a minute, I need to count the cargo."

"After all this time, you don't trust me? I'm so sad." Mac laughed. "Let's go boys."

"Wait a minute!" Digger stared at the side door.

Narrowing his eyes, Mac claimed, "If I didn't know better, I'd say you were purposely delaying my departure."

"Now, why would I do that?"

The soft warble of a thrush sounded outside. Company had arrived.

"I wonder," Mac said. Sliding his hand to his gun, he called to Knox: "Out of here. Now."

"What about you, Captain?"

"I'll be there shortly."

Digger shifted to the end of his wagon, farther away from the side door, the one he'd watched so closely.

"You're behaving quite oddly tonight," Mac accused. "Anything you want to tell me?"

The side door rattled.

Knox hovered at a window on the far wall. "Hurry, Captain."

"Who are they, Digger? Who's knocking at that door?"

"How should I know?" the rat asked. He crouched behind the wagon.

A gunshot sounded from outside. Mac advanced on Digger in three long strides and grabbed him by the throat. "Sorry, but I don't believe you. You're responsible for one of my men being killed. This isn't finished. I'll beat the truth out of you. Then you'll tell me what I want—"

The side door burst open. Mac tossed his torch to the ground and kicked dirt over its flame, then dashed for the window where Knox had escaped. A gunshot ripped through the air behind him.

The clock struck eleven. Grateful for a brief respite from the frantic social schedule set by her mother, Penelope had enthusiastically embraced Joanna's idea and stayed home. Now she, her mother, and most of the servants were abed.

After a trying afternoon listening to Lydia Litmore, Joanna had soaked in a bath and eaten upstairs. Alone. She was not fit company for even her family, and she knew it. Her thoughts lingered with Mac, knowing he was somewhere in the dark, the rain, in danger. True, he was doing what he had done for years, and survived, but her apprehension refused to ebb.

Since sleep eluded her and reading had proven futile, she had dressed to once again search her father's papers. She and Mac agreed that the symbol on the notes, the same as on the pin, had to be the link between the statue and the murderers. She was certain she had seen the design somewhere before. If only she could remember where.

Nestled on the rug beside the fire, Joanna scanned the journals of her father spread before her on the floor. Tossing the fifth book to the side, she pulled another close and began to flip through its pages.

Confucius pranced into the room, his head held high. A mouse struggled for freedom, caught by its tail in the cat's jaws.

"Take that rodent elsewhere, you beast," Joanna snapped. "I have no desire to share your prize tonight."

Of course the cat ignored her. He pranced toward the stack of books on the carpet and there released his catch. Determined to escape death, the mouse scurried for what it deemed safety—Joanna's skirts.

With a squeal, Joanna jumped to her feet, tossing the book in her hands forward in self protection. Confucius leapt to avoid the flying missile, landing on a nearby shelf. Her father's prized tea jar tottered precariously back and forth, finally toppling to the floor.

Joanna stood motionless as it shattered.

A red piece of paper rolled into a cylinder was barely visible in the pieces of broken pottery. Her fingers shook as she bent to her knees. With great care, she pulled the entire scroll case, approximately four inches in length, from its hiding place in what appeared to have been the jar's false bottom. Chinese lettering marked the cylinder's golden clasps. This could only be one thing.

"You blessed cat," she said. "You shall eat kidney pie for a week."

Mac was her next thought. She had to tell him. Truth be told she welcomed the excuse to go to his house, to ensure his safety. Surely he would be home by now. If not, she intended to wait.

She rang for Chang and gathered her cloak.

Chapter Twelve

Mac opened his front door, letting the light from the foyer beyond spill over him. He called back to Knox, "Alert the staff that we had a spot of trouble and gather the supplies you'll need, then come upstairs. Have Cook clean the floor behind us."

Hesitating, the man said, "Do be careful, Captain. You seem frightfully peaked."

"I'll be fine," he assured him.

Knox darted off to the kitchens.

As the clock struck twelve, Mac hobbled across the white marble floor of his foyer toward the staircase. He had been damn lucky, considering. This time had been close. Too blasted close. He'd miscalculated the authorities, and his plan had failed. And he'd been shot.

Blood soaked his temporary bandage, sweat beaded

his brow, and his leg hurt like hell. As far as he could tell, no bones were broken. The bullet had gone through his thigh. Even so, he'd not be standing for long.

The stairs loomed before him, as ominous as a squall off the coast of Africa. Yet he had to reach his bedroom before he collapsed. He balanced several seconds against the oak banister before he managed a step. Then another. From the corner of his eye, he glimpsed a patch of navy blue silk appear through the doorway from the parlor.

"Mac, you're home! I have exciting news. I found the Scroll of Incantations. Chang verified the writing. This is—" Joanna's mouth fell open in shock. The paper in her hands fell to the floor, forgotten. "Dear God, you're bleeding! Is there a surgeon on his way? Why are you just standing there? What happened?"

A dozen questions of his own ran through Mac's muddled brain. He hobbled back down the stairs he'd just managed to climb, a painful undertaking. "What the devil are you doing here? It's nearly midnight."

"I am fine. You, on the other hand, have been injured. And you said nothing would happen tonight. I warned you." She traced a small scratch over his eye before her light touch moved to his thigh. "Now look at you. Were you shot? Stabbed?" She shook her finger in his face. "I distinctly remember telling you this business was dangerous. But would you listen? No. You should be in bed. Can you walk?" She waved her arms in the air. "And would you please tell me what happened?"

"You must first close your mouth long enough to allow me to talk. I'll be fine. Go home. I'll call on you tomorrow and explain everything."

Chang chose that moment to appear through the front door. His brows drew together. He wasted no time moving to Mac's side.

Knox—along with half the staff in their nightgowns—dashed back from the kitchen. His arms laden with bandages and several small vials, he nearly downed Joanna in the process. "Oh, Sweet Hebrides. Good evening, Miss Fenton. Forgive my impertinence, but this is not the best time for a visit."

The stairway was becoming more crowded than Tattersall's on sale day. Mac grimaced as he pivoted and struggled back up two steps. "She's just leaving."

Joanna followed. "I most certainly am not. At least not until I check your wound and assess the damage. There could be an infection."

Mac's leg throbbed. His head suffered persistent buzzing. He needed to lie down. Soon. Or his pride would suffer a terrible blow when Knox had to carry him up the stairs. Sucking in a deep breath of air, he closed his eyes in search of patience. "I assure you, I shall live to see another day. I will contact you tomorrow."

"Father often asked for my assistance, and I have worked in the sickrooms at the orphanage. I can help."

"Stop, Joanna. This is your final warning. I'm going

to climb these stairs, strip naked, then go directly to bed. Now please get the hell out of here."

She sailed past him up the stairs, heedless of his words. "There is no need for profanity. And I doubt you can even make it to your bedroom without Chang's help. An ox-eye daisy has more color than you."

The fact that she was right was infuriating. "I'm not that bad off," he argued.

Joanna ignored him. Over her shoulder, she tossed orders to the staff with an efficiency he began to admire.

To Mac's surprise, the cook, the groom, even the upstairs maid and both Knox and Chang did as she commanded. None of them suggested she return home. None of them suggested the scandal of her presence here. Lack-brains surrounded him. *He* was the one who had been shot, yet only he seemed to be thinking with a clear head—no mean trick, since concentration became more difficult with each passing moment.

Joanna meant well. He knew that. But almost every fiber of his body wanted to protect her from scandal, to remind her of the danger her reputation was in from the *Ton*. Maybe it was because he'd failed to protect her from witnessing Ashford's demise.

Certainly another part of him was simply hesitant to allow her such intimate entrance into his life, his bedroom. He had to protect her from himself. He had surely never imagined her here under these circumstances. Indeed, he'd had far more exciting and lusty fantasies about Joanna and his big four-poster bed. Satin sheets, scented oils, rose petals and their naked bodies. . . . Damn if he wasn't half-aroused at the thought even though bleeding like a stuck pig.

The crazy woman and his first mate had reached the top of the stairs. She'd set herself to playing nursemaid to him and would not be deterred.

A litany of curses froze on his tongue—Joanna had asked that he not curse. "Bloody shark bellies," he growled. Then he glared at Chang. "I thought I told you to keep her home and out of trouble."

"Silly man blame others for problems in own house."

His house was being overrun by lunatics, he was going to bleed to death on his own stairs, and a Chinaman was spouting crazy philosophy at him. "Oh, stuff it," he snapped even as the butler moved to help him.

When they got to his bedroom, Mac saw Knox at the window, peering through the curtains to the street below. The man crossed to the trestle table by the wardrobe and poured Mac a drink, then brought both the glass and the bottle to the bedside table. "Come along now, sir."

Joanna stood in the middle of the wood floor, an unyielding expression on her face. "Remove your trousers. Where is your nightshirt?"

Mac downed his whisky in one gulp. "I don't have one."

Her expression was a mix of curiosity and shock. "What do you wear to bed?"

Not feeling particularly gracious, Mac moved his face inches from hers and, as wickedly as he could muster, whispered, "Nothing. I'm naked. Interested in hearing more?"

The girl turned scarlet.

He gave a harsh laugh. "Good Christ, Joanna. The mere mention of me naked shocks you, and yet you expect to dress my wound?"

She fisted her hands on her hips. "Your foul temperament will not make me leave. Every gentleman owns a nightshirt."

"You keep forgetting I'm not a blasted gentleman," he retorted.

She sighed. "Then we will do the best we can. When I turn my back, you will remove your trousers, sit on the bed, and cover yourself."

Like a flock of sheep, the others stood by waiting for him to comply. They obviously thought Joanna knew what she was about. What choice did he have? He swallowed the rest of his drink, poured and drained another, limped to the bed, and with Knox's aid tugged his clothes off. He tossed those to Chang. He dropped onto the bed and draped the cover over most of his legs, leaving only the wounded part of his lower thigh exposed. "You can look now."

Mac downed another brandy, grimacing, while Joanna prodded, probed, and washed his wound. She found a particularly sensitive spot.

"Ouch! By the saints, woman. Be careful."

"For a man who professes to be able to care for himself, you whine more than the three-year-olds at St. Anne's."

"It makes me feel better," he griped.

As she stitched Mac's wound, Knox stood to one side, testily offering his opinion. He obviously didn't like having his duties usurped. Chang hovered on the other side, muttering nonsense about fools and their counterparts. Mac prayed for an end to the torture.

When his leg was finally wrapped, he slipped on a robe Knox had found, and lay down. All he wanted was to sleep for a week. "Everyone can go now," he said.

Just when he thought he might gain compliance, that everyone might actually leave so he could empty the contents of his stomach and die in peace, his groom darted into the bedroom. The man's face was devoid of any color. "Pardon, sir. The constable's downstairs. He wants to talk to you."

Chaos erupted. Mac tried to talk over the cacophony of everyone jabbering at once, but his efforts proved unsuccessful. He really had no desire to stand, and wasn't even sure he could. Instead, he leaned on his elbows and whistled.

Blessed silence.

"Joanna, where is your carriage?"

"Out front." When he frowned, she added, "I did not expect the authorities to knock down your door. What are you going to do?"

185

There was no hope for it. He pushed himself up and off the bed. Standing seemed even harder than it had a few minutes earlier. He grabbed the wooden bedpost. "I'll simply go down and greet the man. The staff will swear I've been here all night long. With a spot of luck, the constable will believe me."

Her mouth dropped open, snapped shut, then opened again. "That is your idea of a plan? You can barely stand!"

"It's the best I can do on short notice. Knox, take Joanna down the back stairs and round the front. With any luck, no one saw her carriage."

Feet pounded up the stairs.

"Captain," Knox spoke up. "I believe the authorities have arrogated the decision for themselves."

"Bloody hell." Damn, he felt odd. He pointed to the wardrobe in the corner. "You can all hide there."

"That is ridiculous. I have an idea," Joanna said. She grabbed up his bottle of whisky and, ignoring their complaints, splashed the contents onto Knox and Chang. "Pretend you've imbibed. Stall for as long as you can." She shoved them through the door. The groom followed. She added a dash of alcohol to Mac's hair for good measure. After all, a drunken man wouldn't be expected to walk all that well.

"What are you doing?" Mac asked, his pain transforming to disbelief.

The chit said nothing. Instead, she locked the door then extinguished all but two candles. One moment she was standing beside the bed like a sensible rational woman, the next she was yanking pins from her hair like a full-fledged nutter. Honey-brown locks floated to her waist. Her black slippers and white stockings fell to the floor next.

Even in his befuddled mind, Mac had a fair notion of what she planned. "Put your clothes back on!"

"No." Joanna wasn't about to debate the wisdom of her plan. She was already too nervous to form a single syllable—let alone an intelligent sentence. Perhaps this *was* insanity. It certainly was a risk. Yet, beneath Mac's rather green complexion, she'd seen worry and doubt in his eyes. Knox, too, had looked as though the hangman's noose was already tightening about his neck. Neither thought for one moment that the constable would accept their story.

Not only that, Joanna feared that loss of blood was finally taking its toll on Mac. If he tried to walk, the authorities would see the truth for themselves. She couldn't just steal out the back door like a thief when he needed her most.

Surely, her plan had holes, possibly large gaping ones with complications she had yet to consider. Unfortunately, time was short. Angry voices grew closer every second.

She debated how to proceed, whether to climb into Mac's bed, and if she should wear her gown if she did. Likely not. If *he* slept naked, she doubted his partners would wear anything, either—which meant a gown was definitely out of the question. Blood pounded in her temples.

Working the ribbons on the front of her dress, she knotted two in the process. Her fingers simply refused to work. After three deep breaths and one torn ribbon, her gown drifted to the floor. She was dressed only in her shift. Staring across the room, she gulped.

By the Goddess, the bed seemed to have shrunk since last she looked. Maybe it was the muscled chest wrapped in black silk staring back at her or the broad shoulders that occupied most of the mattress, or the fact she was about to climb into bed with a man, one she found wildly attractive. In any case, the bed was definitely smaller.

Mac's expression likely mirrored her own: sheer unadulterated shock. "You don't have to do this," he said. "There's still time to hide in the wardrobe."

Hide in a wardrobe, indeed! How would that help? Now was not the time to turn coward. Not after all Mac had done for her. She'd talk to the constable, vouch for Mac and go home, no one the wiser. She swallowed her panic, shuffled her feet, then jumped beneath the covers and lay flat on her back. She was like a fish, she imagined, floundering on shore.

Mac leaned on one elbow. "Some plan. Now what?"

"Considering your reputation, I assumed you would be able to handle the situation from here on."

"Only you would climb into man's bed to rescue him from himself," Mac said. Sighing, he pressed his forehead to Joanna's. "What am I going to do with you?"

Fortunately or, depending on one's point of view,

unfortunately, a loud yelp postponed that particular discussion. Footsteps clattered from outside. Someone pounded on the door. A bombastic voice quoting Wordsworth, which could only be Knox, countered by Chang reciting Confucius, became a shoving match in the hall. A scuffle of sorts ensued.

"Move in the name of the King!" a voice rang out. Then "Open this door!"

Joanna fought the sudden urge to hide beneath the covers.

"In for a penny, in for a pound." Mac whispered. Then he yelled, "Go away. I'm busy."

His gaze traveled over Joanna's face, settling on her mouth, and suddenly she knew he was going to kiss her. She was in bed with a man she'd had wicked fantasies about, and he was going to kiss her.

"Open the door, or we'll break it down."

"Give me a minute." He rubbed his finger ever-so-slowly across her lip. He lowered his face to hers.

This was not the time to be kissing, she thought. Then again, she *was* supposed to be a woman lost in the throes of passion. She met him halfway. First she noticed the scent of the whisky, then the texture of his lips, their softness. They were also overly warm to the touch. It took little encouragement for her to open her mouth and allow his tongue entrance. His heat flooded through her, to her stomach and lower. It was from his fever, Joanna told herself. Mac seemed content to linger over her mouth, though. There came a crash at the door.

Pressing against his shoulders, she murmured, "I'll let them in."

"Not unless I'm dead," he hissed. "Stay under those covers and keep your mouth closed." He gritted his teeth as he swung his legs to the floor, stood and tested their stability. Wobbling a bit, he managed to stay standing. "They're looking for a wounded man. Our story will appear more credible if I'm the one to answer."

He had a valid point. Besides, the thought of greeting several strangers while wearing nothing more than her muslin shift was anything but appealing.

Hoping to present a more disheveled appearance, she shook out her hair. She tried to look drowsy and bit her lips slightly to redden them, trying her best to present the appearance of a woman seduced—a difficult task since she had limited points of reference. Other than the marble frescoes with naked writhing bodies she'd seen in her travels with her father, she wasn't sure how such a female should appear.

Mac crossed the short space, opened the bolt, and stepped back.

Two over-sized policemen and a man wearing a dark suit shoved their way inside. The enormous gaping hole in Joanna's plan, one neither she nor Mac could have ever anticipated, hovered at their side:

Lord Dorridge, wearing a smug grin.

So much for good intentions. Joanna squeaked and buried herself beneath the linens, praying for divine intervention. She knew it would not come. Someone tugged at the blanket. She tugged back with all her might, but it did no good.

Slack-jawed, Dorridge stared at her. "Miss Fenton. What are you doing here?"

Joanna peeked at Mac. He leaned against the bed-post, seemingly without a care in the world, but the hand fisted at his side was telling. Then again, Lord Dorridge stirred a similar hostile reaction in her. Either way, it was now or never. As Mac had said, *in for a penny, in for a pound.* "Good evening, sir."

"You bastard," Dorridge cried. "Isn't it enough that you covet the wives of the *Ton* you must seduce innocents, as well?"

Mac shuffled lazily back to the bed and kissed Joanna's cheek. "Sorry, darling."

Heat poured off Mac's body in waves. His fever must have risen. Joanna marveled that he could even stand. She slid to the middle of the bed and pulled him down on the edge. "Do not blame Mac. I am a grown woman who takes full responsibility for her actions." She clasped his hand in hers and brought it to her lips, batting her eyelashes in a style she'd seen Penelope use on several occasions.

Mac's eyes widened with shock.

Seized by the devil, Joanna bent one leg in what she hoped was a seductive position, then winked.

Dorridge was a shaken bottle of ale, his head ready to explode from the tiny aperture of his neck. "I warned you that this man was not to be trusted," he cried. He aimed a frigid glare at Mac. "If you think to seduce the dragon away from Miss Fenton, you are sorely mistaken." He grabbed her wrist, pinching the tender skin. "I won't allow it."

The audacity of the man, to think she would fall for such tactics! "I assure you that my being here has nothing to do with Lung Wang Sun. Now, release me."

Dorridge kept a tight grip on her.

Mac growled.

Dorridge released her hand and stepped back from the bed. "By God, Archer, your days are numbered. You *will* pay for this."

"Let *me* worry about my future," Mac responded pleasantly. But deep in his heart he feared Dorridge meant what he said. He shifted on the mattress, leaned against the headboard, and wrapped his arm about Joanna's shoulders. Feeling as if he might collapse at any moment, he turned to the constable. "You seem to have lost your way, gents. What do you want?"

The man stepped forward. "A few words, if you please."

"Come back tomorrow. Can't you see I'm—"

"I must insist, Mr. Archer. It will only take a minute."

Joanna twisted her mouth and made a petulant noise. She drew a line down Mac's chest with her fingernail and whispered in his ear, loud enough for everyone to hear. "Make them leave."

If only he could; he suddenly had a few choice words for Joanna, who'd become a wanton. And while he rather liked having her wrapped about him like a

192

vine—if only their audience would leave—he wasn't sure that it was a good idea. "I will be happy to discuss anything you like . . . in the morning. At a more reasonable hour."

"I'm telling you, Constable," Dorridge snapped. "Archer is the man responsible. Arrest him."

"Enough," Mac said, reaching for the bottle of brandy on the table beside his bed—anything to muffle the pounding in his ears. At least if he collapsed, the alcohol would provide him with an excuse. "You have managed to ruin my evening, so tell me what's on your mind and be on your way."

Squaring his shoulders, the constable cleared his throat. Several times. He was clearly nervous. "We interrupted a group of free traders tonight and believe we shot the leader."

A yawn slipped from Mac's lips. "An interesting tale, but what has that to do with me?"

"We were told you were the person making the delivery."

"I see." Mac let his animosity toward Dorridge show, hoping it would make suspect the man's accusation. "And who, exactly, gave you this information?"

The constable shifted his weight from foot to foot, considering.

"Give over, Archer," Dorridge sneered. "We intercepted your cargo."

"Astonishing! You're truly suggesting that I was smuggling goods tonight?"

Joanna giggled.

Mac laughed, too. The tiny army marching inside his skull added a round of gunfire to their stomping. "Sorry, gents. Someone's toying with you. As you can see, I had better plans for the evening than thrashing about in the dark and the mud. Or at least the mud." He nibbled on Joanna's right ear. She had such an interesting ear. As a matter of fact, she had many interesting parts. "You are quite lovely, Miss Fenton," he whispered.

"He's lying," Dorridge shouted.

"I am not," Mac drawled, even as he fought to clear his head. "She's very attractive."

"Thank you." Joanna smiled. "So are you."

"Good God," Dorridge muttered.

"Are you still here?" Mac asked, squinting. Dorridge seemed to be swaying from side to side. "Do stand still, man."

"He's drunk," the constable said with a sniff.

Dorridge pointed to Joanna. "Ask the girl, then."

Clearly uncomfortable with the entire affair, the constable shoved his hands in his pockets. "Miss, what time did you arrive here tonight?"

"Nine o'clock."

"Have you been here since?"

She nodded.

Like a man who's known the truth all along, Mac leaned back against his pillows and crossed his arms. His head dropped to his chest then rose back up again. "You should know Dorridge hates me. Question him," he mumbled.

"You dare accuse me?" Dorridge snapped.

"Evidently so." He lifted his arm in the air only to have it flop back to the covers. "Or if you don't believe me, ask the Earl of Kerrick of my plans tonight."

Spittle flew from Dorridge's mouth. "Don't think to bring the earl's name into this. His influence won't help you."

"The Earl of Kerrick is an acquaintance of yours?" the constable asked, his skin drawn tight about his lips.

"A very good friend, actually," Joanna spoke up when Mac's eye drifted shut.

Mac opened one heavy lid and yawned. "No need for him to intervene. I've done nothing."

Dorridge launched himself toward the bed. "You liar. I know for a fact you were to be there tonight. A reliable source, one of your own kind, named you specifically. And we have a witness. Dig—" The viscount cut off his words with a snarl.

"You were saying?"

Joanna wasn't fooled by the lazy tone of Mac's voice. A deadly gleam shone in his eyes. Tension coiled in his arm. A small tic vibrated in his cheek. Though he could barely stand, she briefly feared he just might leap for Dorridge's throat.

She pressed her lips to his.

"I believe we have seen enough," the constable said. "I apologize, Mr. Archer, for any inconvenience."

"You can't just let him go," Dorridge shouted, but his two companions escorted him from the room.

Over his shoulder, the viscount yelled, "This isn't finished. I'll see you pay this time, you bastard! One way or another, you'll pay!"

As soon as they had vacated the room, chancing no re-entry by the police, Joanna ran and bolted the door. Mac slid down the headboard, flat on his back, his eyes closed. Sweat dotted his upper lip and brow. His forehead felt like fire. "Oh dear, I was afraid of this," she said. She fetched a glass of water from the nightstand and a wet rag.

Once she was at his side again, Mac grabbed her wrist. "Why?" he murmured. He meant, why had she sacrificed her honor for him?

The question came as no surprise. Why, indeed? "They would have arrested you."

"Is that the only reason?"

She dared not mention that she had been terrified that even that plan would not work, that the thought of Mac in prison had nearly brought her to her knees. At the moment, she was afraid to explore the feelings any deeper. "What other reason could there be?"

Mac seemed to consider her answer. He blinked several times as if the room spun out of focus. "Dorridge won't forget the matter."

"Likely not."

"You'll be ruined."

Mac's assertion was the unavoidable truth. She would worry about it tomorrow, though. Wiping his brow, her movements all business, she said, "I've weathered a scandal before. Perhaps I can do so again."

"Not because of me. Why?" he asked again.

He seemed to resent the fact she had just ruined her reputation to save him from Newgate or the gallows. She sought a suitable response. None was forthcoming.

His eyes drifted close. He lay perfectly still, his hands pressed to his brow as if an anvil rested on his forehead. For a moment she thought he had drifted to sleep. Then he moaned. "Damn me. A bloody lady. I swore I'd never be forced to marry one." A small chuckle followed.

The words had been barely a whisper, but for the hurt they caused they could have been shouted by a town crier. Was he actually suggesting she had purposely climbed in his bed to wrest from him a marriage proposal? A lump the size of the Shrine of Dakini formed in her throat. To her mortification, tears threatened to spill. "I don't remember asking you to marry me."

An odd rumbling came from his chest.

She stood beside the bed. "You were in trouble. You told me to leave. I refused. I will live with whatever consequence I must. Like it or not, just like a family, friends take care of each other."

He didn't look up. "They use you."

"My family needs me."

"You need them to need you. *I* don't need you to need me."

197

Maybe he rambled due to the fever or lack of blood. She no longer cared. The disappointment and pain were too deep. She threw the wet rag to the floor. "You ungrateful wretch."

His eyes flew open. He covered his ears with his hands. "Why are you yelling?"

"For your information, people who care about one another do things without expectations or thought of compensation. No one asked me to climb in your bed tonight. I did so of my own accord. And not with the expectation of a marriage proposal."

His face was no longer flushed but rather green, yet he managed to raise himself to his elbows. "I know. I was here. Calm down."

"Why? So you can insult me further? Did you or did you not just call me a selfless weakling with no life of my own?" Hadn't that been what he meant when he claimed her family used her?

He shook his head as if to clear his thoughts. "I don't think so."

"Oh, never mind! You're in no condition to talk." She fisted her stockings in her hand then tugged her slippers onto her bare feet. "Do not worry about tonight. No one will hear a solitary word from me. I will deal with Dorridge in my own way. And, for your information, I would not marry you for all the roses in Scotland."

"Joanna, wait . . ."

She slammed the door before she could hear another excruciating word.

Chapter Thirteen

"I certainly hope you have a reasonable explanation for the mess you've created," Rebecca said, her face a thundercloud ready to burst.

Adam placed a restraining hand on his wife's arm. "Darling, allow Mac the opportunity to sit before you launch your assault. Remember, he's an injured man."

Mac couldn't recall ever seeing this particular expression on Rebecca's face before: She looked ready to tear limbs from his body while condemning him to hell. He'd barely limped into his study before she'd exploded.

He retreated around the chess table to the chair furthest from her. "And good afternoon to you, Rebecca. In case you're interested, I was shot. Thanks to Knox, who poured laudanum down my throat until my fever cooled and I threatened to burn the library to ashes, the last three days are a blur. I'm not in the best of moods, so before you flay the skin from my body, perhaps you could tell me what I've done wrong."

"Joanna."

Her answer came as no real surprise to Mac, and it elicited half a dozen reactions. Accustomed to positions of such accusation, he knew enough to wait for a detailed accounting of his crimes. Indeed, ignorance was often the best defense, especially when dealing with women. "What has Miss Fenton said?"

Rebecca gurgled like a brook after a heavy rain. "Do not play the innocent in all this."

Acting as mediator, Adam handed Mac a cup of coffee and sat opposite him. "There have been some recent developments you may not be aware of. Joanna called on us this morning, claiming she no longer required your services. She asked that *I* help her in your stead. In spite of constant questioning by my wife, Joanna mentioned only that you had been shot. She offered no other details for her decision. She looked exhausted."

"No small wonder, given her current situation and the lies Dorridge is spreading." Rebecca glared at Mac. "They had best be lies."

Dorridge obviously had kept his promise. Although it was horrid of him to attack Mac through Joanna, he had done so. Mac would have to avenge her. But that was not the problem at the moment. Rebecca was. And she was as single-minded as a vicar in search of sinners. Denial was pointless.

Mac's first impulse was to seek Joanna out, offer her comfort and try to shield her from any nastiness. There were a few lapses in his recollection from the other night, but he remembered enough to know he hadn't exactly been at his best. Joanna would likely toss him from the closest and highest window.

He rubbed at the ache in the back of his head. "What, exactly, is Dorridge saying?"

"That he caught you and Joanna together. In your very own bed." Rebecca paced around the rug, three chairs and the marble chess table to stop in front of Mac. "Lady Litmore—the worst gossip in town, mind you—claims she saw Joanna storm from your house well past midnight. You can imagine the rest. Like starving mongrels, the gossips are devouring every morsel tossed in their path. Lady Fenton is beside herself, fretting over Westcliff's pending offer for Penelope, and Joanna refuses to say a word in her defense. Her silence is damning. I have no idea what transpired here, but you have succeeded in ruining the poor girl. What do you propose to do about it?"

"Kill that ruddy Dorridge."

"A typical male reaction, but that is not what I meant."

"If I can't kill him, then I'll break both his arms."

"That is not what I had in mind, either."

"Blast, Rebecca, what the devil do you suggest?"

"There is only one viable solution guaranteed to eliminate any further scandal." Her lips curled into a triumphant smile of victory for females around the world.

Suddenly he knew.

Marriage.

He felt himself swimming through shark-infested waters.

Adam merely shrugged his shoulders and leaned back in his chair, prepared to watch the show.

So much for support from his fellow man.

Mac wagged a finger in Rebecca's direction. "Do not even think to use this as a means to an end of your little matchmaking scheme. I am not bound by society's rules."

"Joanna is," Rebecca retorted.

"True, but *I* am no protection from the wagging tongues of society. Marrying me would be her worst nightmare. I am scandalous, a bastard. A smuggler. And Joanna deserves far better than a reckless bastard."

"Piff. You are no more reckless than I am," Rebecca argued. "And you underestimate your virtues. You are a man with a healthy purse who already moves within limited circles of society. Certain parlors will always remain closed to you, but they would likely bore you anyway. Many will welcome you, especially with my husband aiding your cause." She shifted to stand beside Adam. "And support from an unexpected source may be possible. It seems . . . We have . . . Yesterday . . ."

Adam kissed his wife's fingers. "Relax, darling. His

bark is far worse than his bite." He then turned to Mac. "There is no easy way to say this, but we believe we have found your father."

A band tightened about Mac's chest. His trembling fingers gripped the arm of his chair. Like a man suffering a blow to his head, images and memories swam before his eyes in a confused mixture of time and place. An ominous chill catapulted him across the parlor where he threw open the French doors. He needed air, a clear thought. Like thunder in the silence, the ticking of the clock marked the passing seconds.

"Please say something," Rebecca whispered softly. "I know this is a shock—"

"That's a bloody understatement. I thought I made my wishes regarding this matter quite clear."

"You did. Father had ideas of his own. In this instance—"

"Your father's a menace! A meddling old man if I ever I met one!"

"True, but—"

"What did he think I'd do? Post a notice in the *Times*? Give three cheers and pour a round of drinks? Thank him?"

A study in composure, Adam joined Mac at the doorway with two glasses of brandy. "Actually, I believe Edward, like me, expected you to react exactly as you are."

"Bloody good for both of you," Mac sneered, hating the fact he wore his emotions on his sleeve for all to see. He grabbed the drink from Adam, downed the brandy in one swallow and welcomed the burning in his throat. "Knowing I would react this way, why bother at all?"

"As my wife was valiantly trying to tell you, her father is not to blame. Ironic as it seems, Edward started this search but is still up North waiting for Lord Fairfax to return home."

"Good Christ. Quit talking in riddles."

"Evidently Fairfax owns a small plantation in the Indies. He visits England in the spring every other year. Even then he spends most of his time up North. Fairfax and Edward met four years ago in Dunbar, hence the reason Edward thought you always looked familiar to him. Fairfax changed his plans this year and came to London first. I met him yesterday at Boodles's, quite by accident, and near fell from my chair. The resemblance to you is uncanny. Since both you and Fairfax are in London, albeit briefly, someone else might put two and two together. I thought you deserved to know beforehand."

Seething emotions continued to rock Mac: anger, regret, shock. Anger toward a man he'd never met. Regret for the decent life his mother never had. Shock that, after all these years, he knew his father's name. Bitterness coated his tongue. He could taste the lost dreams of a young boy taunted by those who believed themselves better, men like Lord Fairfax.

"Did you tell him about me?" Mac asked.

"No."

Unaware he'd even been holding his breath, Mac exhaled. "Thank you for that."

Adam clamped his hand on Mac's shoulder. "I know something of duty and regret, certainly revenge, and can only guess what you're feeling. Though I recommend you talk with Fairfax, I will support whatever decision you make. What you do with this information is completely up to you."

Adam and Rebecca meant well. Hell, Mac begrudgingly admitted, even Edward had acted with good intentions. And how could he blame Fate? She was a fickle bitch to everyone. Still, pride would never allow him to lay claim to this man's heritage.

"Fairfax means nothing to me. His *title* means nothing to me. His money means nothing to me. He used and abandoned my mother. To accept him as my father simply because I resemble him or because I could use his title to make myself more fashionable—even if I could thereby court Joanna and save her from ruin—would make me the worst of hypocrites and disloyal to my mother, God rest her soul."

"Then, where does that leave *Joanna?*" Rebecca asked from her chair.

Where indeed, thought Mac. And what to do about her situation?

As utterly ridiculous as it seemed, he had already considered the possible solution of marriage. But he didn't think it was the right solution.

He marched back across the room, stopping before the wooden model of the *Fleeting Star*. The ship symbolized everything he was, everything he knew; it was the niche he'd carved for himself, alone, from his independence and his dislike of those who looked down on those like himself.

Granted, he could marry Joanna. Even without Lord Fairfax's title, he was somewhat accepted in society. He played the role of gentleman well enough. He had the house in the proper neighborhood, the appropriate number of servants, knew how to dress and the lines to speak, and he even joined in lordly games when it suited him. But when it came down to it, the truth was he could not escape his past. Lady Daphne had proven that.

But that had been because he lacked a title.

He had sworn never to be in that position again, to fall for a woman with such priorities. Yet here he was. A title *was* important to Joanna. Her determination to see Penelope wed to a bloody earl was evidence of that.

Yet Joanna and Lady Daphne were as different as sea and sand. In the corner of Mac's mind, he was again the lonely boy who had stared through the window on Christmas Eve, pretending and daydreaming; he was a boy who wanted to believe.

He cursed. Debating with himself or even Rebecca and Adam resolved nothing. Only one person's opinion mattered.

Joanna's.

*   *   *

Her life had reached an all-time low.

Though dressed in her new pink muslin, the very gown Mac had encouraged her to buy—one of the loveliest dresses Joanna had owned in years—she felt miserable, wholly and thoroughly miserable. Even the pink rosebuds in her hair failed to lift her spirits.

Lord Dorridge, the good-for-naught blackguard, had kept his word and wasted no time spreading the news of her fall from grace. He apparently cared little that he was ruining her reputation to get to Mac. Worse, Lydia Litmore was helping. She was doing what she did best: spreading gossip.

She felt terrible. Her sister's possible marriage was in doubt, her own reputation was practically destroyed, and all for Mac—a man who hadn't had the decency to trust her intentions. Heaven knows what he thought of her now. She hadn't spoken with him for three days.

"Good riddance," she said to her reflection in the vanity mirror.

Liar, her heart countered.

Sighing, she tied a pink ribbon about her neck. It was the very devil arguing with one's heart. It was giving her a headache.

At first she had been angry. Furious, in fact. She'd been seized by an overwhelming rage that threatened to decimate every lesson in etiquette she'd ever learned. But when a few days had passed and her tears had dried, only the hurt caused by Mac's blatant rejection remained. Painful, raw disappointment.

207

And the knowledge that she had herself to blame.

She had lived with loneliness humming in her heart for so long, she had barely recognized her impossible feelings for what they were—the first stirrings of love.

A disastrous circumstance, to be sure. Mac had made his stance on marriage very clear on more than one occasion. Marriage was abhorrent to him, especially with a bride who hailed from society. Her pain at his rejection was irrational—he had never promised anything. All she had to be fairly upset about was his interpretation of her motives.

The bedroom door opened. Penelope hovered there, her gaze averted to the chartreuse floral rug. "Mother sent me to fetch you. Oh, Joanna. I'm terrified Lord Beasley has come with an offer."

"If that's true, then I'd say my luck remains constant."

"You can't marry the man. He's at least sixty and has a dozen children. You always manage to fix things for everyone else. What will you do for yourself?"

"He's thirty-eight and only has six daughters . . . and I am fresh out of ideas. Perhaps I should accept this . . . offer. For whatever reason it comes. Mother would not understand my resistance or accept my argument, if for no other reason than Lord Beasley has an ear to your Lord Westcliff. She probably sees this as an omen of good things to come."

"Piff. If Lord Westcliff is worried about this little nothing of a scandal then I refuse to marry him."

Joanna gave a sad laugh. "Oh, Penelope. You are a

good sister. My predicament is more than a little nothing of a scandal. Dorridge caught me in Mr. Archer's bed." She turned in her chair to study her sister's face. "Do you love Lord Westcliff?"

Penelope squeezed her hand. Her eyes told Joanna everything she needed to know. *Yes.* "If only you could explain to people the truth."

"Impossible." Joanna needed to think of something else. She gathered up the family estate ledgers from the mahogany desk. "Let us not borrow trouble until we see what Lord Beasley wants for certain." And with that, they went downstairs.

When they reached the salon, their mother was pacing back and forth. Pacing was a sure sign of trouble. Her wringing of her hands was even worse.

Seated in the overstuffed chair in the very center of the room, much like Prinny holding court at Brighton, was Lord Beasley. Wearing a white coat over a red and white striped vest that stretched tightly over his large abdomen, he resembled a piece of bloated peppermint candy. He sat in Joanna's father's favorite chair, a fact she noted and resented. The thought of spending her days and, worse yet, her nights with this man sent a shiver down her spine. Sweet Empress, she wasn't sure she could do this.

Seeking obscurity, Penelope slid into a Chinese folding chair she loathed.

Lady Fenton's fan beat the air in short rapid swishes. "Joanna, dear. You have a visitor."

Joanna curtsied, set her account ledgers on a side

table by the door, then moved to a sunny spot closest to the window and furthest away from Lord Beasley. "Good afternoon, sir."

Beasley puffed his chest and gurgled several times. Oh, how she hated that habit of his. "Well, um, unfortunate times these are." Gurgle, gurgle. "There is no point in beating about the bush. Society has a wicked tongue, yes, yes."

Remembering the rumors he'd circulated about her during her first season, Joanna had a brief daydream about throttling the man.

He continued, "Now I realize, m'dear, that you and I have had our disagreements in the past, but that is all water beneath the bridge."

"Of course it is," Lady Fenton chimed in.

"I understand this business is difficult, but I believe I have a suitable solution. My wife died over a year ago. The fact of the matter is, my girls need a mother."

Your girls need a nanny.

Beasley stood, then waddled to Joanna's side and clasped her hand. "There was a time I thought we would suit. I still have hopes. Perhaps with a mature age, you now recognize the rightness of what I say. I am not without the financial and personal resources to help your family. And our marriage would certainly quiet those wagging tongues that even now spread lies that—"

Joanna's mother gulped her tea. "Your proposal certainly bears consideration."

Lord Beasley's hand was dry, almost reptilian. Onions and cigar lingered on his breath. Joanna had thought she could do this—for Penelope, for her mother—but now resentment brewed, overflowing into anger. Nausea churned in her stomach. Joanna wanted to run upstairs. She wanted to scream, "Why me?" She had sworn never to be any man's sacrificial lamb, especially this one, he who was responsible for the failure of her first season four years ago. There *had* to be another solution.

If only Mac—

She refused to rethink the possibility.

Pulling her hand free, she moved to the fireplace. "Let's not be too hasty. I appreciate the offer—"

"Exactly what offer is that?"

It was Mac's voice, and it came from the parlor door with sufficient chill to freeze the Thames in August.

"Oh!" Lady Fenton gasped. "Mr. Archer. What are you doing here?"

"I came to see Joanna."

Lord Beasley raised himself to his full five feet four inches. "Now see here, you cad. You've upset the lady, don't you know. And the rumors . . . I suggest you leave immediately."

"I was going to suggest the same to you." Mac grabbed Beasley by the arm, dragged him across the room, and pushed him toward the door. "Good day." Joanna felt a mixture of shock at his treatment of the lord, and joy at Mac's sudden appearance.

"Oh dear," Lady Fenton cried.

Mac wasn't feeling particularly gracious toward

Joanna's mother. From what he'd overheard, the woman had been ready to pawn her daughter off to a near-sighted small-minded turtle. He shot a nasty glare in her direction.

"Oh, dear me," Lady Fenton repeated.

Treating Lady Fenton much the same as Lord Beasley—albeit more gently—Mac escorted her from the salon. Penelope needed no encouragement; she fled of her own accord.

Chang hovered at the door, a small smile on his lips. He said, "Remember: Cleverest man is one who knows how best to get what he wants."

Mac had no patience to figure out what the butler meant. He said, "No. The cleverest man is he who knows when to ignore people who spout idiotic words of wisdom." He slammed the parlor door in the butler's face and leaned against the cool wood, reining in his emotions. The moment he'd seen Beasley sitting in the parlor, spouting his vulture-like offer of marriage, Mac had wanted to boot the man to Lancashire—along with his title, six daughters and three estates. He'd wanted to pummel the man senseless. These feelings of jealousy were new and wholly overwhelming.

No doubt Joanna would have fled the room with her sister if he'd given her the chance. She wore her new day gown, which displayed far too much flesh above the bodice, considering she'd been entertaining Beasley. Her hair fell loosely down her back. She was remarkable. Beautiful. And standing motionless beside a bronzed and lacquered table, dark circles lining her eyes and wariness filling her gaze, she resembled a rabbit trapped in a snare. It pained Mac to know he was responsible for her current state. "You look lovely," he said.

Her lips twisted into a frown.

He supposed she wasn't in the mood for compliments. "We need to talk," he tried instead.

"Indeed. Mother will be beside herself—and heaven knows what Lord Beasley will do. I have enough problems without additional fodder for the gossips."

Mac felt frustration well up inside him. "I could care less about your mother—or Beasley, either."

She snorted. "Obviously. Please leave. I no longer require your services."

Until she said the words herself, Mac hadn't realized how much her dismissal wounded him—even though he knew and understood the reason for it. "But you do. I talked to Adam this morning and told him. I gave you a promise, and I intend to finish the job. But that is not the matter I meant we should discuss." He paused "I'm sorry for what I said the other night."

"There is no need to apologize. Your observations are not so different from several I have heard before."

Her words were cool, but her shoulders heaved— which did interesting things to her breasts and in turn, given the circumstances, ignited an inappropriate response of certain undisciplined body parts of his. Lord, he'd missed her. "Not from me."

"True. Nonetheless, I think it best that we now part

ways. I will salvage this mess without your help. Good day."

"Playing the martyr and throwing yourself on the mercy of that pompous toad, Beasley? Not a chance."

She looked angry. "What I choose to do or not to do is entirely my decision."

"Not any longer."

"Mac, this is ridiculous. Let me explain, so that you may take your leave—and your arrogance and faulty assumptions with you. I considered the possibility of marrying Lord Beasley, but after all these years of doing for others, I refuse to abandon my entire possibility of happiness for Penelope or my mother. I deserve more. Indirectly, I have you to thank. I'm not sure what this decision says about me, but I shall ponder that later. What's important now is that I resolve the problem of my scandal, find my brother Randolph, and secure Penelope's marriage to Westcliff. Then I will settle in the country. Alone. And quite happily. So you need not worry yourself about me."

As if she recited a shopping list for the cook, her voice was devoid of emotion. The calm acceptance of her fate, of becoming a lonely spinster who lived on her relatives' charity, eliminated any and all reservations Mac had. Beyond a doubt, he knew what he had to do. And it seemed surprisingly simple. "The only solution is for us to marry by special license."

She looked shocked. "That is an utterly absurd notion. I cannot afford to abandon my search for Randolph and plan a wedding right now."

"You can't afford *not* to."

A struggle took place on Joanna's feature's, then she said, "For the sake of argument, supposing we could manage to squeeze a wedding into all that is going on, let us consider the suitability of the match. Since I decided not to marry Lord Beasley for the sake of my happiness, I should take that into consideration. I want a home with walls and furnishings and a garden. That is what I enjoy. I spent the first ten years of my life on ships, in ports and in villages of foreign countries. I want a solid foundation for a family. You, on the other hand, spend half your life on a ship. What does that get me?"

Mac sighed. "I won't lie. The thought of being land-locked holds the same appeal to me as being shot in the leg. The sea is all I know. But you should remember that I *do* have a home—the very one you invaded the other night." He raised his hands in a gesture of conciliation. "This debacle is partly my fault. And I would like to see you happy. Somehow or another we have to find a middle road."

Joanna's face clouded with emotion. She brushed a nonexistent speck of dirt from her sleeve.

"You deserve children," Mac added, feeling a desperate need to convince her.

"I shall be a stellar aunt to Penelope's sons and daughters."

"You expect that to be enough?" Mac found himself grasping at straws. "What about passion?"

"My reputation is already in tatters. Perhaps I'll take a lover."

She had tossed out that comment far too nonchalantly to suit him. "Like hell you will! We will marry in three days. That is the end of this discussion."

"Why do you suddenly want so badly to marry me?"

Why, indeed? Mac had expected to explain his actions from the night before, perhaps grovel a bit, but her disdain wrapped in civility surprised him. He'd assumed he'd make the proposal, she'd waver for a moment, maybe two, then say yes. He hadn't expected to actually explain the reasons for his change of heart. He wasn't sure he understood them himself.

Circling the room, he studied an etching of her family. Everyone seemed so blasted happy. Joanna deserved the same. Whether of not he was capable of such commitment remained to be seen—but he had to try. "If I deserted you, I'd be no better than my own father."

"There is a major difference. I carry no child."

"No matter. This shame and scandal will follow you wherever you settle. I refuse to bear that responsibility." He found himself voicing some of his fears, too: "Your reluctance to wed me comes as no surprise. I cannot begin to be the best man for you. I have a checkered past. Though my friendship with Lord Kerrick provides me some latitude, as does my financial solvency, if we were to marry, I must warn you that you would never be accepted in some of the finer salons of the *Ton*. Still, it seems the best solution."

She looked annoyed. "My reluctance has nothing to do with your social standing, which only proves how little you understand me. Another reason to forget this insanity."

Devil take it, the female refused to listen to reason! He moved closer, trapping her between his body and the wall. "You seem determined to find an excuse not to use me. Why?"

"Perhaps I don't like you."

The muscle is Mac's jaw clenched, but he said nothing.

After a moment, Joanna looked uncomfortable. Finally she said, "There are many reasons I shouldn't marry you. If I tell you the closest to my heart, will you leave?"

"I can't promise that."

Ducking beneath Mac's arm, she placed what she obviously deemed a safe distance between them. Then she admitted, "Women practically swoon when you walk into a room. No doubt you receive improper offers from ladies two or three times a day. As you recall, Lady Dorridge herself thrilled me with details of your liaison—one of many you've admitted to having. I would rather live alone, ostracized, than become your *pity bride*." she looked momentarily vulnerable. "To be honest, though I believe you like and care for me, I *know* you would never be content with me as your wife."

Finally! The real hole in her sail.

And it was something he knew and understood: an

underlying insecurity that she wasn't pretty enough, or smart enough, or some other silly notion she'd come to believe over the years. For the first time that afternoon, Mac stood on solid ground.

"Offers two or three times a day, hmmm? I'm flattered. Although I'm not sure even I have the stamina to live up to such demands." He laughed, then became serious. "Joanna, I can't deny I've known countless women, but I never had sufficient reason to refuse them before."

She leaned her head back against a window. Disbelief lingered, but hope hovered in her gaze as well. "Am I suddenly to believe that I am the woman of your dreams?" She sneered. "Please do not insult me."

Walking up to her, he gripped her chin. "I see I must convince you."

She shook her head. "Your skill as a lover is irrelevant to this discussion."

"On the contrary, since you continue to underestimate yourself, doubt yourself as a woman, I feel compelled to prove the attraction you hold for me."

Mac's breath brushed Joanna's temple, her cheek, then finally the sensitive skin above her lips. Her pulse leaped and her skin tingled where his fingers touched. She felt her limbs thrum with excitement. Then he kissed her.

Restraint, plus a tenderness that made her want to weep, filled his touch. Mac pulled back to nibble the spot behind her right ear, the curve of her neck, then finally returned to her lips. He kissed her more deeply than before, urged their two bodies closer. With surprising gentleness, he commanded her to listen to her body: its yearning for his touch, the blood coursing through her veins.

Desire curled her toes.

Mac raised her hand to his lips. Passion burned in his green eyes, darkening them. He placed a single kiss upon her palm. "Admittedly, I'm a man with a lusty appetite. But it's you who make me hunger. Making love is one of life's greatest pleasures—and nothing would give me greater satisfaction than to make love to you." He shook his head, but did not stop staring into her eyes. "Perhaps passion is not the most solid foundation on which to build a marriage, but it's a start. And it's more than you'd have with someone like Beasley." He paused, took a tortured breath. "If you don't believe me . . ." He placed her hand on the front of his trousers. "Feel what you do to me, Joanna."

Sweet Empress! She could feel his arousal. Her fingertips itched to move, to explore. She felt curious. Scandalized. Her body responded. Such behavior was wicked. Shocking and wanton. And beyond a doubt, thrilling. She attempted to mask her reaction by saying, "A temporary infliction, I'm sure—and from what the maids say, easily cured with any ready female."

"Quit being so damn stubborn about this." A wry grin touched Mac's lips before he placed his forehead on hers. "Trust me. The only reason I would ever leave our marriage bed is if you refused me or turned to another."

Joanna felt herself melt, then she was reminded of her other concerns: "What about Jamaica? Do you intend to marry me then sail away immediately thereafter?" She slid out from beneath his arms and stepped behind a row of potted ferns. "And what of love?"

Mac's face turned somber. "I am not a saint or a martyr, Joanna. If I felt nothing for you, I'd be halfway to Jamaica now and be dammed your reputation. But as for love . . . I enjoy your company and definitely want you. Isn't that enough?"

So love was not part of the package. And there was the distinct possibility Mac might never love her in the way she hoped. The admission was no surprise, but stung nonetheless.

Yet, she realized, she loved him with all her heart. And he offered himself in the only manner he understood. There was no question that she had little to lose—except pride. Others married with far less in common. Even if this didn't work, it would be good for her family. And, if she were willing to risk her feelings on a gamble, she had the vague possibility of being truly happy one day. A new beginning lay at her feet if she was brave enough to reach out and grasp it. Could she?

Ripples of a new self stirred deep within her soul, followed by an inexplicable feeling of rightness. "I agree."

Chapter Fourteen

Life certainly had a way of taking a turn—for better or worse, Joanna had yet to decide. She was now a bride, trussed in white satin and surrounded by family, staff and a select group of friends. Champagne provided by her husband flowed freely. White lilies and purple hyacinth were spread about the parlor. Someone, she suspected Chang, had slipped pink Hollyhocks, a Chinese symbol of fertility, amongst the arrangements.

Her husband—butterflies fluttered in her stomach at the thought—stood across the parlor. Dressed all in black, save the red rose pinned on his lapel, Mac talked with Rebecca and Adam. Rebecca burst into a flurry of words and gestures. Mac's lips thinned. As if he sensed her watching, he turned and smiled.

She doubted she'd ever grow accustomed to calling

Mac her husband. Devilishly handsome, charming men such as Mac simply didn't marry women like herself. Yet she wore a simple gold band on her finger as proof he'd done just that.

He'd allowed her three days to prepare for the wedding, during which they had spent much of their time making social calls in the company of Lord and Lady Kerrick, that pair's seal of approval obvious. While some people still gave her and Mac the cut direct, others now played the game of wait-and-see.

Mac had hired three additional servants for her household, freeing Joanna to spend more of her days and evenings talking with him, riding in Hyde Park, or even tending her flowers. If she hadn't known they were already to be wed, she would have thought he was courting her.

Despite all the pleasantness, Joanna's other difficulties remained: Dorridge was beside himself, Charlie had yet to return from his hidey-hole in the country, and Randolph was still missing. And though the auction was less than a week away, her participation in the search for her father's statue had been temporarily suspended. Mac continued to spread the word along the docks through his connections, hoping someone would hear a rumor or two. At the same time, he said he was intent on finding Digger, the ruffian he suspected of ratting out himself and his crew.

Once her initial shock at his manhandling of her subsided, and once Mac deposited a hefty sum in a special bank account, Joanna's mother had been thrilled with their sudden marriage. Shopping became her first and foremost priority. And now the same woman who buried her problems beneath her pillow and avoided any discussion more serious than the dinner menu, the weather or current fashion, prepared to instruct her daughter about the role of a bride on her wedding night.

The concept was staggering.

Her mind whirling, Joanna gripped the ornately carved arms of the yoke-back chair in which she sat. It was nestled in a corner behind some potted ferns, providing a modicum of privacy, which was why she supposed her mother had led her here.

Sitting beside Joanna, Lady Fenton steepled her fingers as if seeking divine guidance. "I know we have never addressed this subject. Truly, I never saw the need." She cleared her throat. "Relations with . . ." She tipped her head to the left. "A bride . . ." Blinking twice, she finally blurted, "Simply lay perfectly still and your duty will end quickly."

"My duty?" Joanna asked, more than a little disappointed. Although she had heard some things from the maid when she was younger, she had been hoping for greater elaboration from her mother than "lie perfectly still."

Her mother looked embarrassed. "How shall I put this? The man takes his . . ." She tapped her finger on her chin. ". . . object of desire . . ." Her cheeks flushed red. "Then you . . . There's pain . . . usually . . . if a girl is a virgin, which, of course, you—" Her lips pursed into a thoughtful frown. "Dear me, this is more difficult than I imagined."

The woman studied the four corners of the room, spying Cook who was carrying in a tray of blackberry tarts. Her entire body heaved in relief. "Think of Cook when she's prepared a turkey. It's a matter of proper basting and stuffing the cavity, so to speak. If done well, then everyone's satisfied. Mr. Archer will undoubtedly know what he's about." Rising, obviously deciding she'd said enough, her mother kissed Joanna's cheek and escaped to talk to the vicar.

Not a full minute passed before Rebecca slid into her recently vacated chair. "You look frightful. What did your mother say?"

Still in a state of confusion, Joanna murmured, "We talked about turkeys."

"Turkeys?" Rebecca echoed. "How odd." Excitement replaced the bewildered look in her eyes. "I have a surprise, a belated wedding gift—though Mac will likely be furious that I told you." She glanced over her shoulder, then leaned forward. "We believe we have located Mac's father. The man's name is Henry Belgrave, earl of Fairfax. Isn't that wonderfully distinguished? And he's in London. He never married and has no children—therefore if Mac is Fairfax's son, and if Fairfax were to acknowledge Mac, then Mac would be the heir to his estates. You would be Countess Fairfax!"

Joanna stared, speechless, a dozen questions spinning through her mind. Already suspecting the answer, she asked, "Does Mac know?"

"Yes. He's being pigheaded as usual, as if we never discussed the possibility before."

He hadn't said a word to her. Disappointment twisted in Joanna's stomach that he hadn't shared this knowledge of his possible paternity. "He knew you might know his father?"

"He knew my father was looking for him," Rebecca agreed. "When Father first met Mac, he knew he'd seen that same face some other time. Father has been investigating the matter since last year. He was right. Adam pieced the truth together when he accidentally met Lord Fairfax the other day."

"And what did Mac have to say?"

Rebecca looked nonplussed. "His skin turned a ghastly shade of red when he heard the news. He is absolutely furious and wants nothing to do with Lord Fairfax."

Joanna felt sympathetic for Mac. "I imagine discovering who your father is and that he possesses a title as well must be both overwhelming and terrifying." The discovery shocked her, certainly. "Especially when aside from you and Adam and a handful of other lords and ladies, Mac seems to only *tolerate* society." She thought she recalled a reason. "Do you know why?" she asked.

"I asked Adam once," Rebecca answered, studying her fingernails. She seemed locked in some internal debate. Her decision made, she faced Joanna and asked, "Has Mac ever mentioned a woman by the name of Lady Daphne?"

Since Rebecca's expression had turned so horribly grave, the news could not be good. Joanna shook her head, more than curious now.

"When Mac first came to London, he believed himself to be much the same as other men. One night, he met Lady Daphne Renwick. She had come to town for the season to find a husband, and she aligned herself with Mac in a supposedly torrid affair. He fell madly in love with her—or thought so at the time—and proposed. She threw his proposal back in his face. One month later, she married an earl fifteen years older than herself. It seems that all she wanted was the title. And the horrible woman didn't even bother to keep their affair or Mac's proposal a secret. He was humiliated."

At a loss for words, Joanna simply bobbed her head.

"But after that, ladies actively sought his company— for sexual favors, alone. Women whose husbands mostly didn't care. Mac spent the next several years developing a reputation being with them. It is no wonder he has a rather jaded point of view toward society men and women. And I imagine he puts his father in the same category. But I was thinking that perhaps *you* could convince Mac to at least speak with him."

"I can't say I blame Mac about being disgusted by those people," Joanna said, absorbing the knowledge that he had proposed to a woman once before. "As for

Earl Fairfax, I see no harm in suggesting he and Mac meet, but ultimately Mac must decide."

"That is exactly what Adam said," Rebecca snapped. Then she sighed. "I know you both are right, of course. Mac is such a dear, and I simply want the best for him." She peeked over her shoulder again, glanced from side to side, then pursed her lips. "And speaking of husbands, since your mother only mentioned turkeys, do you have any questions about tonight?" Searching once more for anyone within earshot and satisfied they were alone, she blurted, "I mean, you do realize men and women are different than one another—anatomically speaking, that is."

Indeed, thought Joanna. She'd touched that very difference with her hand already. She just wasn't sure what exactly to do about it. She nodded.

Rebecca edged closer. "I assure you, there is nothing to worry about. In fact, when it is done right . . . The French call it *le petit mort*, the little death. I think I screamed the first time," she whispered with a grin.

Sweet Empress, thought Joanna. She was going to be basted, stuffed, then left to die while screaming her lungs out.

"I imagine Mac is much like my husband and well-skilled in these things—a benefit, to be sure. I shudder to think what might have happened had he *not* known what he was about. I knew fairly little. I mean, who would have imagined making love in a chair?"

She was going to be basted and stuffed while stuck in a chair before she died screaming? The image made

Joanna's eyes cross. "I rather hoped we might use a bed," she said weakly.

"Of course you will. Tonight." Rebecca's grin grew to disturbing proportions. "But I would be remiss not to mention the chair or the table or the carriage or the wardrobe. There is also something men seem to be particularly fond of, though you might find it horribly decadent." Rebecca leaned even closer and whispered several suggestions—nay, specific instructions!—into Joanna's ear.

As if guided by the very subject they discussed, her gaze drifted toward her husband—not him exactly, but rather his groin. Joanna's hand flew to her mouth. Dear Goddess! She needed to cancel the wedding night. Immediately. She lifted her eyes to find Mac staring at her, an amused smile on his face. The wicked man probably knew what they were discussing!

He quickly closed the distance between them. Flames of embarrassment burned beneath her skin.

"What are the two most charming ladies in London discussing?" he asked as he arrived.

Joanna lurched from her chair. "Rebecca needed advice on her garden. Petunias."

Giggling, Rebecca stood as well. "Exactly. And don't forget the daisies. If you will excuse me, I believe I shall go discuss petunias with my own husband."

Perhaps if she wished hard enough, Joanna thought, the floor would open and swallow her whole. No, she would never be so lucky. "What else would we possibly discuss on my wedding night?"

With a seductive slide of his lips, Mac kissed the palm of her hand. His eyes glittered with promise. "I can't imagine."

Shivers rippled out and spread from Joanna's fingers up her arm and down to her toes. "I just remembered. We should talk to Lord Harry before he leaves."

"Do you suppose he would like to discuss petunias, too?"

"Oh, be quiet," she muttered, quitting all attempts at prevarication. Since Mac refused to release her arm, she had no choice but to allow him to accompany her.

Leaning over the buffet, a well-stacked plate in his hands, Lord Harry Tatterton alternated nibbles between a goose liver paté and a meat pie. He beamed at Joanna. "Such a lovely bride. Your father would have been proud. He could not have made such a lovely match himself. . . ."

Indirectly, Joanna thought, her father *was* responsible for her current predicament. His ambivalence toward money had led to the family's financial woes. The family's financial woes had led to Joanna selling his statue, and to Randolph's desperation and disappearance. Randolph's disappearance had led Joanna to Mac. She would decide later whether or not to thank him in her prayers. "A day does not go by that I do not think about him."

"I understand," Lord Tatterton said. "Your brother deserves a tongue-lashing the likes of which he has never had. *He* should have walked you down the aisle. Not me."

229

"Considering the short notice and circumstances at the country estate, he simply could not be here."

"The auction is in less than one week. He had best be back by then with that statue in hand. What was he thinking, taking Lung Wang Sun with him?"

She hated lying but, knowing many people attending the wedding would request a private viewing of Lung Wang Sun, Joanna and Mac had agreed upon the excuse Harry had just repeated. "Who can say?" she prevaricated. "But Mac has a drawing he would like you to look at. Do you mind?"

Mac pulled a small paper from his pocket and handed it to Lord Harry.

"A snake?" the man asked. "What would you like to know?"

"Have you seen something like this before? Or perhaps you know of a legend that might be tied to such a design?"

Tatterton set his plate aside. "You're shaking. What is this really about, Joanna?"

"Nothing important. Truly. My curiosity often drove my father wild. I found the drawing in his papers and didn't recognize it. It really is nothing to concern yourself with. The design is familiar to me, but I cannot place it."

Mac drew her closer to his side. "Excuse her rambling, sir. A healthy curiosity mixed with a bride's nervous chatter. Surely you understand."

Tatterton smiled, accepting the lie as some shared and universal male truth. "Well, then. Let me think of the relevant myths. This is clearly a snake coiled to strike. I'm not quite sure what the stake in the middle represents. Hmm . . . St. Patrick drove the snakes from Ireland. Hecate, the Greek goddess of darkness, was often painted with serpents. Then we have Medusa. And Adam and Eve, of course. And snakes grounded Athena to the Earth. The Hindus had their very own snake goddess, too. Is any of that helpful?" he asked.

"It might be," Joanna prompted.

Suddenly Mac put in, "Did Joanna tell you we found the Scroll of Incantations?"

Harry choked on a sugared plum. When he recovered from a fit of coughing, he exclaimed, "No. Shame on you, my dear. Tell me. Where was it hidden?"

She pondered Mac's motivation even as she explained, "Confucius deserves the honors. He accidentally knocked Father's Ming Dynasty tea jar from the shelf. It had a secret bottom."

"Your father always was a clever man. This news will spawn a new wave of interest and speculation. If you include the scroll in the auction, the bidding price of Lung Wang Sun will increase substantially."

"We have not yet decided what we will do," Mac confided. "For now, the scroll is under lock and key at my home."

"Very wise, young man. That object is not something to be left lying around."

Joanna kissed Lord Harry's cheek and hurried away, leaving the man muttering at the buffet. To Mac, who followed, she whispered, "I assume you have a reason for telling him about the scroll."

"I thought it might be interesting to see what develops."

"Do you still consider Harry a suspect?"

"I have not ruled out the possibility—though I can hardly believe the man capable of hurting you or Randolph. He does however have access to a great many ears. It will be interesting to see what develops once the news of the scroll's discovery spreads."

"This could be a very dangerous game," she warned.

"I'm prepared for that."

The deception, the seemingly endless lies, opposed the very morality Joanna had been taught, the same one her brother had obviously forgotten. It was wearisome. The responsibilities of the last year—the financial problems, Penelope's season, her brother's disappearance, this supposed love match, the wedding, the upcoming wedding night—were all too much.

She leaned into Mac, accepting the strength he so unconsciously offered. "I should like to forget Randolph and serpents and Lung Wang Sun for a long while."

Mac pressed a tender kiss to her lips. "I think I can manage that."

The carriage rolled through the fog clinging to the London streets. Joanna couldn't help but remember the last time she and Mac had occupied such a conveyance together, at night; it had been the first time he'd offered her a private lesson in passion. Her body hummed with anticipation.

Why was she surprised? She simply walked into the same room as Mac and her body reacted strangely. On some elemental level, one she didn't quite understand, her body recognized his.

Unfortunately, tonight—one of the most important nights of her life—now that they were actually alone, her mind clung to her fear of the unknown and to the memory of all the women who'd preceded her to Mac's bed. "Where are we going?" she asked as calmly as she could.

"My home. I released most of the staff for the night so we wouldn't be disturbed. Are you nervous?"

"Why would you think that?" Her voice was tremulous.

"No reason, other than you're as white as bleached whalebone and if you grip the handle of the door any tighter, it might just pop off." He waved a finger in her direction. "Come here."

"I am really quite comfortable where I am," she said.

"Then I'll join you."

Her husband, complete with all rights the title implied, slid across the small space that separated them, consuming every inch of leather between her and the door. Before she could blink, he had loosened her cape and tossed the garment to the opposite seat.

Hadn't Rebecca mentioned carriages, naked bodies and lovemaking in the same breath? Now Joanna's cape, one of the last barriers between Mac and her naked flesh, rested on the leather across from her. Panic, curiosity and excitement warred with one another. "What are you doing?"

"Making you more comfortable, less you expire before we even reach our home. But fear not. Nothing shall happen tonight without your full consent."

Her panic eased as Mac's fingers sought, found and circled the small pulse points at the base of her neck, releasing the tension trapped in her muscles. There was nothing sexual about the massage, yet Joanna's heart beat wildly. She moaned.

"Like that, do you?"

Like was too tame a word. His hands brought sheer, unadulterated pleasure. She managed a sigh and dropped her head onto her chest. Massaging and soothing along her spine, across her shoulders, he worked his magic for several long wonderful minutes. When she finally realized he'd managed to free her curls and loosen the buttons at the back of her dress— for surely that was the reason for the cool draft of air and the feel of skin against skin—the sensation was too glorious to ponder.

And when had he placed her on his lap? No matter, she decided. She was certainly more comfortable than on the carriage's hard leather seats.

All the while Mac's hands stroked the muscles in her neck and back. His lips traced a path from her collarbone to her ear, over her jaw to the corner of her mouth. She shuddered. He gave her a kiss as soft as a sigh, caresses promising a heat she'd never before considered. He wanted her. She knew that. And, regardless of her fears, she wanted him.

Her breasts ached with the desire to be held. Her entire body seemed to throb, casting her nervousness away into the shadows of her mind. When his hands drifted lower, dragging her gown with them, when his thumb brushed her nipple, shooting a spark to her stomach and below, an aching need blossomed and Joanna arched her body toward Mac's palm.

"Easy, darling. Relax." He chuckled.

Hah! She thought she might expire on the spot, partly from pleasure and partly from mortification. At least then she wouldn't have to eventually face him in full light.

All fears faded as he bent her over his arm, pulled her body forward, and pressed his mouth to her nipple. Oh, most definitely, she would expire. But she hoped to endure a few minutes more of his wicked assault first.

Mac's breathing turned ragged, his hands more brisk, less controlled. For the first time in her life, Joanna felt the power of being a woman. It brought a wealth of confidence. Pure female instinct tempered her fears. She tugged Mac's face down to hers and pressed her mouth to his, mating their tongues.

Without a doubt, she enjoyed kissing this man. She thought she could linger in their carriage for hours just doing that.

A duel of lips and teeth and tongue ignited whispers

of pleasure from them both. Their passion grew. Their breaths mingled as their fingers sought and found each newly bared expanse of flesh.

Mac lifted his mouth, his breathing as ragged as Joanna's. Then he straightened her clothing and fastened the buttons on her dress. As if hesitant to release her, he kissed her one last time. "We're home, darling."

Her befuddled mind now registered the fact that the carriage had stopped. She peered outside. A lamp glowed at the top of the steps that led to the front door of her new home, a new life. The power of being a woman, the power he'd just shown her, flowed through her body. She would be a good wife. She would make Mac forget all other women. She would make him love her.

Chapter Fourteen

Mac was still in a state of shock that he was about to carry a bride across the threshold of his home. He'd mostly accepted the idea, but it still took him by surprise from time to time. He certainly had no reservations about the upcoming wedding night. He'd thought of little else since she'd agreed to his proposal. Passion lay beneath her shyness, passion he'd already tasted, and he looked forward to devouring it in its entirety.

Hopping down from the carriage, he swung Joanna into his arms, turned and took three steps. The driver took the vehicle around to the carriage house.

"I've a gun," a deep voice growled from the shadows. "Release the lady at once."

"Afraid I can't do that," Mac answered with deadly calm.

Joanna wriggled in Mac's arms. "Let me down."

"Be still," he ordered.

"But, Mac . . ."

"Do as she says," the stranger snapped.

Mac really had no desire to kill a man with Joanna present, it being his wedding night and all, but if he put her down, that's what he'd do. He sought generosity he normally wouldn't extend to such a highwayman stupid enough to pull a gun on him. Dropping his head, Mac fought for patience. "If you value your life, you'll walk away before I lose my temper. I'm in no mood for games tonight."

"This is no game, you blackguard." Though the words promised violence, the voice quavered.

Joanna wriggled free of Mac's hold and managed to peek over his shoulder. "Randolph?" she cried.

"I should have known," Mac muttered.

Randolph jabbed the gun deeper into his back. "I demand that you release her this instant."

The lad confirmed what Mac already suspected: Randolph Fenton had oysters for brains. Eager to meet the person who'd caused more trouble than a green crew on its first voyage, Mac slowly turned.

A scraggly brown beard covered Randolph's chin and much of his cheeks. His hair brushed the collar of a once-grey jacket that was now ragged, stained and loose-fitting. The last few weeks had been hard on the lad, which provided Mac with a small measure of satisfaction. Nevertheless, Randolph needed to learn a lesson. "And what do you propose to do if I don't?"

"Well," Randolph stalled, dismay on his face. "I'll shoot you."

"You most certainly will not," Joanna snapped.

Mac squeezed his wife once for silence. "Tell me, Randolph. Are you hurt? Injured?"

"No. What are you doing with my sister?"

Ignoring the boy's ridiculous assumption that he would answer his questions, Mac asked, "No broken bones? No loss of memory?"

Randolph shook his head, his brows furrowed. "I asked you first."

"No worries, then?"

"I've a great deal to worry about, but I'm not dying or such, if that's what you're asking."

"Splendid." In a whirlwind motion, Mac slid Joanna to the ground and punched Randolph square in the face. "*That* is for scaring your sister half to death and for pulling a gun on me."

The boy dropped to the ground like a stone. Both Joanna and the gun forgotten, he held his hand to his face. "Creepers. I do believe you broke my nose. I ought to shoot you after all. I still might, you know."

"You're certainly welcome to try. A bloodied nose is the least you deserve, pup."

"Pup, you say? I am a grown man."

"Then start acting it, for God's sake!"

"Stop bickering, both of you." Joanna pulled a handkerchief from her bag and handed the white linen to her brother. "Mac, help him inside."

"Why would I do that?"

Her shoulders jerked to rigidity. "Because otherwise I would have no other choice but to take him home and see to his injuries."

Over the boy's dead body, thought Mac. He was glad Randolph was alive. Truly. Watching Joanna smile was reason enough. Mac simply resented the boy's timing. He'd had far more exciting plans for this evening than questioning Randolph. Joanna obviously felt otherwise. Still, arguing with his new bride was even less appealing than interrogating Randolph, so there was no hope for it. He cursed, tugged her brother up from the ground, and shoved him none-too-gently toward the stairs. "You stink," he complained.

"For your information, I've had a rough go of it the last few weeks."

Mac managed a grunt. They clamored up the steps and marched to the study, where Randolph collapsed in the nearest chair—Mac's favorite, which would likely have to be burned first thing in the morning. The stench alone, not to mention the possible stains, would never leave the fabric. Mac stomped to the liquor cabinet.

Kneeling at her brother's feet, Joanna clasped his hands in hers. "Where have you been? I thought you were dead."

"Why would you think that?"

"I found one of those hideous notes."

Immediately he looked contrite. "Golly, sis, I'm sorry."

"And that is supposed to make everything all right?" Mac asked angrily. Now that he knew Randolph was alive and well, he wanted to take his wife to bed—it was his wedding night after all! Yet here she was coddling her pain-in-the-arse brother, who didn't even have the good sense to be groveling with gratitude.

The boy loosened the buttons on his coat. "You don't by chance have an extra spot of whisky, do you?" he asked.

Mac growled.

Joanna shot him a warning scow.

Obviously thinking he'd won a major skirmish, Randolph smiled.

Mac thrust a glass into the boy's face. "Be careful, pup. I can still kick you out—regardless of your sister's wishes."

The boy sobered immediately. "Why are you here, Jo? Do you know who this is?"

"Of course. Mac and I were married today."

Randolph blanched. "But Jo. He's a free trader."

"I know."

"And he hasn't a title. And I've heard nasty rumors about his penchant for violence which, judging from what I've seen tonight, are true. You ought not to have married the man."

"Randolph. You should know better than to believe idle gossip. And Mac would never hurt me."

"Damn right," Mac added from where he now stood by the fireplace. "So, if you weren't hurt, why did you suddenly decide to show up on my doorstep tonight?"

241

The boy scratched at the raw skin above his cravat. "I was tired of running and hiding. I'd decided to talk with Ashford once more, to see if maybe we could work out a different form of payment for my gambling debts—rather than the statue. He was barely alive when I got to see him. Then someone arrived and I hid in a closet near the kitchen."

"That was us," Mac said.

"How was I to know that? All I heard was muffled voices. Blimey. I was afraid someone would find me and think I'd done the poor fellow in! Afterward, I went to warn Charlie. He was terrified, and was leaving for the country. He said you had told him you wanted to help. At first I thought you might be the one who's after me so I decided to follow you. Tonight, when I saw you carrying Joanna, I didn't know what to think. I just reacted."

"It seems that's all you've done ever, leaving chaos in your wake." Mac rubbed his chin. "Where is the statue?"

"I hid Lung Wang Sun in the wall of a nasty rooming house near St. Giles where I've been staying. I'm lucky to be alive." He looked sheepishly toward his sister. "I fell into a spot of trouble."

From his position beside the mantel, Mac snorted. "You likely walked into it with your eyes wide open and your head up your—"

Joanna cleared her throat.

"Never mind," Mac muttered. "I've met your friends and visited Eden. We have a fair idea of your *troubles*,

but there are holes we'd like you to fill. Tomorrow."
He had other things he wanted to do tonight.

"I would prefer he explained now," Joanna said. "I
cannot rest until I know what's going on."

Randolph downed his drink and extended the
empty glass toward Mac. Realizing his host's cordial-
ity was limited to one drink, the boy eventually set the
glass back on the table. He rolled his shoulders several
times. "I'm blasted sorry I caused you trouble, sis. It
was to be a lark, an adventure."

"*What* was?" she asked quietly.

"It all sounds rather ridiculous now, but we thought
to develop our reputations as rakes. Ashford knew the
places to frequent and so we visited them with regularity. In the beginning, the hells were most stimulat-
ing. They were so very different than the stuffier
gentlemen clubs, like nothing I had ever seen. I gambled, too. I won in the beginning, then started to lose.
I swore my luck would change if I kept playing. By
then I owed more than I could afford to pay."

"A common occurrence for those foolish enough to
test their skill at such places," Mac chided. "The dealers at Eden cheat."

"I realized as much. Unfortunately, too late." Randolph leaned his elbow on the arm of his chair and set
his chin in his hand. "When the doorman there
pressed for payment, I became desperate. Ashford
claimed he knew someone who would cover my debts
in exchange for Lung Wang Sun. The idea made sense
at the time. Then you"—he looked at Joanna—

"decided to hold that bloody auction. I stole the blasted statue."

When Joanna frowned, he added, "I changed my mind, which should count for something, but Ashford refused to return the thing. He said the Serpent would never let go of it now. I knew the statue was worth more than what he was willing to pay me. I snagged Lung Wang Sun back from Ashford and decided that if I hid until the day of the auction with the statue, there wouldn't be anything anyone could do to any of us. We'd sell the thing, I'd take part of the money, pay my debts, and that would be that."

"You call that a plan?" Joanna mumbled.

"These people threatened to *kill* me."

"And who, exactly, are these people?" Mac asked.

"That's the rub. I don't know for sure."

"Of course not," Mac snapped. Then he added, "There was one small problem with your plan. In order to protect your sorry hide and prevent a scandal, Joanna told everyone you were sick and recuperating, first in London, then in the country. Whoever wants that statue decided to leave their messages with Joanna."

Alarm spread across Randolph's features. "Were you hurt?"

"No," she answered quickly.

Irritated that she still insisted on protecting her brother from the consequences of his actions, Mac said, "The hell with that." He stomped to the desk in the corner. "You want to know if your sister was harmed. She could have been killed when she ventured into one of the rougher taverns on the docks to solicit help to find you. She watched your friend Ashford die—something a woman should never have to witness. Then she nearly died when a chap delivering a message for you pushed her over a thirty-foot balcony."

"Do not exaggerate," Joanna interrupted. "I told you, after I had time to think the situation through, I believe the villain simply pushed harder than he meant. My near fall was an accident."

"Accident or not, the result would have been the same had you fallen." Mac pulled a velvet bag from a compartment in his liquor cabinet and tossed the pouch into Randolph's lap. "And what about your sister fretting over family heirlooms and gifts given to her by her father?"

The velvet pouch lay untouched in Randolph's lap. "Oh."

"Is that all you have to say?" Mac asked.

Joanna knew the contents even before she reached for the bag. She did so anyway, loosening the silk strings. The locket inside scorched her palm as she stared at the familiar initials engraved upon it. She turned her gaze to Mac. "Where did you find this?"

"I bought it from Annie this morning. I take it the locket *is* yours?" When she nodded, he added, "I thought as much. I was going to show you tomorrow, not wanting to spoil our wedding day. Your brother sold this along with a strand of pearls to Annie yesterday. She couldn't tell me where he went, though."

She whirled on her brother, unwilling to accept his deceit. "You stole and sold my locket? The one gift from father I treasure more than anything? And mother's pearls? How could you?"

"I knew you loved them and saved them until the last. I was desperate, Jo. My money ran out. Why do you think I waited so long to sell that locket in the first place?"

"Your restraint is supposed to make me feel better?"

Shifting in his seat, Randolph tried to shift away some of the blame. "You must admit, some of this is your fault. If you hadn't intervened, none of those accidents would have happened to you. I never imagined you'd tell people I was sick." He shook his head. "Though I should have known."

"Should have known what?" Joanna's words were clipped.

"That you'd interfere somehow or another. It's what you do best."

Joanna felt herself snap. She had been so worried, so hesitant to accept or admit Randolph's duplicity in this entire matter, willing to give him the benefit of the doubt to the bitter end. Her life had been turned upside down because of his weakness for gambling, his irresponsibility, and *he* blamed *her*. Her. The one person who had tried to shield him from scandal and protect her family. And he had stolen from her. Joanna saw red, a blinding fury. Before she even realized her intent, her hand shot across the empty space between them and connected with her brother's cheek.

Mac applauded. "Well done, darling."

Randolph rubbed his reddened cheek, stunned. "Why'd you do that?"

"You inconsiderate ingrate! You have no idea what I have endured. You should have known better."

"Cor, sis. I apologized. Of course you're right. I should have anticipated your interference. You always did take matters into your own hands."

"Interference?" She sputtered like a dying candle. "I tried to protect you. And if I hadn't, who would have? You?" Hysterical laughter spilled from her mouth.

"Maybe I needed the chance to prove myself, which I never seemed to have."

The blood rushed from her face. The disappointment she thought could spread no further infiltrated her memories, those hours spent worrying and doing, while Randolph played at being viscount. "Prove yourself? Where were you when we sold my horse to pay for Penelope's piano lessons? And what were you doing when I was scrubbing the bedroom floors to save money on maids so we could afford a cook? And who shuffled bills about because you needed to 'experience Paris.' How *dare* you tell me you never had a chance to prove your worth! All you ever had to do was tell me you wanted to take control."

Clearly uncomfortable with her accusations, her brother shifted again in his seat. "After what happened with Beasley, you seemed to need something to do more than ever. I never expected you to actually marry, and I didn't want to hurt your feelings."

She shook her head. "So, you made your decision based solely on what you believed best for me. How generous of you. Well, as you can see, I managed to find a man willing to take a chance on such a pitiful spinster as myself."

"You're twisting my words all around."

Joanna didn't want to listen anymore. She let Mac gather her trembling body in his arms. "Shall I shoot him now or wait until tomorrow morning?" her husband asked.

She burrowed into his chest.

Mac glared at Randolph. "Don't forget you are in this house at your sister's request—so I suggest you take care of what you say. Seeing Joanna upset displeases me. I suggest we table this discussion until tomorrow."

The boy yawned. "A bed would be just the thing. A small one will do. A bath and a hot meal, too."

A guest was the last thing Mac wanted on his wedding night. He was tempted to flatten the lad for his presumption, but he couldn't very well send him to the wolves. Until he decided what was to be done, he intended to keep Randolph under lock and key. And though Joanna was angry with her brother, she would not want him to leave tonight. And making Joanna happy had become increasingly important to him.

Chapter Sixteen

Mac's bedroom was prepared for one purpose: Seduction. If Joanna was ever sure of anything, she was sure of that. A scarlet blanket of rose petals covered the huge four-poster bed. A fire crackled in the hearth, and candles flickered on the bedside table, coating the room with a honeyed glow. Joanna's comb and brush and a few other necessities lay beside Mac's belongings on the top of the dresser. Their intimacy did not escape her, and it seemed to proclaim even more grandly that this was not an All Fool's jest; she was married to MacDonald Archer.

His eyes burned with an intensity she now recognized, but she was not sure what to say.

"I have no chambermaid," her husband began, "so tonight the duty of helping you undress falls to my hands. Not that I mind." He kissed her thoroughly, leaving her light-headed, then turned her about and slipped the buttons of her gown free, one by one. His lips traced the same path as his fingers, down her spine until she knew he could go no further, that the buttons had indeed stopped.

Like a shy mouse seeking the nearest hole in which to hide, Joanna scampered behind the privacy screen, a new addition since her last visit. Coward, she accused herself.

"By the way," Mac called. "Rebecca delivered a present for tonight. It should be on the chair back there. I must admit I'm rather anxious to see you in it."

Joanna held up the gown that lay on the chair before her. White satin ribbons tied two scraps of white lace together at the shoulders, beneath her arms, at her hips and at her knees. Otherwise the garment gaped from top to bottom. Surely Mac didn't expect her to wear this? Then again, she knew what he wore to bed. If she didn't wear this, he'd probably prefer she wear what he did. Nothing.

"Would you like some champagne?" he called.

Most definitely, she decided. Tonight seemed a perfect time to start enjoying alcohol. "Yes. Thank you."

Crystal clinked as Mac poured two flutes. The fire in the hearth hissed as a log fell. The mantel clock marked seconds, which stretched to minutes. And Joanna stood in her bare feet, wearing two scraps of fabric better suited to draping a window than covering up her body's flaws. She tried to remember a more horrifying and potentially embarrassing moment in her entire life, but none was forthcoming.

"Do you need any help?" Mac asked, his voice laced with patience and, if she wasn't mistaken, humor.

Peeking around the corner of the screen, she asked, "Do you by chance have a robe?" She swore she heard his brows arch.

"And ruin the moment I have so long anticipated?" He shook his head. "I've seen you in your shift. There is nothing to be nervous about."

"Easy for you to say," she muttered to herself. "You're fully dressed."

He'd had scores, legions, of women in his bed. And while she found a particle of confidence in the fact that he hadn't married any of those women, he hadn't been caught in a public scandal that coerced his hand. Then again, she believed Mac when he'd said he'd never allow himself to be shackled to a woman out of duty alone. The news that he had once proposed to another woman was disturbing, and she could not help but wonder if he had truly loved Lady Daphne.

All this thinking was giving Joanna a headache. She could rethink the marriage 'til her eyes turned brown and still come up with the same answer: Theirs was a marriage of convenience. This enthusiasm she was experiencing was simply because Mac was a passionate man and he expected a wedding night.

She tentatively stepped from behind the screen.

Mac raked his gaze down her torso and back again. An appreciative gleam appeared in his eyes. "Mercy, you are beautiful. I must remember to thank Rebecca someday," he added, as if to himself. Then he slipped a glass into her hand. "Perhaps this will help settle your nerves."

"Thank you."

"You're welcome." He moved beside the fireplace, sipping his champagne, in no apparent rush to claim his husbandly rights. At least he hadn't ripped the gown from her body and thrown her to the bed. Joanna wasn't sure whether to be pleased or disappointed.

Gulping her champagne, she stared first at her toes that curled into the carpet, then the navy blue walls and finally the bed. The bed he'd prepared just for her. His efforts warmed her heart. "Did you know that when Cleopatra seduced Mark Anthony, she met him in a chamber filled knee high with red rose petals?" she asked.

"A smart woman intent on pleasure, I'd say."

"And the Greeks believed that Aphrodite, the goddess of love, created the first red rose."

"Hmmm."

"Truly," she added, bobbing her head. If he was going to be nice enough to pretend he cared about her ramblings, then she was going to return the favor and pretend to believe he was interested. Mercy, now she was rambling in her head. "When her lover, Adonis, had been gored by a boar. Aphrodite rushed to his side, scratching herself on a thorn which forever stained the flower red."

"I rather like the idea of you wearing nothing but a rose." Mac tried to keep his voice composed. Was he still breathing? He wasn't sure. He was too busy staring at his near-naked wife. The glow of the fire painted her every delectable curve in orange and gold.

After the debacle with Lady Daphne, Mac had given marriage little consideration. Yet here he was, married—to a lady of the *Ton* of all things. There were bound to be bumps in this relationship, issues to be resolved, yet at the moment they all seemed implausible. Everything was perfect. He was finally going to make love to Joanna. His wife. From the gentle rounding of her hips, the swell of her breasts, the hardened nipples, and the slender neck meant to be adorned with rubies, hers was a body designed for his caresses. She was his wife. To do with as he pleased.

She looked ready to bolt for the nearest door. He thought he'd eliminated most of her fears in the carriage and that she'd warmed to the idea of making love to him. At least a little bit. *He*'d certainly warmed to idea.

The erotic images filling Mac's brain were going to have to be put on hold. He placed his drink on the mantel. "Do you think, by chance, you're ready to let me hold you?" he asked.

"I am sorry . . . I've never . . . My mother and Rebecca said that . . ."

Her words and evident fear, would challenge any man's peace of mind. Mac moved toward Joanna. "What did they say?"

"Very different things to be sure, yet neither made sense. If you must know, this is horribly embarrassing. I cannot fathom how, but Rebecca said you will make me scream.

He grinned. "I certainly hope so."

"My mother told me to lie very still."

He shook his head, staring into her eyes. "You won't, I promise."

"This entire consummation thing does not sound altogether pleasant," she admitted.

He had to get her settled down. "Consummation is such a cold description. Making love sounds better and far more pleasurable, don't you think?"

She raised her face to his. "I am behaving like a ninny."

"You're behaving like a virgin. And if you must know, I'm equally terrified. I've never bedded a virgin before. I'm wondering if I can manage the task without mucking things up."

Her lips curved slightly. "I have no doubt that you will handle the situation with the greatest of skill."

Finally, a smile, he thought. Thank God. He wasn't sure how long he could just stand there and not touch her. "Do you trust me?" he asked, not sure what he would do if she answered no.

She nodded.

Progress. He held out his arm, pleased that she slid her hand into his and took the three short steps to close the gap between them. "Do you remember the times we've kissed? The way I touched you in the carriage?"

She nodded again.

"Making love is not so different—except of course all of our body parts are involved."

She looked skeptical.

Virgins were certainly a tricky business. And pleasing Joanna was paramount to anything else. But he was sailing in uncharted territory. He said, "Undress me."

She was taking a sip of her champagne, and she choked. "I beg your pardon?"

"As you said, it seems unfair that you have to stand about wearing near nothing. I simply mean to make you more comfortable."

"Somehow the thought of you naked does not make me feel any safer."

"But the evening will be so much more enjoyable. For both of us. Why don't we start with my shirt?"

Her teeth gripped her lower lip as she set about the task of removing his coat. Next came his cravat and the tiny silver studs that kept his shirt closed. Her fingers were a mere whisper brushing across his skin, leaving a trail of heat. Lust almost overcame his resolve. Calling on every ounce of patience, he gritted his teeth and refused to rush.

Her hair smelled of jasmine and sweet femininity. The tiny pulse beat in her neck. His finger slid across that sensitive spot, back and forth. Her fingers faltered at the final button of his shirt. When she tried to speak, he laid a finger across her mouth. "There is nothing to fear tonight," he swore. "I promise only pleasure."

Discarding his shirt, he lifted her onto his bed, lying beside her, braced on one elbow. A fine blush covered her skin. The rose petals he'd strewn there were crushed beneath their weight, and they poured their fragrance into the air. Mac pulled a single rose from the vase on the table. He traced her lips with the bloom, back and forth, as he had done with his finger. His lips replaced his finger, kissing her gently, tenderly, restraining his need to plunder her.

He raised his head. Her gaze held the first stirrings of pleasure. He wanted more. He wanted her desperate, like he was. "Shall we continue?" he asked. When she nodded, he kissed her again, mating his tongue with hers, pouring his ardor into his caresses as his hands ran down her throat and between her breasts. She moved restlessly, seeking something he doubted she understood. He loosened the stings that held her night gown together. "I don't think we need this any longer."

Suddenly Joanna was naked, her negligée discarded like an old sheet.

Mac's trousers had come off as well, and his hand crept up her thighs to cup her intimately. She practically leapt from the bed. His chuckle reverberated on her lips. "Easy, love."

Easy? Just like a man, she thought. *He* knew what *he* was about.

She didn't dare move. The cool texture of the roses

contrasted with Joanna's heated flesh as the room suddenly grew a hundred degrees warmer. Her heart pounded a wild, insistent drumming. It took every ounce of willpower to keep her hands at her sides. With a groan, Mac captured her mouth with his in a blatant possession, and she ceased to question anything.

He seemed to have sprouted eight pairs of hands, for he touched her everywhere, awakening her body to sensations she never suspected were possible. All the while he plied her with kisses: her neck, her lips, her breasts. He whispered in her ear. "Touch me, Joanna."

Of course, he would want her to touch him. Mercy, her hand actually shook. She tentatively spread her fingers across his chest, marveling at the masculinity of his body. He had rocks for muscles. Her hand circled lower, hovering at his hip. They both stopped breathing until Mac guided her hand to the singular most male part of his body.

As light as butterfly wings, she brushed her fingertips across his erection, over and down the length of him. He moaned against her mouth, telling her he liked her boldness, that he welcomed her touches. She grew more confident, driven by the need to give pleasure as well take it. An ache, centered between her legs, expanded and grew. When she felt his finger move to her soft folds, touch the moisture there and penetrate her body, her eyes flew open to lock with his.

"Does that hurt?" he asked, his voice husky.

Surely he didn't expect her to answer. No one had said anything about talking during this. She wasn't sure her lips could move even if she thought of something coherent to say. She simply nodded.

With a grin, he kissed her again. His finger continued to move and tease and torment, for surely that was what he was doing. If possible, the fire in her body grew, the ache intensified.

"Mac? I want . . ."

"I know." He rolled between her legs, adjusted his body so that she could actually feel him at her very core. She might have asked a question or two if she could form the words, but suddenly he was joining their bodies. There was a pressure, a slight burning, a strange tension, and then the feeling of rightness. The sensation was quite extraordinary.

He moved, slowly at first, giving her time to adjust. His breath teased her ear as he invaded and retreated. Her body began to match the rhythm he set even as his busy mouth moved over her neck, her breasts. He stroked her nipples with his tongue even as he pushed her closer to the edge of some unknown place. His clever fingers reached between their bodies, stroked the very place she ached the most. She thought she might burst through her skin. Mac was relentless as he continued to pump his hips, demanding she obey her body's demands. Like a beam of sunlight on a cloudy day, pleasure burst from within her, shooting down her legs and curling her toes.

She screamed Mac's name even as he shouted too, and emptied himself within her.

Dawn peered through the narrow space between the curtains. The scent of their lovemaking and crushed roses hung in the air. Joanna's head nestled in the crook of Mac's shoulder, his muscled arm possessively wrapped about her waist. Even in his sleep, he held her close.

The events of the night before, the hours spent in passion, melted into one glorious memory after another. Mac had been patient, playful, lusty to be sure—gentle one moment, fierce the next. Like a tender new bloom kissed by early spring, she'd never felt so cherished. A warm glow unfurled in her belly and inched toward her heart.

She'd risen before him and now had returned to nestle back down with him. The rhythm of his breathing changed as Mac's hand shifted higher, cupping her breast.

She lifted her head, a smile teasing her lips. "Good morning."

"You should have wakened me."

"I enjoyed watching you sleep." She traced a finger down his forehead, over his nose, stopping at his mouth. "I never thought a man beautiful before."

He grinned. "You told me much the same the morning we met in your conservatory. You especially like my mouth."

"Even more so now." She ran her gaze over the

length of his body. "Among other parts."

His eyes rounded with shock. "Quick. Fetch the constable. A wanton has replaced my shy bride." Laughing at the sudden blush on her cheeks, and the memory of the predicament which had landed him in this wonderful state, he rolled her beneath him. "And I could not be happier. Now, before we see to those other parts, tell me what you've been doing while I slept the morning away."

"I was studying my new home and learning your secrets," she answered.

"What did you discover?"

"To begin with, your bedroom is simple and elegant, a tasteful reflection of you."

"Elegant, eh? Me? I like that, though there are some who would disagree."

"Then you will tell them to talk with your wife."

A blue-grey watercolor of a rocky coastline, the waves pummeling the shore, covered much of the far wall. Another panel hosted an oil painting of a valiant ship's crew, battling the strong hand of Mother Nature. "The ocean is a part of you, especially the beast that lies beneath the calm waters. You much prefer the challenge of a storm than idle seas."

"But if and when my lady wife sails with me, I prefer a calm sea." He nibbled at the sensitive spot behind her right ear. "More time for other delights."

Granting him greater access to her neck, she turned her head toward the bedside table where books by

Wordsworth, Marlowe, and Thomas Fielding lay. "You like to read before going to sleep."

He nibbled her bare shoulder. "I *used* to enjoy reading before bed. I have discovered a far better method to help me relax. What else?"

A beautifully crafted zither sat by itself on a corner shelf. The typical wave-shaped head sported tiny ivory flowers and anchored the strings. "I admit I never imagined you a musician."

His expression clouded. "I'm not. The instrument belonged to my mother. When I was young, she used to play early in the morning. I would lie abed, pretending to sleep, all for the pleasure of hearing her sing."

"What a lovely memory." She touched her hand to his cheek. "You are a complicated man, Mr. Archer, and I have much yet to learn."

He lowered his mouth to within inches of hers. "I shall endeavor to be a patient tutor until you fully understand all of me." He pressed his hips against her, letting her know exactly which "all" he was particularly interested in at the moment. His lips met hers in a soft kiss, but her stomach grumbled. "I see I am already neglecting my duties as a husband," he said.

Obviously thoroughly comfortable in his nakedness, he rolled from the bed, sauntered to the washstand and splashed his face with water. Afraid she might be caught staring, Joanna averted her gaze to the mirror above his dresser.

"Considering all that transpired last night, I can't

believe you have a shy bone left in your body," he remarked.

"A gentleman shouldn't mention such things."

Laughter rumbled from him. "Now, there is the prim and proper lady I married!"

She launched a pillow at his back, leaned against the headboard, and hugged her knees to her chest. "Last night, Rebecca mentioned they found your father. What are you going to do?" She swore he stopped breathing altogether. The towel hovered an inch from Mac's face. "Mac?" she asked hesitantly. "What is the matter?"

Tossing the linen to the table, he grabbed his trousers from the chair. "Forget whatever it was Rebecca told you. I don't give a damn about this man, whoever he is."

"Lord Belgrave, earl of Fairfax."

"Rebecca told you his name? Did she tell you so you could prod me into meeting with him?"

"Of course not. The decision to meet Lord Fairfax is yours alone—but if he is your father, and if he has no sons, you are possibly his heir. Do understand the implications?"

"It means a titled bastard abandoned my mother when he could have and should have found a way to find us but didn't bother."

Mac tried to mask his anger with indifference, but his hostility was evident. Rebecca had mentioned Mac's irrational point of view on this subject, so Joanna had expected the topic to be a difficult one—

emotional issues of any kind usually were, especially for men who considered themselves above such female silliness—but she had not grasped the depth of Mac's anger. Prepared to ride out the storm, she said, "Perhaps if you talked with him, he could explain—"

"As far as I'm concerned, there is no acceptable explanation for his actions." Mac jerked his trousers up his legs. His shirt came next.

"But what about—"

"Listen well. I needed a father when I was six and was learning to sit a horse for the first time. When I was seven, and learning how to plant a facer on a village boy who dared to call me a bastard. By ten, I was older and wiser and had stopped dreaming about this great man I'd fabricated in my mind. I stopped hoping he would magically appear and rescue us from poverty. I no longer cared. And the morning I put my mother in the ground, I cursed the day that man was born. I certainly don't need him now."

"Rebecca said he never married. If that is true, perhaps he had reason. He would likely welcome an heir."

"So I'm his heir—if he finally deems me worthy. Well, I'm not for sale. At any price."

A gentle rapping broke the awkward silence that had claimed the room. "Who is it?" he snapped.

Knox's muffled voice carried through the door. "I have completed the errand you requested yesterday."

Mac crossed the room and yanked open the door. "Where is Fenton?"

"Devouring a plate of Cook's pastry and eggs."

Mac nodded and closed the door. He braced his arms against the wooden frame and stared straight ahead. His spine held rigid like the limbs of an oak preparing for a heavy winter snow. "I don't want to argue, Joanna. Our life has enough entanglements as it is without adding Lord Fairfax to the mix, but let me make this perfectly clear. I want nothing from this man."

The beast lay dormant, leashed for the time being. Mac claimed to not care, but his fierce reaction proved otherwise. Joanna feared he cared too much. For him, hating Lord Fairfax was easier than admitting otherwise. Bitterness rode inside Mac; left unattended, the wound would fester. Something had to be done, but Joanna couldn't very well disregard his wishes. This problem was his to resolve. Hopefully time and logic would clear a path.

Wrapped in the cream-colored sheet, she climbed from the bed and crossed to his side. "I am sorry I raised the subject. You see, I have this terrible habit of trying to rescue people. Maybe you should ask Randolph. I'm sure he could tell you of the dozen or so times I busied myself with his affairs. And if he has by chance forgotten, I know of several other people you could question." She pressed a kiss to his shoulder. The muscles of his back leapt beneath the caress. "Forgive me?"

He pivoted around to face her. "There is nothing to forgive. Rebecca and her father, on the other hand, need to be taken in hand. And Randolph is still an idiot."

"Thank you for that." More than anything, she wanted to erase the haunted look in her husband's eyes, to comfort the man who had once been a little boy who so needed a father's love. She ran a fingernail down his chest, stopping above the waistband of his trousers where his erection pressed against the soft wool of his trousers.

"Careful, darling. I thought to question your brother and feed you breakfast, but sustenance of any kind will be long in coming if you keep that up."

She dropped her sheet to the floor. She had rekindled his pain, the least she could do was give him pleasure. "Randolph can wait, and I fear I am no longer hungry."

With his anger pushed back to where he kept it under lock and key, he swept her into his arms, strode across the room and tossed her onto the bed. "Oh, but I am."

Chapter Seventeen

Contracts, manifests and lists of supplies yet to be purchased for his trip to Jamaica littered Mac's desk. Until a few days ago, his entire happiness had rested on the upcoming voyage. But what would he do now? He was going to have to make a decision regarding the matter soon, but at the moment another, unexpected and complicated piece of his happiness, which was sitting across the study, required his attention. She sat stroking Confucius—the beige monster of a cat had been a belated wedding gift from Lady Fenton—and glared at her brother. She looked ready to knock him over the head.

Randolph, oblivious to Joanna's agitated state, prattled on, all the while popping almonds into his mouth. He had not stopped eating since he'd arrived.

Suddenly Joanna leaned over in her chair and twisted his ear.

Randolph leapt from the settee and yelped. "Cor, sis. You've turned into a brute."

Grinning despite himself, Mac said, "Be happy the guns are tucked away in another room."

He turned to the fourteen-inch-tall snarling dragon Knox had retrieved from the boarding house near St. Giles, the artifact that had turned his life upside down. Blue and green ribbons of color shimmered across his study wall as sunlight reflected off its gem-covered surface. Shimmering pearl eyes gave the artifact an eerie, almost intelligent appearance. Mac looked from the statue to Joanna. "You're certain you have no sentimental attachment to this statue?"

"Other than that my father adored it, none. But even if *I* adored the piece, my feelings would not matter. Family comes first."

"I can pay the debts for you."

"We discussed this before. You married me, not my family. I will not accept your charity for them. We will proceed with the auction as planned."

"Wait a moment," Randolph interjected. "Maybe we should talk about this. I'm still the eldest."

"Do not even think it," Joanna said. "You got us into this, and there are consequences you need to face. If you work extremely hard, watch how you and mother spend money, and listen to Mac's investment plan, you shall have a nice healthy income in no time."

The young man settled in the chair furthest from his sister and gathered his bowl of nuts to his chest. He slumped lower in the chair and swallowed an almond.

The lad was in for it all right, thought Mac. His sister had not yet forgiven him and Randolph had yet to learn restraint. Mac actually looked forward to guiding him down the path to financial cunning, but first things first. "What did Ashford want with the statue?" he asked again.

"All he said was this 'serpent' fellow wanted it."

"And you have no idea who the 'serpent' is."

"None." The boy's expression brightened. "Ashford did have a lady friend. Maybe we could find out who she is and ask her."

"How do you know he had a lady friend?"

"He spouted this and that about his lady love all the time—it was his grand secret because she was married. The night I broke in to retrieve the statue, I heard voices in his parlor. Ashford was going to show her the statue. She was thrilled and promised to express her gratitude"—he glanced at his sister—"in 'grand style' later . . . if you understand my meaning. I grabbed Lung Wang Sun and hurried out as quickly as I came."

"Would you recognize her voice if you heard it again?"

"To be sure. It was pure sin, laced with honey and whisky. You know, the type that puts ideas into your heads just by saying your name. I kept thinking Ashford was one lucky devil—" Randolph caught Joanna's frown out of the corner of his eyes and cleared his throat. "But, um . . . yes, I'm sure I'd remember her voice."

"That's a start," Mac mused. "Did Ashford ever mention a Lord Dorridge?"

Yawning, Randolph said, "Never."

Joanna moved to stand beside Mac. She studied the papers on his desk. "Do you believe Lord Dorridge is behind the threats to my brother?"

Overcome by his new bride's proximity, he dropped into his chair and toppled her onto his lap. She laughed as he said, "He's certainly capable of such villainy, but I can't imagine his reasons. And his methods are usually far more direct." He turned his attention to nuzzling the tender spot behind Joanna's left ear. A moment later he asked Randolph, "What about Jinx?"

Joanna's brother waved his hand in the air. "He's a nasty bugger . . . not someone you want to tangle with in a dark alley, that's for certain. But he doesn't make the decisions."

"We're basically back where we started," Joanna complained, tipping her head to give Mac's lips full access to her neck.

"Not quite," Mac argued, but his mind had started to drift from Oriental statues to more pressing matters like making love to Joanna again. He tried to focus. "We now know Randolph is alive, and we have the statue. We know the person called the serpent owns

Eden and wants Lung Wang Sun. I suggest we circulate another rumor."

"Such as?" Joanna settled herself more tightly against his lap. The minx was actually teasing him. Two could play this game. He placed his hand directly below her breast, moving his thumb back and forth across her ribs. "Since everyone from Lord Tatterton's seems to think I married you to get my hands on Lung Wang Sun, I suggest we encourage their thoughts in that direction. Of course, if we do that, you will bear the brunt of it."

Joanna looked sad but willing. "The *Ton* has used me for target practice before. What do we hope to gain?"

"The serpent's attention."

"In other words, we'll shift the danger from Randolph and myself to you. It's a dangerous game you play, husband."

"The closer we get to the auction, the more desperate this person will become. I am better equipped to deal with threats to my life than either of you—and I'm not about to let anyone do me in. I have yet to fully enjoy a honeymoon." He kissed her then, pressed her closer on his lap.

"Cor," Randolph muttered as he averted his eyes. "A brother shouldn't have to witness his sister with a man's tongue down her throat."

Mac lifted his lips away long enough to say, "True. Why don't you go find something to eat and close the door behind you?"

Joanna flushed a lovely shade of red, but didn't argue. In fact, she seemed rather intrigued by his suggestion.

Knox cleared his throat from a spot near the door. "Excuse me, Captain, but I have news of that tainted scrap of humanity known as Digger."

Mac reluctantly withdrew his hands from Joanna's waist and accepted the envelope his first mate proffered. Unfolding then reading the missive, he felt a surge of anticipation. "Digger claims he has some important information for me. He wants to have a meeting."

Mac lingered in the doorway of the Pig-'N'-Whistle, taking stock of the boisterous crowd gathered around the tables sharing lies, drinks and cards. Tavern wenches served booze and food, and an occasional brisk slap to those who took more than was offered. To Mac's way of thinking, it was a typical Saturday night.

Digger sat near the back door, trying his best to blend with the woodwork. His fingers tugged nervously on his beard, which he hadn't bothered to braid. That alone was telling. Digger's three-braided beard was his trademark. The rat was definitely running scared. The thought made Mac smile.

He turned to Knox. "I don't expect trouble here, but stay put and keep your eyes open."

"Aye, Captain. Do be careful. This vermin possesses

absolutely no scruples." The man moved to the shadows to watch and wait.

In no hurry, Mac sauntered across the taproom. A part of him wanted to tear this rat into little pieces. His more rational side knew enough to wait and see what Digger had to say. He sat down and laid his pistol on the table.

Digger held his hands in the air. "Ye wouldn't 'urt an unarmed man, now would ye? Certainly not in front of so many people."

"The night is young. And I doubt anyone would care if *you* turned up dead. You took a chance in contacting me. I'm not very happy with you these days."

"That's not very friendly-like."

"Don't delude yourself. You and I were never friends. I have little time and even less patience, so let's get on with this. How much was Lord Dorridge paying you?"

"Not as much as you think." Digger hunched over his glass. "A few months back, while you were in the Indies, Dorridge started snooping round the docks. 'e found out about me business and threatened to 'ave me arrested unless I gave him information about ye. He 'ad me by the balls. I had no choice. And I didn't know 'e meant to have you hanged."

"Of course, had you known his intentions, you never would have taken his money," Mac sneered. He didn't bother to conceal his disgust. "I'm not an idiot, Digger."

"Wasn't saying you was." The man took a swig of

ale. "But now Dorridge thinks I been playing 'im a fool. 'e has the authorities lookin' for me and a bounty on me head. I need to leave London. I hear you have a ship leaving for Jamaica soon."

Mac snorted. "And you think I'd allow your scurvy hide aboard the *Fleeting Star*? Not in this lifetime."

Leaning forward, Digger whispered, "Not even if I 'ave information ye've been wantin'?"

Mac felt a rush of adrenaline. The rat wanted to deal. But it certainly wouldn't do to let Digger think he was overly interested. He leaned back in his chair, crossing his arms. "That depends on what you know."

"I want yer word ye'll get me out of London before I say anything."

Mac flattened his hand across the handle of his pistol. "I could just shoot you."

"Wait a bloody minute!" Digger interrupted. "Cripes." He glanced over his shoulder to make sure no one was listening. "Word has it you been lookin' to find out about a fancy statue."

"And if I am?"

"Maybe I knows where it is. Maybe I knows who killed that Ashford bloke. Maybe I knows who wants a certain statue badly enough to kill for it."

"You're saying you have that information?" Mac prodded.

Digger shook his head. "Not as such. But there's this 'serpent' berk what's been running a game out of Eden, baiting young lords and blackmailing 'em."

"Old news, Digger. Certainly not deserving of passage to Jamaica."

"I got more. I got a name. I even got the proof." Digger leaned forward on his elbows. "Do I got yer word?"

The last thing Mac wanted to do was take Digger aboard the *Star*. Lord only knew the trouble the scurvy rodent would cause. But if the man did in fact know who the serpent was, a free ride to Jamaica would be a fair exchange. Mac tempered his excitement by reminding himself to consider the source. "You're a greedy, self-serving liar, but perhaps this time that will work in my favor. Depending on the name and this supposed proof, we have a deal."

Digger grinned. "Oh, ye'll like the proof. I—"

The window on the far side of the room shattered. One of the wenches screamed. Dishes and furniture crashed to the floor as everyone scrambled to safety. Knox rushed out the front door to see what had happened. Looking around, Mac saw that Digger had toppled from his chair. Cursing, he lifted his pistol from the table and dropped to his knees.

Once he was certain the threat had passed, he got to his feet and cautiously slid along the wall, opening the back door to peer into the alley. Nothing stirred in either direction.

A moment later, Knox appeared around the east side of the tavern. Whoever had shot Digger was gone. "Damn," Mac muttered as he made his way back inside.

Digger, his eyes wide with shock, lay perfectly still on the wooden floor. Blood oozed from a hole in his chest. He was not long for this world.

Mac knelt down beside the dying man. "Talk to me. Before you die, tell me." He leaned closer yet, a scant inch from Digger's mouth. "Who's the serpent?"

The man's chest rose violently in a cough. Then he exhaled his last breath with a shudder. "Dorridge."

The dead rat's word was worthless. Mac had already known that Dorridge was behind the raids on his shipments; he'd figured that out for himself the night Dorridge invaded his bedroom. Yet now that Mac was officially done free-trading, the viscount's efforts in that respect were a moot point.

Mac had suspected Dorridge of wanting to steal Joanna's statue, too. But he had never believed the man so foolhardy or greedy as to perpetrate such nastiness at Eden as blackmail and murder—and now all he had to go on was the finger-pointing of a criminal. He needed proof. Frustration filled him as he climbed down from his carriage.

Lights shone through the curtained windows of his home like beacons on a distant shore. An odd calm settled over him as he thought of Joanna waiting for him inside. She'd probably worried the entire time he was gone. He rather liked the idea. Not because of her distress, but rather because someone cared enough to think about him.

Granted, Knox played nursemaid to Mac when at

sea, and sometimes tried when the *Fleeting Star* was docked. They were good friends. But Mac's feelings for Joanna went beyond friendship. Maybe they even bordered on love. He wondered.

Either way, a warm passionate woman—his wife—waited for him inside. Anticipating a delightful end to a disappointing evening, he took the stairs two at a time.

Laughter drifted into his foyer, now adorned with two lush floral arrangements courtesy of Joanna. Mac grabbed a pink rose from the vase nearest the doorway but stopped in his tracks when he heard an unfamiliar and notably male voice. Rounding the doorway to the parlor, he felt as though his ship had been rammed by a frigate.

Seated in the chair opposite his wife, sipping Mac's brandy as if he had every right, laughing, was the man Mac had never meant to meet: Lord Fairfax.

His father?

There was no denying the fact. Staring at the man was like staring into a mirror.

Memories of his bastard heritage, his fatherless youth, his mother's painful death, all swarmed together into a collage of anguish. Ice-cold rage poured through Mac's veins. He tore the rose in his hands to pieces, not feeling the thorns. With a calm he couldn't explain he said, "Well, isn't this cozy."

Joanna practically leapt from her chair. "I did not hear you come in. This is—"

"Trust me, my dear, I know who your visitor is."

Fairfax stood as well. He was an inch or two shorter than Mac and barrel chested. Grey lined his temples, but the rest of his hair was a rich mahogany. Shock filled his eyes, shock and something else Mac refused to acknowledge.

The two men stared at one another, the tension thick as early morning fog off the coast of Scotland. Mac clung to the image of his mother dying from consumption, her frail callused hands clinging to him as she took her last breath, all because he hadn't the money to care for her. He forced breath into his lungs and turned to Joanna. "What is he doing here?"

Fairfax widened his stance and placed his hands behind his back in a manner Mac often used himself when addressing his crew. "I can explain. I arrived in town a few days ago to be greeted by the strangest rumors. I had to know the truth, if the possibility existed. Your delightful wife was kind enough to let me wait."

Mac ignored the hope in Fairfax's voice. Seemingly indifferent, he shrugged. "The fact that you and I share a face means nothing."

"True—though the betting books at White's would likely say otherwise." The man paused. "And your mother, Rachel Elizabeth Archer, would certainly disagree with you."

"Don't expect for me to call you Papa just because you know her name. Your blood may run in mine, but you are not my father. You abandoned all rights the day you left my mother alone and pregnant."

Joanna clasped her hands. "Perhaps if we all sat down and discussed this calmly—"

"No," Mac interrupted. "The choice is quite simple. Either he goes or I do."

"I have no wish to cause trouble. I'll leave." Fairfax moved toward the door. "I loved your mother very much. I never knew she was with child, would never have . . ." Emotion swallowed whatever he was going to say. He stopped by the mandolin hanging on the wall as familiar to Mac as his mother's name. "She played beautifully, Rachel did. She owned another instrument—a zither, I believe. I gave her this the day I sailed . . . along with my solemn pledge to return as soon as I resigned my commission. There were complications."

There was no missing the sorrow, the years of regret, in his voice, but Mac wasn't buying it. He didn't dare. He bound his temper with a slender thread. "How inconvenient for you."

Joanna handed Lord Fairfax his coat and hat. "I am sorry."

"As am I. Thank you for your generosity." He turned to leave, stopped. "I understand the *Fleeting Star* sails for Jamaica soon."

"And if it does?"

"I was curious if you intended to sail as well."

"I have not finalized my plans as of yet."

Fairfax nodded. "Your wife has my direction. I intend to stay in London indefinitely. Make no mistake, while I lost your mother, I shan't lose you. Not without a fight." The man's bootheels clicked across the marble floor of the foyer as he departed. The closing of the front door blasted in the silence like a cannon shot at sea.

Mac's anger was a volatile thing, a dangerous living beast, gorging on old memories and outrage. He stomped to the liquor cabinet and poured himself a brandy, ashamed to see his hands tremble. He flung the glass across the room. A fine mist sprayed the air and dripped down the damask-covered wall. He loosened his fury on Joanna. "What were you thinking?"

She visibly flinched. "I am not sure I was. I was too busy marveling at the resemblance. Once I recovered from the shock, I couldn't very well slam the door in his face."

"Couldn't you?" he snapped.

"No, I couldn't. Do you want me to admit I was curious, that I wanted to hear his story? That I think you should give him the opportunity to explain? Fine. I admit it."

She'd purposely invited Fairfax in for a brandy! And damned if she wasn't taking his side! Mac stomped about the room, trapped and outraged. He stopped before the mandolin, its cherished memory forever tarnished.

Joanna placed a tentative hand on his arm. "Mac, everyone makes mistakes. Fairfax seems a very nice man."

"That does not make the fact he seduced my mother then left her any more palatable. Why did he come

279

here? How can I possibly mean anything to him?"

"You are a connection to the woman he loved. He is a part of you whether you choose to accept that or not. Do you think to pretend this has never happened, that he doesn't exist?"

He spun on his heel. "Yes."

"Now who is fooling himself? And there is no need to yell. I am standing right beside you."

"I'll bloody well yell if I feel like it. You never met this man before today, never knew he even existed before yesterday. Why do you suddenly care?"

"I see your pain whenever we discuss the subject of your mother or your birth. Oh, you try to mask your emotions with humor or anger or even disdain. And I believe Lord Fairfax suffers as well. Given time, you could help heal one another. He never married and looks to claim you as his heir."

Suddenly Mac was twenty again. He knelt beside a bench in a moonlight garden, wearing his heart on his sleeve, the diamond ring that had eaten a large chunk of his savings tucked away in his pocket. And Lady Daphne was blithely explaining she could never marry him. He'd been an exciting diversion, an incredible lover, but certainly not husband material. Her father would never allow a union with someone of his birth. For that matter, she wouldn't either.

Mac couldn't believe Joanna was cut from the same cloth, but her eagerness to force this issue burned like bad gin in his gut. His disappointment was hard to swallow. "Are you sorry you married such a simple man as me? A man of trade? A man of passions? Are you so anxious to be a countess that you cannot see that—"

His wife had turned ash white. "Excuse me?"

"You knew my feelings, yet you disregarded my wishes and invited that man into my home to lounge in my chair and sip my brandy as if he had every right."

Stiffening as if physically struck, Joanna dropped to the edge of the settee. Her hand tightened on the curved armrest. "Do you honestly believe I invited Lord Fairfax in because I have designs on his title?"

He dragged a hand over his face. "I don't know what the hell I think." Mac was so damned disappointed, so bloody confused. He needed fresh air, needed to leave, afraid of what he might say if he stayed. He marched to the door.

"Where are you going?" Joanna asked.

"Out. I have to go out."

Chapter Eighteen

She had been married all of a day and a half and had managed to send her husband stomping from their home. Not that Joanna considered the problem entirely her fault. No, indeed. In some ways, her husband was a blind fool. And pig-headed. Mac could wish his father to perdition all he wanted; that would not erase Lord Fairfax from the Earth. Or even from London. The man appeared set on a reconciliation and looked to be as stubborn as her husband.

Of course she, too, possessed something of a stubborn streak. Had she to do it over, she would again invite Lord Fairfax to wait for Mac.

She sighed and burrowed deeper beneath her quilts. Her attempts to sleep had proved futile thus far. Until her husband returned home, she would not rest.

The mantel clock chimed twice. The doorknob rattled. Something or someone, likely Mac, thudded against the door.

Confucius perked his ears, then stood and stretched, watching the door as if he expected some sort of show.

Joanna considered pulling the covers over her head and feigning sleep, but playing coward would only delay the inevitable. She sat up and leaned against the headboard.

The brass knob turned, the door opened, and Mac swaggered into the bedroom. To Joanna he looked tall, dangerous and still as wildly appealing as ever—even though her temper hadn't fully cooled. A lock of hair spilled onto his forehead. His coat hung crookedly off one shoulder. A nasty bruise purpled one cheek. Evidently, he'd found someone upon which to exact punishment. And likely the arrogant, albeit handsome, sod had decided to drown his troubles in a bottle of alcohol.

She ignored the tripping of her heart. "I see you managed to find your way home, drunk as a loon."

"Why I drank, I don't know," he admitted. "I learned long ago that spirits do little to solve one's problems." He threw back his shoulders and pointed to the bed. "Are there any unexpected guests in there I need to know about besides the cat?"

Joanna fought the urge to launch the table lamp at his head. Instead, she crossed her arms over her chest. "Well, when my husband left in a huff this evening I invited the gentleman next door over for a quick tumble. However, the chap—a very accommodating man—left hours ago."

Mac's eyes flashed. "Impudent wench. That isn't something to joke about, especially with a husband who hates to share his toys."

"Share his toys?" she repeated with an audible gasp. "What a flattering sentiment. Is that all we are to mean to each other, then?"

He lowered his voice to a whisper. "I haven't quite figured that one through."

She felt as though he'd slapped her. But what had she expected, a bold declaration of love? He had married her out of duty, and she was a fool for loving him.

Love. It was a staggering thought, especially in the light of this conversation. She had panicked when she first acknowledged her feelings, then had accepted them for what they were. Mac could be arrogant and domineering, yet was tender and kind and charming and funny. And she had hoped that his love would grow over the life of their marriage. That was how it worked with many couples, she knew. But her love for Mac had come suddenly, and it had grown to frightening proportions in such a short time. . . .

She sighed. She could not expect him to feel the same way she did just because she willed it, but neither would she let him trample her feelings. "Be sure to let me know when you have 'figured it through.' "

Her husband gave an anguished sigh. "You know I care, Joanna. I wouldn't have married you if I didn't." He leaned against the bedpost and worked at removing his boots. It seemed to be a major chore.

"Oh, for goodness sakes." Taking pity on him, Joanna climbed from the bed and began to help him undress.

He grinned. "Now here's a dutiful wife."

"More like a wife who hopes to sleep yet this night."

He brushed his lips against her ear. "I have just the remedy in mind."

"Do you?" She pulled his shirt free of his trousers, loosened the buttons, and tossed the garment to the floor. "In your condition, I doubt you could remedy your way out of a burlap bag."

"Careful, sweetness. You know how I love a challenge."

Confucius seemed to sense a pending battle and escaped out into the hallway.

"Sit down and be quiet," she snapped. When he plopped onto the bed with a bounce, she added, "You think you can insult me, stomp from this house, come back hours later after carousing heaven knows where, then climb into bed and expect me to welcome you with open arms? You behaved like a foul-mouthed bully." She lowered her head and whispered, "You hurt me."

He tumbled her down on top of him. "I'm sorry for that."

"Mac!"

"Shhh." He pressed a finger to her lips. "I'm trying my best to understand."

"There are things we need to discuss."

"I know. But can we leave it alone for now?"

"If you run away whenever life becomes complicated, Mac, you will never remain in one place very long."

"Perhaps that's why I always loved the sea."

He seemed to speak more to himself than her. His eyes were distant, as if he harbored troubles the size of Lambeth Palace and had no idea how to resolve them.

She had troubles too, though. His accusation that she sought Lord Fairfax's title for her own gain still grated. Goodness, the fact he'd even thought such a thing was infuriating. And then there was the unresolved issue of the trip to Jamaica. She had been telling herself that their lovemaking would be enough to hold him here. But the weariness in Mac's voice rendered her helpless to do anything except comfort him.

Now was probably not the best time to discuss difficult matters anyway. Not with a drunk husband who had only one thing on his mind, if his wandering hands were any indication. And, truth be told, she wanted to feel those hands on her. Yet she could not capitulate quite so easily.

She wrinkled her nose. "You stink, Mr. Archer. I suggest you wash away the stench before you climb in this bed."

He bent his head and sniffed at himself. "Why, I do believe you're right. But I have an even better solution. A dutiful wife would bathe her husband."

Bathe him? Her? The suggestion was scandalous.

The man was a libertine with all sorts of wicked notions. And she was apparently as wicked, for the suggestion made heat pool in her lower body and her breasts ache.

A devilish gleam burned in her husband's emerald gaze. "Afraid?"

Terrified, she thought woefully. But his smug grin coerced her nervousness back behind her pride. Let the rooster crow, she thought furiously. Two could play at this game of licentiousness. At least, she hoped they could. She tossed her hair over her shoulder and familiar words back at him, "Careful, sweetness. You know how I love a challenge."

His brows leapt high on his forehead.

She rose, lifted her chin in the air, closed the bedroom door, gathered the bowl of clean water, a rag and a towel, and carried them to the bedside table. Mac watched her, beneath heavy lidded eyes, from the middle of his huge bed. One might even think he was oblivious to his surroundings had it not been for his obvious arousal. Thank heavens she'd left his trousers on.

Hesitating, she pondered where one normally began when bathing a man. She settled for the face. After all, it seemed the logical thing to do; sort of the top to bottom theory. His face was also the least intimidating part of him. She could also safely start with his feet, but one thing was certain: she could not start in the middle.

At this rate, dawn would come and she'd still be

debating where to begin! The gauntlet had been thrown, so without another thought she climbed onto the bed and straddled his body. Her nightgown climbed high on her thighs but that was the least of her worries. Washing his face brought her intimately against Mac's erection—not that the position was uncomfortable so much as . . . disconcerting.

"Problem?" he asked.

"Of course not. What could possibly be wrong?" She gently washed the sweat and grime from his face, paying extra care to the bruise on his cheek. "I see you found someone foolish enough to test your temper."

"There's always someone willing to go a round or two in the places I went tonight."

"Considering your mood, I doubt you gave the man a choice." She slid the cloth down his chin and over his chest. Lean muscle rippled beneath her touch. To her surprised delight, his nipples hardened. "Oh my."

"See? We're not so different, you and I," her husband drawled lazily. He stared at her breasts, visible through the sheer fabric of her gown. And, Sweet Empress, her nipples stood at attention as if Queen Bess had marched through the room. Her skin flushed with fiery color. Her heart raced.

And her rogue of a husband chuckled.

He enjoyed her discomfort far too much. She made quick work of washing the rest of his upper torso, stopping just short of the waistband of his trousers. Then she paused.

She'd removed his shirt. She'd removed his boots.

288

There was no reason she couldn't remove his trousers . . . other than the fact he would then be naked and expect her to—Well, she wouldn't even consider what he might expect her to do. Her breath hitched in her throat.

"Dare you continue?" he asked.

Her gaze flew to his face. There was no mistaking the raw need in his eyes, the tension in his body and desire in his voice. She laid her palm over his heart, whose hammering was steady beneath the rapid rise and fall of his chest. Her pulse answered.

She bent to kiss first one of his male nipples, then the other. She felt his swift intake of air, his slow exhalation as he fought for control. The heady sense of feminine power again rose within her. She nibbled her way to his mouth. She flicked her tongue against his lips. He lay perfectly still. A thrill rippled through her body. She gazed into her husband's smoldering eyes, licked her lips, and smiled seductively. "Afraid?" she asked.

Need swamped Mac like a tidal wave. He groaned deep in his chest even as his hand tangled in his wife's hair and he dragged her down to him. "We can finish the bath later."

Desperation filled him, a desperate lust. He tugged his trousers off and tossed them to the floor. There was no finesse as he rolled Joanna beneath him, spread her legs, and thrust himself home. Thank the heavens, she was as ready as he. The demons temporarily bested, Mac stilled his lower body and drowned his wife with kisses, a deep mating of their tongues. Again and again, he kissed her until their breaths came in ragged gasps, their hearts pounded against one another, and their bodies again crashed together in a storm of passion.

He rolled, settling Joanna atop him. Her mouth was swollen, her gaze alight with desire. When he first rotated his hips, her eyes widened with surprise—they had not done it this way yet. His hands gripped her waist, pulling her toward him as he thrust into her. Thanking the saints that his wife was a quick learner, he watched as Joanna's body pushed down, taking all of him, using his body to achieve the pleasure he'd taught her she could find. She began to rise and fall on him, her eyes drifting closed.

"No," Mac cried. "Look at me. I want to watch you."

Her gaze met his, held. Like a choreographed ballet, their movements matched, their rhythm increasing, slowing, their passion growing. Mac's heart thundered. He could feel Joanna's release building, the subtle tightening of her muscles, the short little gasps. He filled his palms with her breasts, squeezed. She continued to pump. He swallowed her cry of release with his mouth even as a powerful shudder seized his body and he poured himself into her.

Joanna folded onto his chest and was still. Mac lay there, too. For a long while he stared at the ceiling, awake, pondering his future with the passionate woman beside him.

*　　*　　*

Joanna woke with a start. One moment she'd been dreaming of Christmas in Suffolk, roast goose and bread pudding, next she was wide awake. And starving, the result of going to bed without supper then expending endless amounts of energy satisfying her husband. Not that she minded. Mac had ensured her pleasure as well.

She snuggled beneath the covers and contemplated raiding the kitchen pantry. Her stomach grumbled in approval. Glancing to Mac, who slept peacefully, she decided to let him sleep. Perhaps she would find a book to read until dawn when the household would begin to stir.

A chill clung to the stairway. She drew the robe she'd pulled on tighter about her waist. A floorboard creaked from the hallway below. Peeking over the side of the banister, she caught the flicker of a beige tail in the small beam of light cast by the wall lamp in the foyer. With a sigh, she marched down the stairs to the entrance to Mac's study. Confucius sat perfectly still, his eyes trained on the darkened room. She bent to scratch his ear. "Hunting, I see. Good for you. Come along. You can help me find something to read, then we shall see what we can find in Cook's pantry."

Holding her candle in the air, she managed two steps, stopped and stared. The room was an utter disaster. She'd barely come to that realization when her candle flickered and died—but not before she'd caught sight of a shadow passing just inside the open window. And the shadow, a familiar hulking form, was heading directly toward her.

Joanna knew she had to move, to do something, anything. She had no intention of dying this soon after becoming a bride. A scream ripped from her very heart even as a different man's hands, covered with leather gloves, emerged from nowhere and wrapped about her throat. She fought then, tugging with all her might.

A hissing mass of angry feline, Confucius leapt through the air and attached himself to her assailant's back. Joanna whirled and raked her nails across the man's flesh. She caught sight of a gold ring on his finger even as he cursed. Suddenly Joanna was alone, the pounding of feet seemingly coming and going in all directions. She crumpled to her knees and dragged air into her lungs.

Mac appeared.

He rounded the corner of the study, bellowing her name, his voice filled with both fury and terror. In that moment, she knew that he was the most wonderful man in the world, and that deep down he cared about her, maybe even loved her.

Her body quaked even as he enveloped her in his embrace. She fitted herself against him, absorbing his strength, his scent. Her breathing slowed and her heart settled.

He dragged his hands through her hair and tipped her head, searching her face. "Are you all right?"

She felt his hands tremble. It seemed her husband needed reassurance as much as she. Nodding, she said,

"Your plan to divert the attention from my family to you obviously worked. I fear your study suffered horribly."

"The hell with my study," he said.

Knox scrambled into the room, his grey hair sticking out in all directions from beneath a red sleeping cap. "Sweet Hebrides, sir. I . . ." He never finished his sentence. He circled round, gaping at the destruction.

Rousted from their beds by her scream and Mac's bellow, Cook and the rest of the household hovered in the doorway in varying states of dress, staring open-mouthed like a ragged choir.

"Doesn't anyone sleep around here?" Randolph asked with a yawn as he appeared in the doorway. "Creepers. What happened now?" He finally noticed Joanna sitting on the floor with Mac wrapped around her like a shield. "Cor, sis. Are you all right?"

"Does she look all right to you?" Mac snapped.

"I am perfectly fine," she said, though her voice sounded strained.

Mac called out orders for lamps to be lit and tea to be brewed. He ordered Knox to search the grounds and sent Randolph back to bed. Then he dragged Joanna against him and gazed over her shoulder, commanding his own heart to calm.

Books had been pulled from the shelves and carelessly tossed to the floor. The drawers in his desk had been opened, their contents dumped. As if destroyed by an angry sea, his model of the *Fleeting Star* lay broken on the deep blue carpet. The window to the garden was open, the escape route of whoever had done this deed.

Following was pointless.

But Mac would find out who was responsible, and he would pay. No one broke into his home and attacked his wife. No one.

He carried Joanna to the one chair in the room left standing upright. "Tell me what happened."

"When I came downstairs—"

"Why did you come downstairs by yourself in the first place?" he asked.

She busied her hands in the folds of her robe. "I was hungry. I certainly didn't expect visitors at five in the morning. And don't you dare snap at me or I'm liable to cry—and you know how I feel about emotional outbursts. And my throat hurts." She looked overwhelmed. "This is all because of Randolph and that statue. I am sorry I ever asked you to help us. I know I'm rambling, but your house would be intact, you wouldn't be married to me, and—"

"Have you heard me complain once?" He wanted to shake her. "I am a grown man who makes his own decisions. Do you truly believe anyone could force me to do something I truly didn't want to do?"

"No," she admitted. "Still, whether you like it or not, I cannot help but feel somewhat responsible."

He thought he might strangle her then and there. After he kissed her a few dozen times then made love to her a few dozen more. What was he to do about her desire to be martyred?

"Good Christ, Joanna. Do not make me angrier than I already am," he said finally. He dropped his forehead to hers. "When I heard you scream, I had visions of . . . well, never mind what I thought. Since I met you, I have lost more years from my life than all my years at sea combined. If ever you want anything to eat in the middle of the night, you will wake me and I will come with you."

She gave a small smile. "You may regret your offer. You have no idea how often I wake in the middle of the night."

"No matter. I will simply have to make myself available to you."

She smiled more fully. "I rather like the sound of that." Her expression grew serious. "There were *two* people in this room tonight—aside from myself, of course. One person was the man from Lord Westcliff's ball. I am sure of it."

Joanna was about to continue when Cook delivered the tea, which was promptly poured and given to her. Mac poured himself some scotch and moved to sit on the corner of his desk. Once they were alone again, he said, "You better start at the beginning."

He listened as she explained each detail, amazed by her composure as she related the events that had transpired. Since he'd known her, Joanna had consistently dealt with danger and threats and near financial ruin, and done so with unshakable determination. The woman was a rare prize.

When she had finished, Mac felt a rage unlike any

he could remember. The thought of someone touching Joanna—let alone strangling her—clenched his stomach into knots a third-class seaman would appreciate. Mac waded through his scattered papers, stopped to retrieve his copy of *Don Quixote*, and reverently set the book on the mantel. He plucked the main mast of his model *Fleeting Star*, now bent at a right angle, from the floor and laid it on his desk. He placed both his hands on the cool mahogany and stood perfectly still. He heard the whisper of silk as his wife approached, felt the gentle brush of her fingers on his arm.

"Condemning yourself for not being able to stop this incident tonight will not help find the person responsible," she said.

Turning, he laughed—though he felt anything but jolly. "And yet *you* tried to take the blame not ten minutes ago."

She leaned her head against his chest. "Perhaps we should place the blame where it belongs."

His hand slid up and down her back, pulling her closer to him. "And where would that be?"

"On the person who broke into the house. Do you think that Digger had anything to do with it?"

Mac felt her scent drift over him, fill him. He sighed. "That would be rather difficult. The man is dead."

"Did *you*—"

"No, darling, I did not kill the man. Not that I feel overly concerned with his demise. He claimed he knew the identity of the serpent, though. Even said he had proof."

She leaned back in his arms. "Truly! Did he give you the name?"

"Lord Dorridge."

Joanna's eyes filled with shock. He didn't blame her. He was still reeling from the information.

"What of proof?" she asked.

"Unfortunately. Digger died before he told me where to find it."

Knox marched into the room, his cheeks dotted with color. "Thanks to the rain, Captain, we have two distinct sets of footprints. Judging from the depth of the first set, one intruder was a very large man. The other set is much smaller and lighter, perhaps belonging to the snakesman who gained entrance to the house. They both escaped over the garden wall."

"Thank you, Knox," Mac said.

"What is a snakesman?" Joanna asked, as the other man nodded and left the room.

Mac grimaced. "A young boy trained to enter a home through the smallest possible opening. He unlocks the door for the thief, locks up when the thief is finished, and sneaks back out the way he came. Common practice for burglars."

"The other person was not a young boy," she argued.

"How can you be sure? The room was dark—and certainly you were frightened."

"Terrified. But my mental faculties did not cease to work." She stared across the room, trying to remember. "The person who attacked me wore a gold ring."

297

Mac felt her tremble, pulled her to his chest and lay his chin on top of her head as he considered that information. Snakesmen did not usually go about sporting jewelry, and skilled thieves considered what they wore carefully. Which led him to him back to the belief that these intruders were not your typical burglars.

"Where does that leave us, then?" Joanna murmured against his throat.

His mind had already begun to calculate the odds, the pros and cons of an idea taking shape. He kissed the tip of her nose and grinned. "I have the perfect plan."

Chapter Nineteen

It was simple, dangerous and challenging, but not deadly. Or so Mac had claimed, several times in fact, until Joanna acquiesced. Not that she was happy with her decision, she simply realized Mac would have found a way to implement his scheme without her agreement. She shifted in her seat, oblivious to the performance taking place on the stage, her thoughts only on her husband.

He had sent a note to Lord Dorridge naming a place and time to meet. The reason for the supposed rendezvous was negotiating the sale of Lung Wang Sun. There was no doubt that Dorridge would come. And while the viscount waited on the other side of London for Mac to make his appearance, Mac and Knox would slink through Dorridge's parlor window. Inside, they would find the evidence needed to prove his guilt.

Apprehension, a feeling that they were somehow missing an important piece of the puzzle, had gnawed at Joanna ever since the attack the night before. No matter how many times she replayed the events of the last few weeks, she felt uneasy. Like a specter in the shadows, a memory, a clue, something she believed mattered, something she knew she should remember, hovered just out of reach.

It was wholly frustrating.

Even now, as the actors on stage spewed their lines with enthusiasm, Joanna paid them little attention. She had abandoned watching the play when Mac left their box over an hour and a half ago.

Applause jerked her from contemplation.

"Time for refreshments," her mother announced.

Joanna really had no desire to leave the box and chatter with nosy matrons who only wanted to ask her pointed and embarrassing questions about her marriage—for most of which Joanna had no answer. "Was it a love match?" "Rumor has it Mr. Archer is sailing for Jamaica soon." "What of you, m'dear? Are you sailing with him?" "Are you with child?"

Responding to the questions was exhausting. She toyed with the yellow primrose pinned to her gown and asked, "Must we go down?"

"Most assuredly," her mother answered. "Penelope must make herself available for Lord Westcliff. Come along."

Clucking like a hen, the woman shooed her girls from the box and down the narrow corridor to the lobby, which was already filled with bodies. Resigned to do as her mother said, Joanna followed with half a heart. She had realized long ago that society came to the theatre to watch one another, not the play, and the greatest performances took place between acts.

Her mother waved her fan in the air when she saw Lord Harry Tatterton. And lo and behold, Lord Westcliff happened to be standing beside him. Lady Fenton marched through the crowd, making a path for herself and her daughters. In no time at all, Penelope and Lord Westcliff were speaking in hushed tones, while Harry and Lady Fenton debated their favorite topic: original sin.

Joanna hovered nearby to wait until the time came to shift back upstairs for the remainder of the play. Her thoughts drifted from the serpent to Lung Wang Sun to her husband to Eden.

Fact number one: The serpent owned Eden and used the hell as a trap to blackmail unsuspecting lords— normally for money. So why did he want Lung Wang Sun?

Harry leaned both hands on his cane. "Why else were Adam and Eve driven from the Garden of Eden but for Eve's machinations?"

Eden. Adam and Eve. Temptation. The serpent. Dorridge. Lung Wang Sun. Randolph. Ashford. Murder. Sin. Eve. All these thoughts whirled in Joanna's head.

"Your opinion comes as no surprise," Joanna's mother muttered. "Men look to blame women for their

301

problems whenever it suits them. The next moment they'll believe us incapable of crossing the street without their aid."

Eve. A woman.

"Unlike ordinary men," Harry said with a wink, "I have never underestimated women, m'dear. Adam, though, misjudged. He believed Eve incapable of sin. Look what happened to him."

A woman? Joanna shoved herself from the pillar, shaking with the absurdity of her idea. Yet . . . Barely able to contain her excitement, she asked, "Harry, what of Adam's role?"

"A pawn in the ultimate game of life," Harry said melodramatically. "The poor man had no idea he was being manipulated, led down the path to ruin."

Joanna's mind whirled with possibilities. *A woman who would tempt a man, her lover or maybe many lovers, to do her bidding. A woman who wanted ultimate control and power over men, a woman who held men in disdain.* A distant memory surfaced with frightening clarity. And she knew.

Joanna had to reach Mac immediately.

She kissed Harry on the lips and said, "You are a blessed genius! Be a dear, and escort mother home. I am leaving."

Clearly mortified by Joanna's behavior, her mother cried, "What of your cape? And do calm down. You are drawing attention to yourself."

Joanna waved as she hurried through the crowd, apologizing as she trampled feet and disrupted conversations. In her haste, she nearly knocked Lydia Litmore to the floor. Joanna again apologized, whirled and collided with Lady Dorridge.

"Where are you off to in such a hurry, Miss Fenton? Or, should I say, Mrs. Archer?"

Lady Dorridge wore an emerald green scarf about her neck. Her face seemed paler, and she had lost weight. Her eyes shone with an over-bright gleam. She carried a red cape over one arm as if preparing to leave, herself. A shiver of panic rippled down Joanna's spine. "I just remembered I was to meet my husband. If you will excuse me."

"My carriage is right outside. Allow me to give you a ride."

"No, thank you. My driver will be easy to locate."

"In this crowd?" Lady Dorridge laughed: a harsh brittle sound. "I insist."

Joanna felt something prod her side. She glanced down to see that Lady Dorridge's arm, hidden beneath her long velvet cape, was pressed against Joanna's waist.

"In case you're wondering, I have a pistol pointed at you. It would be a pity if I accidentally pulled the trigger."

Joanna glanced behind her. Harry still debated with her mother while Penelope mooned over Lord Westcliff. There would be no help from either quarter.

"Do not think to raise the alarm. There happens to be a fellow standing beside the pillar nearest your family. I believe you made his acquaintance at Lord Westcliff's ball. I must apologize for that incident. Jinx was overzealous in relaying his message. But I digress. One wrong move and he will put a knife through your sister's heart. Feel free to take a peek if you doubt me."

Joanna didn't doubt Lady Dorridge. Oh, no. The woman was obviously not altogether sane. She scanned the crowded room until her eyes locked upon the man in question. He stood a mere two feet from Penelope. In this crush, he could accomplish the deed and melt into nothing before anyone could stop him. Joanna was well and goodly trapped. "I see you planned for every circumstance."

"Actually, I had not planned to kidnap you here. Then your husband dashed out." She paused meaningfully. "I am not one to pass up an opportunity."

"Someone will surely see us and wonder," Joanna protested with false bravado. They were moving toward the side entrance. Chang had been told to guard the front door of the theatre. In an instant, things had gone from bad to worse.

Trying to stall, Joanna stumbled. As she gathered herself up off the floor, she saw that Lord Fairfax stood before her, watching closely.

Lady Dorridge grabbed Joanna's arm with one hand and jabbed her gun into Joanna's side with the other— a not-so-subtle reminder of who held the weapon.

Lord Fairfax bowed. "Good evening, my lady. A moment, please."

"Good evening, sir. I am terribly sorry. I am just

304

leaving." When she tried to pass, Lord Fairfax stepped in front of her.

"Is your husband here tonight?"

Her mind raced to find a plausible means to convey her dire circumstance. One possibility came to mind, but even if Fairfax correctly interpreted her message, considering the way Mac had thrown the man from their house, she wasn't sure he would be the right one to help. She had to try, though. "Mac wasn't feeling well and left early, but perhaps you could drop by tomorrow. I know Mac would be thrilled. *The two of you had such a lovely visit the last time.*"

Against all hope, Lord Fairfax kept his face blank. "Perhaps I shall," he agreed. Bowing to both ladies, he then casually drifted off in the opposite direction. Joanna didn't dare turn to see where he went or what he did. For all she knew, he thought she'd lost a shingle.

Just as she was stealing herself to peek, Joanna was shoved by Lady Dorridge out the door, down the steps, and toward her waiting carriage.

"How do I know my sister is going to be all right?" Joanna asked.

"You worry needlessly. I have no designs on your family, only your family's possessions. Move along. I prefer no further interruptions."

All pretense evaporated the moment the carriage door closed behind them—the roles shifted immediately to captor and captive. Lady Dorridge draped her cape over her lap and aimed her pistol directly at

Joanna's chest. Dark leather gloves covered her hands. A gold ring glittered in the dim light provided by the lantern. Lady Dorridge glanced from her hand back to Joanna, and while Joanna despaired, Lady Dorridge gloated. "I was quite furious last night with your untimely interruption. Wearing the ring was an error on my part . . . but I grow tired of this game, anyway."

Joanna folded her arms in her lap. The carriage shifted as someone climbed into the box overhead.

"That will be Jinx," Lady Dorridge explained.

The reins cracked and the horses lurched forward, speeding away from the theatre. Panic gripped Joanna, but she tipped her head in the air, using every ounce of bravado her mother had ever instilled in her. "Where are you taking me?"

"The place I have in mind guarantees our privacy while we wait for your husband to come and play your valiant rescuer."

"And what makes you think Mac will come?"

Lady Dorridge's lips contorted into an obscene smile as cold as winter's first frost. "Oh, he'll come. And if he hopes to see you alive again, he'll do exactly as I say."

Mac managed the window with ease. A highwayman depended on bold courage and intimidation. A footpad used much the same approach. But a burglar, that was a man with patience and a cool head: two attributes Mac had acquired and honed to a fine edge by an early age.

Sneaking into Lord Dorridge's parlor was as easy as climbing a fallen tree, especially since he knew which room to enter. The young boy whom Mac had sent to deliver the message to the viscount earlier in the day had studied the man's house and managed to unlock the correct window with no one the wiser.

Mac tugged Knox over the sill, closed the window and the curtains, then crept across the room and placed his ear against the closed door. Voices came from somewhere in the house, likely the kitchens. Mac tested the doorknob, pleased to discover that Dorridge kept his private room locked from the outside and a key on the inside.

He felt another wave of satisfaction at the thought of Dorridge waiting at the Pig-'N'-Whistle. The longer Dorridge waited, the more the pompous ass would stew. When he realized Mac wasn't coming, he would be bloody furious.

And this time Mac didn't have to worry about Joanna. She was safely tucked away at the theatre with her mother and sister. He remembered the fear he saw in her eyes, the tender kiss they'd shared which had turned so hot as he was leaving. Once this evening ended, he intended to show her exactly how much he appreciated that concern.

Too, Chang was acting as guard dog for her, and if everything went as planned, Mac would be home before Joanna.

He lit his small lantern.

Dorridge's study was typical of most lords, elegantly

furnished in shades of grey and navy blue. A black lacquer cabinet embellished with serpents and flying birds sat against one wall, a rosewood roll-top desk against the other. Jade statuettes and ivory carvings nestled on a shelf in the corner. Fine leather chairs faced the fireplace. The other usual trappings com- -pleted the room.

"What precisely, Captain, am I to look for?" Knox whispered as his lantern flared to life.

"Digger said he had proof, but it wasn't on his body or in his room. We can only hope there is something here in Dorridge's study. Start with the cabinet. Look for anything that might incriminate Dorridge or tie him to Eden or the serpent."

Mac unlocked the desk's cover with a small pick. Inside, chubbyholes contained stationary, seals and wax. There were lists of quarterly revenues from Dorridge's estates, a letter to the House of Lords regarding the matter of low crime in the city, general correspondence to the Viscount's solicitor, but certainly nothing illegal.

Knox emptied the cabinet, glanced behind paintings, and even peeked beneath the expensive Indian carpet. Mac knocked along the wall, searching for a safe or secret room. Knox studied every piece of bric-a-brac. Max tested the stones of the fireplace. Everything seemed in perfect order.

"Are you certain this is the correct room?" he asked Knox.

His first mate appeared as perplexed as Mac felt.

"Robbie was very specific about his directions. The cook confirmed his discovery while she fed him milk and crackers."

Mac crossed the study to another door. "Where does this lead?"

"Robbie did not say."

Beyond was a smaller version of the last room, yet one which had an entirely different feel. Its furnishings were simpler, without a single piece of Oriental art in sight. Mac felt a new surge of hope. "This could very well be the place."

He moved to the small writing table. The rectangular desk had only one drawer and an inkwell. If one had documents and ledgers to conceal, he doubted they would be hidden in this desk. Red velvet lined the interior, upon which lay a neat stack of stationary, a box of sealing wax and seals. Mac knew before he even looked that he would not find the serpentine seal he needed.

Disgusted, he shoved the drawer back into place. A peculiar noise sounded. He jiggled the desk again, noting that this particular noise came from one of the front legs. His fingers slid down the tapered wood and back up again. Nothing. Rubbing his chin he studied the design of the desk more closely. There could only be one other possibility.

He reopened the drawer, pried the velvet aside and discovered a small square opening directly above the leg of the desk. "Knox, bring the other lantern."

"What did you find, Captain."

"Buried treasure, I hope."

Mac eased his fingers into the space. A paper inside rustled. He could barely contain his excitement. Wasting no time at all, he pulled free a sheet of paper rolled into a scroll. He reached into the opening again and felt a small box. Inside the box, nestled on red velvet as well, was a stick of red sealing wax and a golden seal. Engraved in the top was a serpent coiled around a stake.

"Why, sir, you were right. This certainly proves that Dorridge is the fiend responsible for all those misdeeds."

Nodding, Mac spread the paper on the desk and scanned the names. "So it would seem."

Knox whistled from over his shoulder. "Sweet Barbados, even I recognize some of those names. This man was draining the coffers of a great many young nobles."

"So it would seem." Mac studied the neatly penned accounting of months and months of blackmail. There were columns for each name, the amount of money owed, the calculated various interest, and the date each debt was paid. A fortune had been made at the expense of some of the finer families of society.

The evidence clearly pointed to Lord Dorridge.

Mac held the proof in his very own hands.

Yet . . .

Dorridge was a womanizer. Rumors had even surfaced about his preference for rough sex with whores. He was not a gambler. He never drank himself to oblivion. According to the ledgers in the other desk, the man was financially solvent with much coin to spare. Why was he blackmailing young lords of London? And even if he was, why hadn't he waited to simply buy Lung Wang Sun?

Aside from all the other strange gaps in the equation, those two questions caused Mac the greatest worry. Yet he held proof in his hands, discoursed in Dorridge's very own home.

"I say this has been a fine night's work," Knox announced as he prepared to leave. "Let us tidy up and be off."

Mac sat down in the desk's chair, his hands behind his head, and stared at the paper before him. The handwriting was neat, almost dainty. Something wasn't right. He looked around the room.

Knox stared at him. "Pardon me, Captain, but if you don't mind, I'd just as soon we take our leave before someone discovers our presence. It would be most difficult to explain."

Mac nodded. "Look around, Knox. Tell me what you see."

His first mate's brows furrowed in confusion, but he did as asked and looked about. Studying the room with a keen eye Mac had come to trust over the years he said, "The room is designed for one person only and not for social calls. The furniture is delicate, almost feminine."

"Exactly."

"Pardon me for saying, sir, but the last time I saw

that particular expression on your face, we spent three interminable days in a Turkish prison. What exactly does it mean?"

Mac glanced to the numbers again. "Damn." He leapt from the chair, rushed into the other room, and pulled the estate ledgers from their drawer. He laid the scroll beside one ledger and stared long and hard at the numbers. A horrible feeling settled in his stomach.

"Take a look," he stated.

Knox studied the writing. "It would appear to be penned by two different people."

"Exactly."

"A secretary, perhaps?"

"The serpent would not hire someone else to record these numbers. No. He would see to the task himself." Mac pulled out a letter being drafted to the House of Lords by Dorridge.

"Possible but . . . Oh dear Lord. Do you mean—"

Mac dashed for the locked door, turned the key, marched into the foyer and started shouting.

"We shall be shot at dawn," Knox called as he followed.

Two servants scurried down the stairs, wearing similar expressions of shock and wariness at seeing men they had never seen before standing in the foyer of Lord Dorridge's home, uninvited.

"Who uses this study?" Mac snapped.

"L-l-lord Dorridge," the maid stuttered.

"And the other?" Mac pointed in the general direction of the second room.

The poor girl quaked in her slippers. "Why, *Lady* Dorridge uses that room."

How could he have been so blind? An even more troubling thought came to mind. He remembered sitting beside Joanna at the theatre, biding his time until he could sneak away, when he had seen a familiar face in the crowd. Lady Dorridge. Fear seized Mac. "Son of a bitch."

He sprinted for the door, knowing Knox would automatically give chase, and collided with Lord Dorridge.

The viscount's expression transformed from confusion to fury. "What are you doing in my home?"

"Get out of my way," Mac snapped. He didn't have time to explain.

"Not until you tell me what you are doing here."

"Did you kill Digger?"

"The man's dead?" Dorridge asked, genuinely surprised. The reaction only increased Mac's apprehension.

"When was the last time you saw him?" he asked. "And don't bother denying that you were using him to gather information about me."

"According to my butler, the blighter came here several nights ago. I was not home, so he waited in my study. When I finally returned, he was gone." Dorridge slammed his cane onto the marble floor. "I demand you tell me what this is about."

313

Mac shoved the scroll of numbers he held into Dorridge's hands.

The viscount's face went white with shock and developed patches of scarlet. "Do you think to blackmail me?"

"Those numbers were penned by your wife. She's been having a fine time with some of your friends, it seems. And if she harms Joanna, I'll—" Mac stormed from the house, sprinting for his horse where it was tucked away in the alley with his groom. He didn't bother waiting for Knox, who hobbled behind as quickly as his thin legs would manage; he had one purpose and one purpose only. To reach his home and find Joanna.

The ride was a blur. When Mac saw the lights burning in the parlor windows, he felt a spark of hope. He burst through the front door, stopped at the bottom stair and shouted, "Joanna!"

Lord Fairfax appeared, striding from the parlor with Randolph on his heels.

Mac drew up short. He didn't have time to deal with this man he had no desire to know in the first place. He snarled. "What are you doing here? I thought I made my position clear on your last visit."

"You did. Perfectly. I am here on a different matter. I believe I have a message for you from your wife."

Mac's hands clenched at his side. "Tell me."

Fairfax detailed the odd conversation, the strange woman, and Joanna's odd behavior. He finished with, "I followed as best I could, but I lost the conveyance near the docks. From there I came directly here."

Randolph's eyes rounded with the telling. "Do you mean to say someone has kidnapped my sister? Cor, Archer, why aren't you rescuing her?"

"All in good time, my boy. If you recall, I just discovered she was missing." Mac rubbed his hands over his face. Joanna could be almost anywhere, but instinct told him Lady Dorridge had taken his wife to Eden. He forced himself to breathe.

Knox rushed in, his face flushed. He held an envelope in his hand. "Captain, this just came as I arrived."

Mac steadied his hand as he read the note:

Mr. Archer—
If you wish to see your wife alive, bring Lung Wang Sun and the Red Scroll of Incantations to Eden. You will be met. Come alone or your wife dies.
—The Serpent.

Mac turned the envelope upside down and three crumpled primroses tied with a blue ribbon fell into his hand. He'd last seen these same flowers pinned to his wife's new gown. She'd lectured him about his excessive expenditures on her new wardrobe all while she'd dressed. He'd pinned the flowers on her himself. *Primroses for hope,* she'd said.

He gave the note to Randolph, who passed it to Fairfax.

"I assume you know this place," Fairfax said with

complete calm. "What do you intend to do?"

"I intend to retrieve my wife."

"Of that I had no doubt," Fairfax answered.

Mac narrowed his eyes, ignoring the tug at his conscience to offer a crumb of acceptance to this man. Instead he said, "Fetch your coat, Randolph. I need all the information you can give me about Eden. You are about to have that chance to prove yourself that you seemed to want so badly. Knox, find Adam and tell him what has happened." he turned toward the stairs.

Fairfax grabbed his arm. "How do you know the serpent will let either of you live?"

"I don't."

"I can help. She will not be prepared for my presence. We can take my carriage."

Mac wanted nothing from this man, least of all *his* help. Yet Fairfax had correctly interpreted Joanna's message and come to Mac's aid when he'd already been treated miserably by him. An even greater shock, Fairfax seemed an honorable sort willing to add his support though it might mean physical danger. The man was obviously accustomed to dealing with such difficult situations, and recognized the need for a clear head. He would be useful to have about if something went wrong.

The resolve in his father's green eyes, the evident desire to see the matter to the end, triggered an emotion that felt suspiciously like admiration deep within Mac's heart. He nodded consent.

Chapter Twenty

Joanna tugged on the ropes binding her hands behind her back, but to no avail; Jinx had secured them after carrying her up a dark stairway and dumping her in a chair in a room which obviously served as a private retreat from the debauchery downstairs. Judging from the bawdy voices and the occasional female shrieks, Joanna guessed she was at Eden.

Lady Dorridge sat nearby, beside a glowing fire, sipping a drink from a dainty china teacup any lady might own, a contradiction to everything Joanna had once believed of the nobility. Her face showed signs of indescribable fatigue. Her shoulders shook as she coughed. Retrieving a small vial from her purse, she poured a clear liquid into her drink. Peppermint filled the air.

In that instant, the reason for this entire nasty affair

became clear. Joanna had worked in orphanages and seen such death amongst the children. She'd used the herbs and medicines to try and ease the coughing, the pain. Softly, she said, "Consumption, I gather. You went to great lengths to obtain my statue."

Lady Dorridge's eyes flashed with bitterness. "Aren't you the clever one." She rose from her chair, distracted and agitated. Her pistol swayed with the movement of her arm. As she glanced at the small clock on the table beside the bed, she added, "Yes. I need that statue. But I created this place long before I knew I was dying. And I was so very close . . ."

"Close to what?" Joanna asked.

"To what I wanted. I planned to leave my husband. And this place—I discovered early on that young lords of the *Ton* are easily tempted and so wonderfully gullible. They seek a place to taste the side of life that nullifies their very existence. I give them what they want and what many of them deserve."

Lady Dorridge's voice held a dream-like faraway quality which made Joanna wonder what exactly her vial contained. She worked the ropes of her bonds against the back of the chair and continued to talk, trying to gather all the pieces of the puzzle and a possible means of escape. Her fingers were beginning to grow numb. "So, you created Eden."

"The plan was quite brilliant, I must say. Men never credit women for their intelligence, but this was truly ingenious. The down fall of men by a woman. I have my husband to thank for the name. He is the most unchristian man I have ever known, yet he was forever tossing biblical references in my face. Since I intended to destroy the young lords of the *Ton*, lure coins from their pockets with the apples of debauchery, Eden seemed a particularly fitting name."

"Why use the serpent and not Eve?" Joanna prodded, sawing at her bonds.

"It added to the illusion. Everyone suspected the serpent was a man." She laughed at some secret joke.

"If you had so much money, why didn't you wait for the auction? You could have bought Lung Wang Sun, taken the thing, then sailed wherever you wished to go."

"It was all I could do maintain the façade of the good wife. My husband would never have allowed me to go to your auction, and I could not risk someone else winning."

"So you used Ashford to lure Randolph to this place," Joanna asked.

"No reflection on your family, dear, but your brother made for an easy mark."

"And Ashford?"

"A pawn in my game, yet one no different than any man. Once he realized I was ill, he decided he would be better off without me. I had no choice but to be rid of him." Her emotionless declaration was frightening.

Joanna shivered. "Not all men have ulterior motives."

"Still the idealistic miss, I see. You'll sing a different tune after a year or so of marriage, once your husband tires of you and parades his mistresses in front of you as if your feelings were inconsequential. You ignored my advice and married. A mistake." The woman paused. "I must say I am surprised Mac proposed, though."

"I imagine there were a great many who were as surprised as you, but thank your husband. He was directly responsible."

"My husband is a repulsive hypocritical bore." Malice filled her every word.

"Do you love Mac?"

Lady Dorridge's question took Joanna by surprise. She considered how best to answer and finally settled on the truth. Which made her wonder, why had she kept these words from her husband? Her insecurities seemed a paltry excuse not to have recognized how she felt—especially when she was no longer sure she would ever have the chance to tell him. "Yes. I love him with all my heart."

"Tsk. Tsk." Lady Dorridge waved her pistol in the air. "You forgot what I told you. Never confuse lust for love. Love gives power to the *man*. Men, in turn, abuse that power and it pollutes everything they touch. Use *them*: take their money, their status, enjoy their bodies for your own pleasure, but never give them your heart. You're better served to cut theirs out."

Joanna was shocked. Lady Dorridge wore her own evil like a corsage. Without a doubt, the woman was insane, ruled by a dark heart that Joanna doubted had sprung up from her mortal illness. The realization was terrifying. Cold sweat trickled down Joanna's back. Fear coated her tongue.

Ruled by a greater desperation, she studied the tiny room. When Mac arrived, they would need every advantage as well as a hefty dose of luck if they hoped to leave this place alive.

A shout came from below. Lady Fairfax moved to the wall, pushed the red silk aside and peered through a small hole. She smiled, reminding Joanna of Confucius when he'd just trapped a mouse. "If nothing else, Man is constant. I see your brother is returned from the country and anxious to see his lady-love. Care to see for yourself?"

"My brother is here?" Joanna crossed to the wall, baffled. Standing on her toes, she peeked through the small spy hole and saw the entire lower floor of the gambling hell. Her eyes widened as she saw a drunken Randolph stagger into the room on the arm of another man whose face was hidden. Randolph shouted a woman's name and started to climb a set of stairs opposite. When he stumbled, Joanna saw the familiar jaw line of Randolph's companion. *Lord Fairfax.* She had barely made that observation when Mac strode into view, Jinx at his side.

Joanna considered screaming, but she doubted Mac would hear her above the noise of the establishment. And to anyone else, her scream would be taken as sport. Lady Dorridge would not appreciate the action, either. However, if Randolph and Lord Fairfax were here, she could only assume her husband had a plan. She felt the stirrings of hope.

"Your husband is prompt, if nothing else," Lady Dorridge said. She watched from a similar opening in the wall a few feet away. Turning, she aimed her gun at Joanna. "Move back to the chair and sit down."

The gleam in the woman's eyes turned fevered as she herself edged into a dark corner and waited.

Joanna could do nothing but wait as well.

After what seemed in interminable amount of time, the door's brass knob turned. The door slowly opened and Mac entered, his shoulders cocked backward, his chin high in the air. He held a brown package under his arm. Showing absolutely no fear, he exuded a confidence that bordered on arrogance. Joanna's heart leapt at the sight of him, yet she was furious about his open display of disdain. He had no idea he was dealing with a madwoman!

He spied Joanna and stepped in her direction.

"My gun is aimed at your wife's pretty blond head," Lady Dorridge said. "Stay exactly where you are and no one will be hurt."

"No need to hide in the shadows, Lady Dorridge."

There was no mistaking the contempt in Mac's voice. Joanna started as she realized he'd called Lady Dorridge by name, that he knew she was the serpent.

"I shouldn't be surprised that you discovered my identity." She stepped from the darkness. "Besides a fine lover, you were always an intelligent man. If we have time, you will have to tell me how you made the connection. Is that both the statue and the scroll?"

Mac nodded.

"Put them on the desk and step over to the empty chair beside your wife."

"How do I know you will let us leave once I hand over the artifacts?"

Joanna had wondered much the same thing.

"You don't. But as long as you have complied with my instructions and do as I say, I shall keep my words. I shall sail to Italy tonight, and you and your wife can live happily ever after—if such a thing exists. Otherwise, I will kill you."

"Let's hope it doesn't come to that, then," Mac said. There was no missing the calculated gleam in Lady Dorridge's eyes, so he did as directed. He allowed Jinx to tie his wrists behind his back in the same manner as Joanna's, then sat.

Judging by the yelling below that suddenly began, Randolph was enjoying his role in this drama—and doing an excellent job. It wouldn't be long now. The boy's voice grew closer and even more boisterous.

Lady Dorridge glared at Jinx. "Find Bliss and shut that fool up before he rousts every person from their rooms. Then find that sailor who speaks Chinese and bring him back here." She rushed to the desk. Her fingers shook as she unrolled the scroll. Her breath was labored as she scanned its contents, then she removed the cloth from the statue.

Lung Wang Sun's shadow appeared on the wall behind Mac.

"Are you all right?" he asked Joanna now that Lady Dorridge was distracted. He was unable to wait another minute to hear his wife's voice.

"Yes."

"Randolph is here."

"I know."

"How?"

"The small spy holes in the far wall." Her expression softened. "Mac, I need to tell you—"

"Be quiet," Lady Dorridge snapped from where she sat. "Both of you." She clutched the red scroll to her chest with one hand, her pistol in the other, and circled the desk. She stopped in the middle of the room.

More than anything, Mac wanted to take this woman down. He had no doubt he could do it alone, but he dared not take a chance with Joanna sitting so close to him. There was no telling who the bullet might hit if Lady Dorridge's weapon went off. Instead, he watched the door, awaiting Fairfax and Randolph, praying that Jinx was disposed of by now. He willed Lady Dorridge to step closer to him. She seemed frozen, staring at Joanna in a way Mac found most unsettling.

He lounged against the back of his chair. "I've figured out a good portion of this, but have a few questions. Do you mind?"

"We have a moment before Jinx returns."

"Were you aiming at Digger or me the other night?" Mac asked.

"Digger, of course. He was not a very nice man. He

tried to blackmail me. I gave him a bullet instead."

So Digger had played Lord and Lady Dorridge and Mac as fools, and for that he'd died. Greed had sealed his fate. Yet Mac frowned at the easy manner in which Lady Dorridge had confessed the murder.

Evil laughter spilled from her mouth. "Mac, darling, don't look so disheartened. Digger had less use than a fourteen-year-old cur."

A commotion erupted outside the door. Mac readied himself to push Joanna to the floor with the weight of his body. He stared in shock as Lord Dorridge burst into the room, waving a pistol in the air, his face mottled with rage.

"Where is she? What have you done with her?" he cried.

Where the devil were Randolph and Fairfax? Mac wondered.

Dorridge glared at his wife, obviously surprised by what he'd found here. "Have you lost your mind? Put down that gun."

Even with a pistol pointed at his chest, the man hadn't the good sense to stop giving orders. "I'd shut up, Dorridge," Mac suggested.

"I think you should do as Mac says, darling. But I am so glad you came to pay your respects before I left."

"You're going nowhere." Lord Dorridge stepped forward. It was a miscalculation. The cocking of his wife's pistol sounded like thunder on a clear day.

Fairfax and Randolph appeared in the doorway, saying nothing as they took in the bizarre scene before them. No one had anticipated this occurrence.

"You can't shoot all of us," Lord Dorridge said.

"But I can shoot one of you," Lady Dorridge responded. She directed her gun toward Joanna. "And I will kill her. Do you wish to be responsible for that? However would you explain it to your lofty friends in the House of Lords—being the cause of Miss Joanna . . . Archer's death?"

Mac saw red. "If you so much as blink, Dorridge," he snarled, "I'll kill you myself."

"Oooooo," Lady Dorridge cooed. "I daresay he means it." She took a moment, savoring, then ordered, "Step back all of you and drop your pistols."

Fairfax and Randolph looked frantic, but they did as the woman commanded. Lord Dorridge hesitated, but Fairfax settled the decision by yanking the man's gun away and tossing it next to the others on the floor.

"Lady Dorridge," Mac said, his voice deceptively calm. "Miriam. You have the statue *and* the scroll. No one will try to stop you if you wish to leave."

"I must first make sure the scroll is authentic. We shall wait together." The woman kept her eyes on Mac, her gun on Joanna, and she slithered toward the fireplace. All the while she clutched the scroll against her bosom. Her shoulders shook as she began to cough. Then she said, "If you have deceived me, I shall shoot your wife. Foolish girl, I warned her not to give you her heart. She loves you, you know."

Intense hope filled Mac. Was it true? But now was not the time to wonder at sentiments of love. Sparing

Joanna one passing glance, wishing he could hear the words from her own lips, he stood. He had to save them. He moved slowly, cautiously, his hands still tied behind his back. "Joanna has done nothing wrong, Miriam. If you wish to harm me, do so, but not my wife."

"Shall I shoot you, then, if this scroll turns out to be a fake?" Lady Dorridge's gaze burned with crazed amusement. "Tell me why. Give me one good reason to let *her* live. Restore my faith in men."

Mac wasn't sure what to do. He settled on the truth, for his conscience would allow nothing else. If he were going to die, he wanted Joanna to know it. "I love her. My life was empty before I met her, and I was too stupid to know better. She is my heart, my soul."

Lady Dorridge blinked several times as if her mind refused to accept his words.

Mac stepped closer, placing himself between the two women. "The scroll is authentic. I would not risk my wife's life for it. And if you need to shoot someone, shoot me."

"Mac," Joanna cried as she lurched from her chair.

"Sit down," he snapped. "For once, do as I ask." He ignored the plea on his wife's face, ignored the tears streaming down her cheeks, and turned back to Lady Dorridge. "If someone needs to pay for the sins of those who hurt you, hurt me. You *could* shoot Joanna—but is she really the one who deserves to suffer for the sins of men?"

The wild panic disappeared in Lady Dorridge's eyes,

replaced by an eerie acceptance. She aimed the gun at Mac.

A hush settled over the room.

Mac sighed, accepting his fate but feeling an acute sense of loss. He heard Joanna whimper. Fairfax cursed and Randolph muttered. Lord Dorridge demanded his wife obey him and drop her weapon.

Lady Dorridge pulled the trigger.

"No!" Joanna screamed.

Collective gasps filled the air.

The pistol had exploded, but Mac stood firm. Lady Dorridge had changed her mark. Lord Dorridge clutched his chest, his eyes wide with shock. His wife stood, staring at what she had done.

Suddenly, everyone was talking and moving at once. All Mac wanted was to hold Joanna, who sat frozen in her chair. "Would someone cut these ropes?" he asked.

Randolph made short work of Joanna's bindings as Fairfax tended to Mac's. Freed at last, Mac scooped his wife into his arms. He felt her shudder, heard the tears catch in her throat. "Hush, sweetness. You're fine."

Another scream pierced Mac's ears. He turned to find that Lord Dorridge had somehow managed to reach his wife. He wrapped his hands about her neck. The Red Scroll of Incantations was knocked loose and fluttered into the fireplace.

Lady Dorridge broke free of her husband's grip, knocking the dying man away. "No!" she cried. She dropped to her knees and shoved her hands into the fire. "No!" She pulled her hands back out, scorched, clutching the burning remnants of her last chance at life. Flames were licking their way up her sleeves. She scrambled to the corner of the room, flailing her arms. A keening wail escaped her lips even as the fire leapt from her gown to the curtains along the wall. The silk drapes burst into flame, and the fire licked up towards the wooden ceiling.

"Sweet Goddess," Joanna cried out. "Help her!"

Mac sighed. "We must move quickly. This place is a bloody tinderbox." He moved toward Lady Dorridge, who was still spinning and flapping. "Miriam," he called. "Let us help you."

Fairfax tried to reach for her, too. Beyond rational thought, the woman escaped out into the hallway, spreading flames and shrieking.

Smoke filled the room in which they stood. Mac swung Joanna into his arms. "We have to get out of here, too," he called to the others.

Fairfax pushed at him. "Go on," he shouted. "We're right behind you."

"The statue!" Joanna cried. But Randolph had already grabbed Lung Wang Sun and headed toward the door.

Outside, bodies crowded the hallway. People from the bedrooms had smelled the smoke and grasped its meaning. Lady Dorridge had managed to set quite a few of the draperies afire along the corridor. It wouldn't be long before the entire building was alight.

Mac shoved his way through the throng, glancing over his shoulder every few feet to see if Lord Fairfax followed. As he neared the stairs, before he rounded the corner, he saw the man struggling along with a body draped over his shoulder. Lord Dorridge.

The stairs creaked under the weight of the crowd dashing to safety. Mac was the first to burst outside. He sucked fresh air into his lungs and staggered across the street, his knees buckling as he dropped to the ground.

Joanna barely moved. Mac ran his hands over her hair, her face. His mouth found hers in a desperate kiss that seemed to startle her back to life. She responded with a whimper, then clung to him and kissed him back.

When he finally managed to lift his head, Mac saw Randolph leaning against the wheel of their carriage. Nearby, Fairfax knelt beside two bodies. One was that of Lady Dorridge. Fairfax shook his head. Both Lady Dorridge and her husband were dead.

"She was dying," Joanna whispered against Mac's neck. "She honestly believed Lung Wang Sun could save her."

Mac exhaled loudly and grasped his wife's face between his hands. "I thought *you* were going to die."

"Me? I was not the one offering himself up as a sacrificial lamb!" She ran her thumb across her lip. "About what you said—"

"I meant every bloody word. I love you. God knows I don't deserve you, but you have me, and I'll be damned if I'll ever let you go. I promise I will love you until the day I die."

"I am so glad to hear it. You see, I have a secret. Lady Dorridge was right. I love you, too." Tears of joy pooled in her eyes. She let them fall. "Does this mean you won't be sailing for Jamaica after the auction?"

She loved him, too! Joanna had said it! Mac's heart ached with an intensity that threatened to consume him. In that moment, as Eden burned and people dashed to safety, he thought himself the luckiest man in the world. "Not unless you want your honeymoon aboard a merchant ship. I don't want to give up the sea forever, but I promise to find a solution suitable for us both."

"I swore to never set foot on a ship ever again," Joanna said, moving her lips close to his. "But for you, I would sail around the world."

Epilogue

One year later.

The scoundrel was late.

Tonight promised to be one of the most significant events of Joanna's life, second only to her wedding, of course, and her husband was conspicuously missing. Joanna had purposely arranged to meet him at the Litmore ball because she had what she considered a wonderful surprise. He had readily agreed, claiming he had a surprise of his own for her and would join her shortly. It was now an hour and a half later.

People already fought for space in the long narrow ballroom, and still revelers arrived. With the exception of her husband. Dancers crowded the marble floor, the gilt chairs surrounding the room were near full, voices rose above the din of the orchestra, and the butler called the list of new arrivals with annoying regularity: *Lord and Lady Brunger . . . Lord Marguart . . . His Grace, Duke of Elsegood.*

Joanna tugged at the bodice of her gown.

"Do stop fidgeting," her mother muttered, her gaze hawk-like on Penelope and Lord Westcliff, as was the duty of any soon-to-be mother-law. "Patience, dear. Patience."

"Easy for you to say," Joanna responded. "Your gown has a bodice. Mine is a strip of fabric better suited as a sash."

Only Mac would fully understand and appreciate what it cost Joanna to stand amongst her peers, dressed in this outrageous scarlet satin gown, making what she considered a public spectacle of herself. She was declaring her ability to ignore the gossips of the *Ton*, her distaste for their mores. Aside from the trinkets she had purchased for him, she felt this public declaration was the most meaningful gift worth giving Mac on their anniversary. She loved him for whom he was, more than any other man, titled or not. And the *Ton* be damned.

"Your gown is gorgeous," Rebecca said, appearing. She grinned wickedly. "Shocking, but truly gorgeous. I wager Mac will take one look at you and demand you go home . . . with him." She smiled and patted Joanna on the shoulder. "Relax and enjoy yourself."

"Hah! They should have been here by now."

Another litany of names echoed from the hall: *The*

Earl of Lansdown . . . Lord and Lady Giles . . . Count and Countess Ramsdell.

"Cor, sis. Wait until Mac takes a look at you." Randolph had appeared from nowhere.

Joanna spared a quick glance over her brother's shoulder. Finding no one remotely resembling her husband, she turned her full attention to Randolph. "I distinctly remember leaving you in the company of my husband with precise orders to deliver him in a timely fashion. You are here. He is not. Do you care to explain?"

"You never were one to wait for gifts with good grace." Randolph rubbed his hands together. "All in good time. Just wait."

"If one more person tells me to be patient or to wait or to relax, I swear I will scream."

Lady Cosgrove . . . Lord Tottingham . . . Lord and Lady Eddols.

Joanna took a glass of champagne from a passing servant as yet another matron sauntered by with eyebrows arched to her hairline and her lips curled in disapproval. The woman's husband, who had a face like a parrot, had the audacity to wink.

Enough was enough.

"I am going home. You may relay the message to my husband, if and when he bothers to arrive. He will simply have to accept his gift there."

"Um, Joanna," Rebecca said, barely containing her laughter.

"If I have any sense I will turn this gown to rags.

Granted, Mac dislikes these affairs, but showing on time once would not kill the man."

Rebecca tapped Joanna on the shoulder. "Um, my dear, you might wish to turn around."

"He's probably locked in his study, poring over his newfound wealth with that blasted tobacco trade of his. If I—"

"For goodness sakes, turn around," Lady Fenton ordered, in her motherly not-to-be-ignored tone of voice.

Joanna didn't want to turn around. She wanted her husband. She spun on her heel.

The Earl of Fairfax . . . Lord Kerrick.

Adam and Lord Fairfax proceeded down the marble stairway into the ballroom.

And Joanna swallowed her tongue.

Behind them on the landing stood Mac, dressed all in black, one hand behind his back, his head tipped arrogantly in the air. She'd barely grasped that he was there when the butler cried:

Lord Belgrave

Blinking several times, Joanna tried to assimilate what she saw, what she heard. Lord Fairfax was publicly claiming Mac his heir? Even more startling was the fact that Mac had somehow come to terms with the fact.

Perhaps it was not so strange, on second thought. The death of Lady and Lord Dorridge had rocked society for weeks—as had revelation of their misdeeds. Fairfax had been a staunch supporter of Joanna and Mac during the subsequent investigation. Perhaps that had earned him her husband's gratitude. Certainly as soon as the auction of Lung Wang Sun had ended, Lord Fairfax had pressed an assault of reconciliation the likes of which Joanna had never seen. Now, it seemed, the two men had reconciled their differences and learned to respect one another for who they were, not what they could or should have been. The past was buried.

Murmurs swept across room like waves on the shore. The crowd parted. Composed and determined, Mac strode to Joanna's side with natural grace.

Her heart pattered wildly against her chest, a common occurrence when her husband was about. Her palms dampened.

Mac raked his gaze over her bare shoulders, the snug fit of her meager bodice, lingering on her breasts overly long, then swept back to her face. His delicious mouth parted in a wicked grin that promised hours of recreation and pleasure for both of them. Joanna's toes curled and her skin flushed. Knowing her husband, he was likely considering how best to remove her dress from her body. She was having similar thoughts about his clothing.

He bowed. "You're looking lovely tonight, *my lady*."

"Thank you." She curtsied and flashed him a smile. "*My lord*."

"My father called me an ass for taking so long to come to terms with my decision. What do you think of that?"

A Rogue's Promise

Lord Fairfax flashed his teeth in a broad grin. The fact that Mac had said *father* did not go unnoticed by Joanna. "I see," she said.

"Adam and your brother seconded the notion."

"Did they now?"

"M-hmmm," Mac added casually. "I had to admit they were right. This title thing can't be all too difficult to manage. After all, I seem to manage you just fine."

"You think so, do you?"

Pressing a tender kiss to her lips, he said, "I do." He pulled a bouquet of yellow tulips from behind his back and said, "Joanna, I am utterly and hopelessly in love with you. You are my life, my heart. Do you think you can stand to be married another hundred years or so to a lord if I promise not to grow all pompous and arrogant?"

A love she thought could not possibly deepen, did just that. Not because of Mac's acceptance of the title—Sweet Empress, no—and not because of his blatant display of affection. He was forever kissing her and touching her in public. It was because she knew what it cost him to set aside his pride and officially join the ranks of society. And she knew he'd done it for her. Tears streaked down her cheek.

Panic crossed Mac's face, and he looked at the flowers he held. "Dear God. Don't cry. Chang said these were exactly the flowers I needed, spouted something about man at his best knowing when not to be stupid anymore. I told him I wanted something that showed how I felt . . . If he lied, I'll kill the—"

She pressed a finger to his lips. "Chang was correct." They're perfect. And I believe I have already learned to deal with your arrogance."

"In that case, sweetness, I know exactly why you wore that dress—and it does stir a man's soul. I thought to linger, perhaps dance, but now that you and I have given the gossipmongers sufficient fat to chew, I believe we can find a better way to end the evening. You see, I'm in a bit of a hurry to see exactly what you have on beneath these fancy trappings."

Unable to resist, she leaned on her tiptoes and told him in excruciating detail what she wore . . . and what she expected him to do about it.

His gaze caught fire. He swept her into his arms and marched toward the exit, his lips molded to hers in a kiss that was only a foretaste of the pleasure to come.

Joanna considered objecting for all of a moment about this spectacle, but then she wrapped her arms about him and kissed him back with all the love in her heart. No doubt the London tongues would wag tonight. And, in truth, she rather hoped they did.

PEGGY WAIDE
POTENT CHARMS

She is the most frustrating woman Stephen Lambert has ever met—and the most beguiling. But a Gypsy curse has doomed the esteemed duke of Badrick to a life without a happy marriage, and not even a strong-willed colonial heiress with a tendency to find trouble can change that. Stephen decides that since he cannot have her for a wife, he will convince her to be the next best thing: his mistress. But Phoebe Rafferty needs a husband, and fast. She has four weeks to get married and claim her inheritance. Phoebe only has eyes for the most wildly attractive and equally aggravating duke. But he refuses to marry her, mumbling nonsense about a curse. With time running out, Phoebe vows to persuade the stubborn aristocrat that curses are poppycock and the only spell he has fallen under is love.

____4694-6 $4.99 US/$5.99 CAN

Duchess For A Day
Peggy Waide

To save her life and her inheritance, Mary Jocelyn Garnett does what she must. She marries Reynolds Blackburn—without his knowledge. And all goes well, until the Duke of Wilcott returns to find he is no longer the king of bachelors. As long as the marriage is never consummated, Jocelyn knows, it can be annulled—just as soon as she has avenged her family and reacquired her birthright. Unfortunately, her blasted husband appears to be attracted to her! Worse, Reyn is handsome and clever, and she fears her husband might assume that she is one of many women who are simply after his title. After one breathless kiss, however, Jocelyn swears that she will not be duchess for a day, but Reyn's for a lifetime.

___4554-0 $4.99 US/$5.99 CAN

Dorchester Publishing Co., Inc.
P.O. Box 6640
Wayne, PA 19087-8640

Please add $1.75 for shipping and handling for the first book and $.50 for each book thereafter. NY, NYC, and PA residents, please add appropriate sales tax. No cash, stamps, or C.O.D.s. All orders shipped within 6 weeks via postal service book rate. Canadian orders require $2.00 extra postage and must be paid in U.S. dollars through a U.S. banking facility.

Name_____
Address_____
City_____State_____Zip_____
I have enclosed $_____ in payment for the checked book(s).
Payment <u>must</u> accompany all orders. ❑ Please send a free catalog.
CHECK OUT OUR WEBSITE! www.dorchesterpub.com

FOR THE LOVE
OF LILA
JENNIFER MALIN

Tristan Wyndam envisions his late mentor's daughter as a bespectacled spinster, not a youthful beauty. He anticipates helping to secure her inheritance, not escorting her—unchaperoned—to Paris. But Lila Covington defies all his expectations—and society's conventions. She does, however, promise to protect his reputation on their illicit journey, striking the Englishman speechless. Then she dons britches to play the part of a boy and her enticing legs render him breathless. But it is her performance as his wife that leaves him senseless with desire and longing for all the trappings of a real marriage. Luckily the befuddled barrister suspects he possesses the only lure strong enough to snare a liberated lady: true love.

Dorchester Publishing Co., Inc.
P.O. Box 6640   ___4997-X
Wayne, PA 19087-8640 $5.99 US/ $7.99 CAN

Please add $2.50 for shipping and handling for the first book and $.75 for each additional book. NY and PA residents, add appropriate sales tax. No cash, stamps, or CODs. Canadian orders require $5.00 for shipping and handling and must be paid in U.S. dollars. Prices and availability subject to change. **Payment must accompany all orders.**

Name: _____

Address: _____

City: _____ State: _____ Zip: _____

E-mail: _____

I have enclosed $_____ in payment for the checked book(s).

For more information on these books, check out our website at www.dorchesterpub.com.
_____ *Please send me a free catalog.*
COMING MAY 2002

Rules For A Lady

Katherine Greyle

A lady does not attempt to come out in London society disguised as her deceased half-sister. A lady does not become enamored of her guardian, even though his masterful kisses and whispered words of affection tempt her beyond all endurance. A lady may not climb barefoot from her bedroom on a rose trellis, nor engage in fisticuffs with riffraff in order to rescue street urchins. No matter how impossible the odds, a lady always gives her hand and her heart—though not necessarily in that order—to the one man who sees her as she truly is and loves her despite her flagrant disobedience of every one of the rules for a lady.

___4818-3 $4.99 US/$5.99 CAN

Dorchester Publishing Co., Inc.
P.O. Box 6640
Wayne, PA 19087-8640

Please add $2.50 for shipping and handling for the first book and $.75 for each book thereafter. NY, NYC, and PA residents, please add appropriate sales tax. No cash, stamps, or C.O.D.s. All orders shipped within 6 weeks via postal service book rate. Canadian orders require $2.00 extra postage and must be paid in U.S. dollars through a U.S. banking facility.

Name_____
Address_____
City_____ State_____ Zip_____
I have enclosed $ _____ in payment for the checked book(s).
Payment <u>must</u> accompany all orders.☐Please send a free catalog.
    CHECK OUT OUR WEBSITE! www.dorchesterpub.com

Major Wyclyff's Campaign
KATHERINE GREYLE

Pity, plain and simple, makes Sophia accept the offer of marriage from the dying Major Anthony Wyclyff. He is wildly handsome, but nothing will overcome her happiness at being "shelved." Then the blasted man recovers! Not that she wishes anyone ill, but Sophia expected to bury the earl's son along with all her childish hopes and dreams—not tumble with him in the dirt. He is resolved to claim his bride, though, and he forces her into a strategic retreat, to act in ways she never dreamed. His flanking attack brings him closer than ever—into her manor, her parlor, her bedroom—and the infuriating officer wagers he'll have terms of surrender within the month! Yet when his fiery kiss saps her defenses, Sophia swears the only terms she'll hear are those of love.

Dorchester Publishing Co., Inc.
P.O. Box 6640
Wayne, PA 19087-8640

_4920-1
$4.99 US/$5.99

Please add $2.50 for shipping and handling for the first book and $.75 for each additional book. NY and PA residents, add appropriate sales tax. No cash, stamps, or CODs. Canadian orders require $5.00 for shipping and handling and must be paid in U.S. dollars. Prices and availability subject to change. **Payment must accompany all orders.**

Name: _____

Address: _____

City: _____ State: _____ Zip: _____

E-mail: _____

I have enclosed $_____ in payment for the checked book(s).

For more information on these books, check out our website at www.dorchesterpub.com.
____ _Please send me a free catalog._